A SPRING
OF LOVE

A SPRING OF LOVE

CELIA DALE

With an introduction by Sheena Patel

DAUNT BOOKS

This edition first published in the United Kingdom in 2024 by
Daunt Books
83 Marylebone High Street
London W1U 4QW

1

Copyright © Celia Dale, 1960
Introduction copyright © Sheena Patel, 2024

A CIP catalogue record for this title is
available from the British Library.

ISBN 978-1-914198-94-6

Typeset by Marsha Swan
Printed and bound in Great Britain by
Clays Ltd, Elcograf S.pA.

www.dauntbookspublishing.co.uk

O happy living things! no tongue
Their beauty might declare:
A spring of love gush'd from my heart,
And I bless'd them unaware:
Sure my kind saint took pity on me,
And I bless'd them unaware.

Samuel Taylor Coleridge:
The Rime of the Ancient Mariner

INTRODUCTION

When Celia Dale's A *Helping Hand* was passed on
to me, I was told I would love it, but I was only half
paying attention. It languished in a pile of other books
that I keep by the side of my bed, which patiently wait
to be read. During the summer of 2022, needing something to keep me company while I was on the tube,
I picked it up and tucked it into my bag. Dale hooked
me from the first page.

I'm not normally a reader of crime fiction but there
is something in the way that Dale conjures mount-
ing dread that draws me in. She builds excruciating
dramatic tension, as she keeps one step ahead of the
reader, and in turn keeps her readers one step ahead
of the characters. This creates a delicious friction –

will the characters find out what you already know? However, will you *ever* know as much as Dale? She holds on tight to the reins of information, loosening her grip to reveal just enough to make you gasp and turn the page. Then, like a slap, there is a kicker-twist.

Little is known about Celia Dale and scouring the internet does not reveal much except a standard brief biography. She was born in 1912 and was familiar with the creative industries as her father, James Dale, was a notable actor, and her husband was a journalist. She herself was an assistant to the novelist Rumer Godden and worked in publishing. She had eleven books published in her lifetime, all well received – a few even adapted for television and radio but then slipped into obscurity. In today's chronically online world, where every morsel of life can be farmed for content and social media rules all, where after writing alone for months (sweating in your joggers, scavenging for snacks like a rat), suddenly, come publication, you need to *know your angles* in front of the camera and are expected to smize down the lens like a model. And so it feels curious that there is seemingly so little material on Dale, photos or otherwise. Although we can probably blame the patriarchy for her falling out of the memory of the canon, it does enable this revival of interest in her writing to be solely grounded in the work.

—

I was staying with my parents when I first read *A Spring of Love*. I would tell my mother, as she lay spread out, watching TV, what was happening to the novel's protagonist, Esther, as if she were a friend of mine. It was as if each encounter with the novel was a phone call, with Esther telling me what was going on in her life. Esther's life is made up of 'gentle, small routines'. She is single and lives with her overbearing but well-meaning grandmother; she has a steady job and because of her grandfather's will has been left with a considerable financial inheritance; she owns her home, in the 'pounding heart of Camden Town', lets the flat upstairs, and also owns a shop managed by a competent couple called the Grovers. 'She had been nowhere, done nothing, loved no one but her grandfather', so Esther feels an intense longing: for something to happen to her, for life. She tries to suppress this hunger and shield herself from the happiness and drama of others, for perhaps, she thinks, life is easier with only her grandmother and her work to fill her hours. However, a crack appears. In a small attempt to disrupt the mundanity of her routine, much to her grandmother's consternation, Esther starts to set aside Thursday evenings for herself. This crack is what opens the door to a chance encounter.

Suddenly there is an interruption to Esther's staid routine. Enter the man: 'Nothing extraordinary had ever happened to Esther in all her life until now.' The narrative shifts gear. Raymond starts chatting to Esther in the tearoom she frequents every Thursday, politely but persistently. He is there the next Thursday and the next and the next after that and his insistence breaks down her carefully constructed walls. One day, he proposes. Dale announces Esther's engagement as if Raymond were Jesus himself, 'he had come'. As if God has anointed her, 'the sun had risen' and life finally opens itself up to Esther. She is in the mix.

Esther and Raymond's love story is not an over-blown, dramatic one. It instead builds over time and is expressed through acts of devotion. After a while, Raymond begins to suggest, lightly at first and then with some insistence, that 'Ett' could separate the upstairs flat into two rooms, and lease them to two professional women who would be quieter than her current tenants, a noisy couple with a new baby. This way, Esther could also charge more money, make double the amount. Esther pulls against this sugges-tion, it's hard out there, for a young family, she doesn't want to kick them out and for a while, Raymond drops it. Esther is a housewife now and Raymond is away for work a lot but that's OK, isn't it? Small warnings pile up, red flags in Raymond's behaviour – Esther is happy but is she in danger? I felt myself holding my breath, willing her to trust her intuition. Dale consistently makes us second-guess our reading of what is happening – for when Raymond is home, everything seems so beautiful for the pair. Are our suspicions of him justified? Is Raymond who he says he is?

All Esther's relationships alter and have to adjust to the masculine presence in her life, to this new romance; even if it is only subconsciously, everyone must accept her, a married woman, as a sexual being. The idea of Esther being 'possessed', not her own person, makes the Grovers become nervous – will Raymond wrest control of the shop? Will they lose their home? The grandmother is resentful when she perceives herself as left out, nervous of being banished from Esther's thoughts. As Esther moves from single to engaged, the question arises: what does it feel like to be unclaimed, what is the value of womanhood on its own and how does it change when attached to a man? Who do we belong to when we belong to no one other than ourselves? What is it to have 'male protection' – does this even exist?

In A Spring of Love, we encounter threads that also run through A Helping Hand and Sheep's Clothing. Like them, A Spring of Love is set in a London that does not feel entirely different to today's. The city is vast, lending itself to an anonymity that creates fertile ground for chance encounters, for grifters and scammers. People collide into one another like whole planets with no context. The city is a black hole to the truth, the bustling activity of its overcrowded streets disguising something wonderful but sinister and unknowable about its inhabitants. This expansive urban cityscape is juxtaposed with the cloistered feel of the home. Her grandfather left Esther property, so she has more financial agency than the other characters. She is a landlord while the other characters in A *Spring of Love* are tenants, living in temporary housing. In the city, the solid, safe idea of the family home disintegrates into 'maisonettes or single rooms', people become transient and fragmentary. Any sense of privacy is a sham, as each neighbour eavesdrops on those next door. Each character overhears the truth and is in turn found out for speaking a lie. It's much harder to keep up appearances when you can hear the truth through the walls.

Raymond's presence in Esther's life destabilises the foundations other people have built in her world and he makes their position much more tenuous as he anchors her finally into the great flow of life. With Raymond, the 'home's' engine revs, splitting the air with sound and purpose . It is no longer the somnolent home that Gran and Esther previously maintained;

suddenly it is a hive of activity. Christmas usually passes them by but with Raymond's arrival comes a whirlwind of purpose. As Raymond increasingly exerts his power over the women, Esther's initial pleasure in being courted threatens to curdle and unknown to Esther, the home becomes unstable, pulsing with the threat of violence. Ambiguities seed doubt – is Raymond's anger controlling? Is Esther's need to acquiesce, to fold to Raymond's demands and ease his rageful fits, the compromise one must make for the sake of love? The home threatens to go from sanctuary to prison, and while Esther's once mundane life may now be filled with excitement, is it the right kind? As Esther embraces married life she becomes more remote to those who once had full access to her, and to the reader, the threat of manipulation looms larger. With this fear, Dale masterfully keeps us turning the pages. She sets up the story much like an authorial mega-spider, weaving an intricate web for her readers and her characters. It is with a dark relish that we watch these points of tension close in on one another and it makes for addictive reading. Who will win?

Dale has much to say about urban living and scam culture all while representing womanhood as far from clichéd or passive or twee but instead as something I recognise – women who are bolshy, brusque, tender and who have to look after themselves. That these characters live and breathe off the page is a testament to Dale's skill. The city Dale portrays is one that is populated by ordinary people, it is not aspirational and so is far more recognisable to me. However, the London that is portrayed is one that is only populated by white people. There is the assumption in art that whiteness is the base upon which all experience is universal and this is simply not true. My one criticism (and it is fundamental) is that in Dale's London, there are no speaking Black or Brown characters or any acknowledgement of an ethnically diverse city. Though it could be argued that she was writing within her experience, in the early 1960s, Britain was coming to the end of its Empire (something that certain factions of our political and cultural classes still mourn), while new waves of immigrants most notably from the Windrush generation and from the other colonies across the world – who were told to come to Britain to build the country back, who truly believed they were returning to the Motherland – were creating great change across the country, especially in London. This had brought in people of colour by the thousands, so where are they in Dale's books and where is the acknowledgement that this seismic change was even happening? Surely this would have been an era ripe for creative exploration but there is a same-ness to the city portrayed that

I just do not believe was the reality on the ground. It is an omission that is glaringly obvious and disappointing.

Ultimately, Esther is a person that I would like to know in real life. She is quietly one of the strong heroines in literature. Lonely characters are my favourite kinds of characters, and it is heart-warming to watch Esther expand in the love she finds with Raymond, to watch her hands move 'zestfully . . . even her reveries were full of tenderness . . . in which, without words, she was grateful for all she now possessed'. It feels slightly odd to admit that despite Esther giving up her working life to become a tradwife, I admire the deep joy she draws from this change. It makes the end of A *Spring of Love* all the more devastating. It left me feeling as if I had pins and needles all across my body. When Esther's life is shattered by a revelation, she makes a choice that I find difficult to stomach as it jars against my idea of Esther as morally robust. I didn't expect it of her and I am still struggling to reconcile this with my understanding of her; to me, as she does to the people in her life, she becomes sphinx-like.

By the end of the book, Dale has circled back to the beginning. It's my favourite type of ending: Esther is back where she started. She is sitting alone in a church, contemplative, but is she the same person? She recalls her relationship with Raymond: 'Not only

ugly things were real.' I wanted some sort of emanci-
pation, or solidarity with the other women in the novel,
but Dale does not give us this easy ending. Instead,
she delivers something else, something realistic and
uncomfortable; something that, if Esther were my
friend, I would find hard to accept.

Sheena Patel
London, 2024

PART ONE

ONE

THE FLOOR with waitress service was always crowded between four and seven o'clock and Esther often had to stand in a queue on the staircase that led up from the ground floor. There was never long to wait. Under the signpost that ordered 'This Side Up' the queue obediently ascended on the right side of the rail that divided the staircase like a crush barrier, alert to advance briskly or even enter, if the commissionaire on the landing above them so willed it. People came out through the swing-doors from the tea-room, replete, buttoning their coats, letting loose with their egress a wafer of Puccini and the smell of teapots. Esther shifted two steps upwards, leaning comfortably against the burnished rail. She was in no hurry. Thursdays were her evenings out.

Once within, passed with the speed of a conveyor belt from commissionaire to head waiter, head waiter to the destined, vacant place, warm still from its last occupant, she took off her gloves, undid her coat. *Madame Butterfly*'s selections had just come to an end and the soft clamour of crockery and voices filled the huge, hideous hall. Women's voices mostly, for women predominated, middle-aged women with parcels and the sated look of hunters. Here and there a child sat aghast before a towering orange torch of squash, bemused by the luxurious carpet, the luxurious teapots, milk jugs, sugar tongs; the luxurious silken slave-master in sleek tails whose smile was silver beneath eyes of slate; the impersonal luxurious women in pink uniforms and pale green aprons who sped and bent over them, did sums with captive pencils, bore monstrous towering trays imperviously through the warm, music-scented, luxurious air.

Esther had been put at a table for two. It was not customary to acknowledge the presence of fellow-eaters, and she did not glance at the elderly female person finishing a peach Melba opposite her. She chose her own meal slowly, set the menu neatly back between sugar bowl and salt cellar, and looked about her in content.

She came here every Thursday. On Thursdays the store stayed open until seven and she stayed on alone in the Invoice Department until half past six or more so that there should not be too much to get through the following morning. She had offered to do it when the late opening first started, for Miss Burroughs was older than she and liked to get home, and Jacqueline was very much younger and liked to get out. Esther enjoyed working quietly in the office that had become so familiar to her in the last fifteen years, from whose windows she could look out over the roofs of London and see on a clear day the tips of Tower Bridge and the top of St. Paul's. Five floors below, the traffic clogged and sweated in the streets; but up here, on a Thursday, the only sounds were the oiled slither of the filing cabinet drawers, the crunch and ping of the adding machine or Esther humming to herself.

No one bothered her. They knew she would do all that was necessary. When she was ready she closed and locked the machines, took her towel and soap-box to the deserted Ladies'. There she washed, combed her brownish, longish hair, dusted her pale skin with powder, touched her mouth with a little pale lipstick, put on her plain brown coat. Coming out of the staff entrance she turned, on Thursdays, not to the bus stop and home but to the clangour of the Charing Cross Road.

On the dais the musicians roused themselves and, as Esther's plaice and chips, roll, butter and pot of tea were set before her, launched into a medley from *The Boy Friend*. The room was not so crowded now, with here and there a vacant table from which the waitress flicked gratuity and crumbs. The elderly female person opposite crashed together great paper bags, reared to her feet and in a sudden loud voice said, 'Good evening,' and was gone. Esther looked after her abashed; perhaps after all she would have liked to talk? Well, it was too late now. She folded the newspaper open at 'Points from Letters' and began to read.

It was interesting what people wrote about. There was someone complaining that weeds seeding themselves from neglected gardens were destroying the nation's heritage; certainly, Esther thought, it was queer how year after year that plant of willowherb flowered in the wall at the back of the kitchen yard. There was someone else complaining that migrating birds no longer appeared to be nesting in the trees of Hampstead Heath; Esther had never seen anything but ducks and sparrows there, but perhaps she didn't go often enough. And there was an MP denying that he ever said something the paper's reporter had said he said; but this Esther didn't read. Then she turned to the Women's Page, and as she ate the last of the plaice and chips studied a 3-column picture of a girl stretched out on a hearthrug wearing 'Zebra-striped matador tights with fur-topped jersey sheath, fine for informal evenings at home'. The article was about how Young Marrieds could make one room seem like three by the clever placing of bamboo screens; and although at thirty Esther did not consider herself young, and had never been married, she read this carefully, for she liked domesticated things.

Someone else was sitting opposite now, a man, but without paying him any attention she looked at the menu and decided on gateau. The waitress was standing by the table, looking dubiously at the newcomer.

'You were at my table over there, weren't you, sir?'

'That's right.'

'They don't really like customers shifting theirselves.'

'Not without permission from Big Brother, eh?' He nodded his head towards the head waiter.

The waitress softened a little. 'Well, not really.'

'Well, you don't tell him and he won't know. And I'll start all over again with a pot of tea and some pastries.' He smiled persuasively.

'Well . . .' The waitress looked at Esther, 'If the lady doesn't mind . . .'

Embarrassed at finding herself drawn in, Esther said, 'No, I don't mind.'

'Well, all right then. Only they don't like it. Pot of tea and pastries, was it? And you, miss . . .?'

'Some gateau, please.'

The waitress went away.

'Sorry to disturb you like that,' the young man said, 'only the fact is I can't stand to sit facing the orchestra. They give me the willies.'

She looked across to the platform where the three musicians, with their white jackets and indoor faces, twitched to their own rhythms.

'See what I mean?' he asked.

She smiled, picking up her newspaper again. 'Oh well, they're doing their best,' she said and began to read; for you did not get into conversation with people sitting at the same table, leastways only sometimes and if it was a woman like the woman who had just gone. Not with a man, ever.

There was an inquest on a poor girl found strangled in Bristol; and a TV star who had been married for eighteen months was divorcing her husband. Gran would be pleased; Gran stored up the discreditable deeds of celebrities as a squirrel stores nuts. A good divorce was better than a good murder to Gran, but best of all was a good breach of promise case. You didn't get many of those now. Esther remembered when she was a child sitting eating her tea in the kitchen while Gran read out all the evidence and all the love letters that were printed in the papers then, rolling out the endearments and the admissions as though she were back on the stage at the Metropole, but with one ear cocked for Grandad's step down the area, when she'd whisk up and off and be cooking his fish in the scullery with a face as clear and wholesome as a two-year-old's . . .

She became aware that the man was speaking to her. 'I wonder if I might trouble you for a loan of your paper?' he was saying. 'That is, if you've done with it?'

'Yes, of course.' She handed it to him over the teapots.

'That's ever so good of you. There's just something I have to have a look at.' He turned to the Small Ads pages and skimmed down them. Esther went on with her tea, but from a glance as the newspaper changed hands she had reassured herself that he was not at all a flashy type. Quietly dressed, pale, with nice fair hair worn a little long perhaps, but that was the fashion now. You could see he took care of it. He had a pleasant voice, and a pleasant smile as he refolded the pages before returning the paper to her.

'Thanks very much,' he said. 'I just put in an ad to sell my car and I wanted to check it was there all right.' She smiled faintly but said nothing, eating the last of the gateau. 'It's a 1946 Vauxhall,' he continued, breaking the back of an éclair with his fork. 'Perfect condition. Well . . .' he munched and swallowed, 'perfect that is for a car that's been flogged up and down little old England for the last few years by yours truly. But I know about cars, mind.'

She still said nothing and he gave her an apologetic bob of the head. 'You'll think I've a sauce, speaking to you. It's just start me on cars and I'm away. I'm ever so sorry.'

'That's all right.' Her pale skin coloured a little. In the silence she lifted the lid of the teapot and looked inside. There was a little tea and she poured it out.

'I've plenty of hot water,' he said.

'Oh – thanks. I've finished really.'

'Like our friends, the symphony orchestra.' He jerked his head towards the musicians' dais, which was now deserted. Many of the tables were empty too, and an air of relaxation, of calm after storm, filled the huge room. 'My word, I wouldn't like their job,' he went on. 'Having to play against all that clatter and talk. I suppose some people listen. I mean, I suppose they give pleasure to someone.'

'Yes, I suppose so.'

The conversation died again before he said, 'You fond of music?'

'Well, quite. I used to listen to the wireless sometimes before we had the telly.'

His eyes brightened. 'You keen on TV?'

'I got it for Gran, really. That's my grandmother I live with. I'd rather get out and be among people, myself.'

'Me, too. People, eh? That's what I like about a place like this. Plenty of people, yet quiet and homey too. If you live by yourself like I do, you appreciate a nice place like this.'

'Yes.' She was putting on her gloves, buttoning her coat.

'Whenever I'm in London I come here. Maybe in time the waitresses might even get to know me.'

She smiled, picking up her bill. 'Oh I don't think so. They've never any of them got to know me.' She got up.

He rose too, and for a flurried moment she thought he was coming with her; but he was only being polite. He stood with a hand on the back of the chair, smiling. He had a nice smile.

'Well, perhaps we'll meet again,' he said. 'And thank you for the read of your paper.'

'Good night.'

'Good night.'

She made her way to the cash desk and paid. Relaxed now, the commissionaire held open the door and even smiled at her as she went out. Downstairs she hesitated. She always went along to the Dominion but she had a sudden fear that the man might after all be following her and she did not want to seem to be hanging about where he could find her. She was not going home yet, for Thursday was always her evening

11

out, so she took the tube to Leicester Square and went to the Empire instead.

It was of such gentle, small routines that Esther's life consisted: going to work each morning, coming back each night, the fortnight with Gran at the seaside every summer, the small rituals of their birthdays, of Easter and Christmas, her Thursdays free, her Tuesdays at the Gaumont with Gran whatever was showing, the regular watching of Gran's favourite television programmes, Gran's charabanc outing every August with the old age pensioners, the annual visit to Grandad's grave at Kensal Green. Year after year since Esther grew up and the war ended the same things recurred smoothly, reassuringly, so that even the things that were different became unremarkable. The lodgers changed in the top half of their house, for instance (it was Esther's house, for Grandad had left it to her), but the lodgers seemed always very much the same. Sometimes business went down at the newsagent's shop which had also been Grandad's and for which Esther had a manager, or the front of it needed repainting, or a new line in chewing-gum or greeting cards was tried out. Sometimes Gran got bronchitis; sometimes Monty, the cat, would have to have his ear sewn together again or his blood purged with powders.

But whatever deviations there might be, they were

all so small and so familiar that when you looked back you could not tell one year from another, as though all violence had exhausted itself for Victoria and Esther Wilson by the time the war ended.

Esther always got home about half past ten after her Thursday and Gran was always waiting for her, watching the television in the basement front room with her feet on the hassock and the centre light on, her tea not cleared away and her supper not got and the mending basket as full as it always was. Cigarette butts were crushed into her saucer and ash had been brushed carelessly into the tablecloth and off her squashed old bosom. She twisted round in her chair when Esther came in, the light striking greenly on her dyed black hair, her monkey eyes bright.

'Etty? You're back late.'

'No I'm not, dear, just the usual.'

'Did you see something good?'

'Not bad – a musical with Gene Kelly.' She took off her coat and laid it over a chair. 'Haven't you had your supper?'

'I couldn't be fagged.' She turned right round in the chair to have a good look at Esther. 'Gene Kelly wasn't at the Dominion, I looked it up special to see what it was and it was one of them Xs.'

'I didn't go to the Dominion.' She began to clear the tea things.

'Where'd you go then?'

'To the Empire. Will you have some supper now?'

'I'll just have a bit of cheese.'

'You'll have dreams if you do.' She carried the crockery out and down the passage to the scullery.

Gran raised her voice above the television. 'Why didn't you go to the Dominion? You always do.'

'Thought I'd like a change.'

'Well, that's a surprise.' She crouched back in the chair again, putting her feet in their grubby pink slippers snugly up on the hassock where the warmth from the stove caught them. The bluish mannikins on the television screen continued to gesture and speak winningly.

Esther came back. 'You've let the stove get clogged up,' she said, knelt and began to rake it vigorously.

'Blooming thing. Why can't we have a nice coal fire like we used to? I remember the Empire before it had pictures. Shame it was, when they changed it. And the Alhambra too, all gold and oriental. Oh, them were the days and the Strand all lit up, with Romanos and the old Lyceum, and Tom Walls at the Aldwych and Stanley Lupino at the Gaiety and Robertson Hare and that big bald man at the Strand . . . Oh my, you got your money's worth then. Did you meet anyone?'

Esther went out to the scullery again, saying, 'Who should I meet?'

'Oh, I don't know.' Gran dug herself farther back into the chair. 'P'raps some day you'll meet someone and come back with something new to tell me. Might as well be in our graves for all that ever happens here. Oh shut up, you silly cat!' She pulled a face at the television hostess who was smilingly describing the next part of the programme, but did not bother to turn it off. From the scullery Esther called, 'Get some teaspoons out, will you, and a couple of knives.'

Gran got up and did as she was asked. She moved dartingly, a shapeless untidy little figure with the grooved face of a monkey and eyes brightly black as her hair, glass diamonds dangling at her ears, stockings wrinkled on trim legs. By one of the chairs she halted and whisked up the tablecloth as though she were looking under somebody's skirts.

'Monty's got your chair again,' she called.

'Well, he'll have to move.'

'Ooh, you bad boy,' Gran murmured, caressing the motionless mound of black fur. 'Aren't you a lovely chap, eh? Aren't you a beauty?' She dropped the tablecloth. 'Etty?'

'What?'

'That Gloria's been at it again. No sooner'd he come home and got upstairs than I heard her going on at him.'

'Don't shout, Gran, they'll hear.'

'Not them. Gone out and good luck to 'em. If you don't get out when you're young, when will you?' She perched on the edge of the chair again, feet on the hassock, looked furtively over her shoulder to see if Esther were in the doorway, then flicked open the two doors of the stove. The coal was blazing up and with a breath of contentment she stretched out her hands to it, staring unblinkingly at the fire from between nar-rowed lids as a cat is sometimes struck immobile by the warmth.

Esther came back with the tray. 'I've done you an egg,' she said.

Gran scowled. 'I said cheese.'

'Cheese plays you up, this time of night. You don't want nightmares.'

'You're just like your grandad, you never let anyone have a bit of what they fancy.' Sulkily she hitched the chair nearer the table while Esther, seated opposite, poured out the tea. She had brought in some biscuits for herself and took one as she half listened to Gran, remembering the tunes in the film she had seen and then the musicians in the tea place and how that young man had said they gave him the willies. Now that was something she could have told Gran, an item of news she could have given her as you throw a stick for a dog: a nice young man, spoken to in a teashop, what did he look like, what did he say? My goodness, thought Esther, Gran could make something out of that for weeks! She looked across the table, half-smiling, half about to tell her, but Gran had started off again on Gloria and Terry Mason who lodged in the top part of the house and whose marriage, Gran suspected, dated from the onset of Gloria's morning sickness. They had moved in two months ago and the loss of Gloria's figure filled the upper floors with lamentation every day. 'My goodness, I bet he wishes he'd kept his trousers buttoned,' said Gran gleefully, scraping out the last of the boiled egg, 'but there you are, that's men – act first, think afterwards. Ah well, he's paying for it now.'

Esther loved Gran as she would have loved a mischievous child or an intelligent chimpanzee which she had reared from a baby. She knew almost exactly what Gran would do, but never what she might say or think. Gran's mind was a kaleidoscope of bright sharp memories, a ragbag among which she rooted busily, avid for a brighter colour, a newer shape, absorbed as a child or a chimpanzee in its own experience. You could ask Gran to do the shopping and she would – if her attention were not deflected by meeting someone or seeing something more attractive to her at that moment. She was not forgetful but wayward, not careless but deliberate. She indulged herself in life, and what she was not given she would snatch, if she could.

Interposing himself between Gran and her own character had always been Grandad. Protesting but subservient, Gran had lived in the shadow of his authority; but between George Wilson and his granddaughter there had always been perfect understanding. She had grown up as orderly, as practical as he but without the vein of hardness that had made him Gran's master. His photograph stood on the kitchen mantelpiece, a stern virile elderly face with bristling eyebrows and moustache and grey hair rising strongly from a square head. At the other end of the mantelpiece was a picture of Esther's mother dressed as one of the chorus in *The Gondoliers*. It was while on a D'Oyly Carte tour that she had been killed by a car when Esther was seven. 'Winnie Delair' the photograph was signed. She too, on the brief occasions when she had been at home, had lived in Grandad's shadow.

Esther could not remember her mother, and the flounced, smiling figure holding a tambourine meant nothing to her. But she often looked at and remembered Grandad's strong face, his tobaccoey smell, the comfort of his lap, the serge of his trousers rough and warm against the underside of her thighs. He had taught her to cut patterns from folded pads of paper, to whistle like a blackbird, to say her catechism, and the dates of the kings of England. He had sung her songs from the 1914 war – 'Grandad's war' – and told her stories of the young fierce fearless fellows who had been himself and his comrades. St Omer and Béthune, Poperinghe and Ypres were fabled places to her; and for a long time she grew nasturtiums each year in the German helmet hung upside down from a nail in the back-yard wall. As she grew older and heard the stories over and over again she realised that they sprang from a nostalgia almost past bearing for the hard company of men, a protest against the female life of peace and a paean for the simplicity of war, uncluttered, unclinging, hard. When the second war came, the stories stopped. There were plenty of new ones, no doubt, as Grandad was an ARP warden, but he never told them, for this was not his war; this war did cling and clutter, invade the female world and mix battle with domesticity. He died in 1948, a silent stern old man whom Esther had loved.

He left her the house, the shop, and eight hundred pounds. He also left her Gran.

The house was one of a row of three-storeyed early Victorian houses in a wide North London street. Trolley-buses ran at the street's end and beyond was the pounding heart of Camden Town, but Handel Street was quiet. The proportions of the road, the plain flat faces of the houses with their four steps to the front door, were so elegant that they gave beauty to what had been designed as a row of workmen's dwellings. Buff and cream and grey, in rain or in the luminous London sunshine, the street had a unity the more arresting for the slabs of yellow-brick flats with which it was being surrounded on ground cleared by the bombs of 1940. Some of the houses were shabby, many were honeycombed into lodging-houses, but outwardly all was still decent.

The road had been built in Grandad's grandfather's time; the Wilsons were the aristocracy of Handel Street. They and two or three other families had been in that small area of North London for four generations or more and the streets which to a stranger were simply anonymous veins in the great body of London had been in reality a village, with a hierarchy and a folk-lore. Old Mrs Bromwich next door, for instance, had hardly been into the centre of London more than half a dozen times in all her eighty-three years. Many old people still remembered when the yellow horse buses were the only transport, and Hampstead at the top of its hill still almost as remote a village as when footpads prowled its bushy slopes. The old families of Handel Street and the surrounding streets had gone to the same school, attended the same Bible classes, intermarried. People who lived a mile away had been foreigners.

That was changed now. The young ones had gone off into the Forces or into the city to work and were citizens of London; what had been family houses were now split up into maisonettes, or single rooms. At one end of the street there were West Indians, at the other turquoise paint proclaimed impecunious intellectuals. Mrs Bromwich and her elderly daughter had lodgers, and who lived the other side of the Wilsons it would be hard to say, they came and went so often.

But this was since the war; in Esther's childhood there was an atmosphere of permanence and the great bulwark of Grandad, so that whatever happened to Esther seemed perfectly ordinary. Perhaps other children were not fatherless; their mothers were not sopranos in an opera company, seldom at home, and killed in street accidents; their grandmothers were gentle, wise women, which Gran had never been; but these peculiarities had been so dominated by Grandad and by the background of Handel Street that they were lost in the unvarying passage of the days. Esther had been evacuated to Devon for two years of the war; but so had all the other children at her school. Most of them were married by now, and she was not; but that was not really an extraordinary difference.

Like everyone else she left the house each morning at eight-fifteen. Gran would be up and dressed, for she did not sleep much in the nights now, hunched at the big table with a third cup of tea and the *Daily Mirror*. On the hearth-rug Monty performed the ritual half-hour's grooming with which he closed the night's secret episodes, before leaping on to Esther's chair under the table to sleep through the day. It was left to Gran to clear and wash the breakfast things, make her own bed, dust and sweep a little, go to the shops. Once a week she went to the launderette, garnering there a treasure of gossip and medical grand-guignol which she passed on to Esther in the evening. Three nights a week Esther turned out a room after she had eaten her supper. On Tuesdays they went to the Gaumont, at the weekends they watched television, on Thursdays she was free.

It was a freedom fought for and held obstinately in the face of all that Gran could think of doing. It drove Gran mad to think that there was something she was left out of, that Esther had even one thing private from her. She had wheedled, reviled, wept, sulked; she had lamented the lost gay days of her youth before she became a prisoner of these killjoy Wilsons; she had wept for a poor old woman thrown on the dust-heap, unwanted, a burden; she had accused Esther of nameless shames each Thursday too terrible for a decent woman to hear. Finally she had subsided into grumbles lit only occasionally by a shaft of malice. She gave up complaining except in a covert way, but by neglecting herself on Thursdays implied that it was Esther who was doing so.

There was nothing so very special about Thursdays after all, as Esther had told her; she knew exactly what Esther did and where she went. But both of them knew that Thursdays were the symbol of Gran's impotence and that although she might snatch at Esther's life, she would always find her hands half empty.

Now, when Esther tidied up the office, washed, combed her brown hair, put on her brown coat, the break in routine had itself become routine, and she looked forward placidly, almost without thought to the tea-shop, the cinema, the bus ride home.

She was later than usual this week, and it was nearly seven by the time she reached the restaurant; the musicians were playing their last selection. She had a table to herself, and because it was late and she was therefore hungrier than usual, perhaps also out of a half-realised impatience with routine, she ordered a mixed grill instead of the usual plaice and chips. She had finished it and the evening paper, when a voice exclaimed, 'Well, good evening! If this isn't the long arm of coincidence!' She looked up to find the young man of the previous week standing by the table.

'Fancy meeting you again!' he exclaimed. 'I was just on my way out when I spotted you. What a coincidence!'

She smiled, not knowing what to say, flustered and yet in an odd way not surprised to see him. Gran had asked, 'Did you meet anyone?' and she never had, until this man last week, and it had stuck in her mind somewhere, behind the habitual thoughts of home and business.

'Well, never tell me the world's a big place after this! Ten million people in London and we run into each other again! Why, thousands of people must come in and out of here every day. It makes you believe in fate, doesn't it?'

She murmured something, looking down at her empty plate. He hesitated for a moment, then asked diffidently, 'Would you think me cheeky if I joined you for a minute – that is, if you're not expecting someone?'

'No – please . . .' She felt hot and shy and could think of nothing to say. He sat down, resting an elbow on the table, eager to talk.

'I only got back to London this morning. To run into practically the only friendly face I know in the whole place is what I call luck. I don't live in London, see – leastways, I don't really live anywhere, kind of a bird of passage, you might say. I'm a traveller – not a fellow-traveller, mind! – I sell novelties for a big firm in Clerkenwell – well, not sell, show samples, get orders, you know the kind of thing. It's interesting, you see a lot of the country. But of course you don't hardly ever get to know people.'

A waitress came up to clear away Esther's plate. 'Here,' he said, 'I'm interrupting your meal.'

'No. I've nearly finished.'

'But you'll have something else – some gateau, an ice-cream? Go on, have an ice-cream and I'll join you with it.'

'Well . . .'

'Go on – have a chocolate sundae, they're smashing here. That's what I'll have, miss,' he smiled up at the waitress, 'I've got a sweet tooth.'

'All right,' Esther said. She heard herself with amazement yet it was all so natural, so friendly. He was obviously so pleased to have found her, a lonely, nice-spoken young man with no friends; and she – after all, what was she herself but a lonely, nice-spoken young woman in just the same case? There could be no harm in it. You could see he wasn't a nasty type at all.

'I just can't get over my luck in bumping into you again,' he said, looking across the table at her with pleasure. He had an open face with eyes of the surprising thick, bright blue of Wedgwood china. His hair was brushed carefully in a wave and was receding slightly at each temple. He had no hat, his raincoat was neat, a scarf folded smoothly inside the collar.

'Is it just coincidence or d'you come here often?'

'Every Thursday – that is, usually.'

'And I'm usually in London Thursdays – you know, call in at the office and report on Fridays, hang about the weekend and Sunday night off on my travels again. I've been round the south coast this week – lovely it was, you could sit out with your coat off last Tuesday in Eastbourne – that is, if you could spare the time. Me, I keep on the go. Never was one to sit down and put my feet up. Perhaps that's because I never had much place to put them up in. My dad and mum died when I was a nipper.'

'My mother died too.'

'And you live on your own?'

'With my gran.'

'In London?'

'Yes – near Camden Town.'

'Well I never – just the two of you on your own? Still, you're better off than what I am – I've got no family at all. My dad was in the Regular Army and got gassed in the first war. They invalided him out, of course, but his lungs was never really much good after that and he passed on when I was three. Mum carried on the best she could – she taught the piano, I can see her now sitting there in the evenings, strumming – but then one winter she caught the flu. She was always delicate, see, and I don't think she ever really got over my dad's going.'

Esther made a sympathetic noise.

He smiled wryly, 'So I lived with my auntie for a bit, till I went to school – my dad's sister that was. She was married to a parson up in Scarborough and I don't think they either of them hardly knew what children was. Even school seemed more fun than being at Auntie's. But my word, whatever must you be thinking of me, running on talking about myself like this? I must be off my rocker!'

'No – it's interesting. You've had a sad life.'

'No more than you, all alone with your grandma.'

'Well, it was Grandad brought me up really. He was a wonderful man. He was in the first war too.'

'A Regular?'

'No. He had a business, a shop.'

'And that's where you work?'

'No. I work at Winters'.'

'What, Winters' round the corner?' She nodded. 'So that's why you come here regular, nice and handy. Well, we certainly have found out a lot about each other. Perhaps we ought to introduce ourselves – my name's Raymond Banks.'

'I'm Miss Wilson, Esther Wilson.'

'Esther – that's a pretty name. Unusual too. In the Bible, isn't it?'

'Yes.'

'I was called after my father – it's kind of a family name, Raymond. Although so far it looks as if I'm going to be the last one to answer to it – the end of the line, you might say.'

'You mustn't say that. Why, you're only young yet.'

'I'm close on thirty. Still, while there's life there's hope, eh?'

The ice-creams had arrived and been eaten while they talked. Now, faced with the empty dishes and the empty tables around them, a sudden self-consciousness possessed them. For the first time the young man's spate of conversation ceased and Esther, looking down, fidgeted with her gloves and handbag. The waitress came, completed the bill and laid it non-committally in the middle of the table. Raymond picked it up.

'Oh no, you mustn't,' exclaimed Esther. She blushed deeply.

'It's a privilege.'

'No, no, I couldn't possibly! You must let me pay for myself.' She began fumbling urgently for her purse.

'Please, Miss Wilson, it'd be a pleasure.'

'No, really. I was here long before you came. I couldn't possibly . . .'

He looked at her closely, weighing her embarrassment and determination, and yielded. 'Well OK – if you insist. Yours comes to seven and threepence.'

She got out the coins and passed them over to him in her closed hand so that no one should notice. Then they stood up and went together to the door.

As he paid, Esther's thoughts were in confusion. She could not see how she was to get rid of him, or he of her; and she did not know what she would say whether he left her or came with her. She had no experience of this kind of thing – indeed, she did not know quite what kind of thing it was. When she was younger she had sometimes been followed in the street; and sometimes still a man would edge up to her in a queue or the dark of a cinema. These things, though they displeased her, were easily dealt with; her air of almost prim composure was soon seen to be unpromising. But this young man was completely different, polite and natural as if they had met at a social and been properly introduced. She could not feel that this was a 'pick-up', for obviously he did not so consider it. Yet supposing he was tired of it now, and wished to be rid of her? How could they separate with dignity?

He smiled as he joined her, holding the door open for her to go through, for the commissionaire by this time was off duty. They went down the steps in silence. Just inside the swing doors to the street they halted.

'Well – I mustn't keep you,' he said.

'No.'

'You go back to your gran now, do you?'

'No. Well, yes – that is, sometimes I do.'

She never did so and the lie made her blush again. He looked at her closely.

'Where do you go when you don't?' he asked.

'Well – usually I go to the pictures.'

He turned his head and looked out through the glass doors across the black and glittering road to the glowing façade of the shops and traffic beyond. His eyes seemed extremely blue when he looked back at her.

'That's just what I thought of doing myself,' he said.

When the programme was ended he came with her to the bus stop and saw her onto the bus. He had suggested going somewhere for a cup of coffee, but all through the film a growing agitation had consumed her and she had refused abruptly. He had looked at her in that keen way he had, and acquiesced at once. As they waited for the bus he had chatted about the film and other films he had seen with the same players in them. Only when a 24 came in sight had he been silent for a moment before saying, 'I can't remember when I've enjoyed an evening so much.'

'Yes – I'm so glad.' She really did not know what she was saying.

'I'll be there next Thursday,' he said, 'just in case I'm in luck again.'

'Oh – I don't know – I mean . . .' The bus was here and she was moving on to it.

He smiled suddenly and touched her elbow lightly before stepping back from the kerb. 'About six-thirty,' he called. And then she was sitting alone in a bus that moved north in the direction of her home, paying her fare, and staring out at the dark reflection of herself mirrored against the streets.

She really did not know what her thoughts were. She felt as though all the firm ground she was used to treading upon had turned into a bog. She had been picked up, had supper with and been taken to the pictures by a completely strange man, a perfect stranger. Why, he might be anyone – a murderer, a confidence trickster, a pickpocket, anyone! Four hours ago she hadn't known him from Adam – and here she was almost engaged to meet him again next week.

Please God, she prayed, clasping her hands in her lap, don't let Gran catch on. Don't let my face give me away. She stared at her face in the window, dispassionately. It was the same pale uninteresting face she had always known, with the same uninteresting brown hair and the air of reserve that gave nothing away. Let it not give me away now, she prayed, not till I've got my mind clear about this evening and have decided how much, if anything, to tell.

I won't go next week. Then I need never tell anything. It can just be one of the things that Gran never knew about, a queer incident, an odd break in routine, that after a bit I shan't even remember. I shall just remember the name, for you don't forget names. And his very blue eyes.

He was waiting for her outside the tea-room when she arrived just before half past six the following Thursday.

'I thought I'd better not go in and risk our not being let sit together,' he smiled, taking her elbow to pilot her through the obsequiously opened door. 'Two, please – and not too near the band,' he said.

The head waiter gestured them through the warm air to a corner table.

'All right?' Raymond asked her.

'Yes.'

They sat opposite each other and he picked up the menu at once, giving her no time for awkwardness. So far she had hardly spoken, borne along on his masculine authority as someone is towed passively to the safety of a shore. No time to think, no time to consider her actions as other than those she had always performed, coming here, ordering, eating, hearing the music; save that now it was he, fresh-faced, confident yet deferential, who set it all in motion. For the first time in many years it was not she who was in charge. She sat helpless, glowing, confused. She had not meant to come.

Through the past week this young man had ceased to be real; he was something dreamed, or an image she had seen on a screen. Not that there was anything peculiar about him; he was ordinary enough. But the fact that he should exist within the quiet limits of Esther's life was so extraordinary that, as during the first few days she thought of him so much, he grew implausible. He could not have happened. It was not possible that she should have supped and spent the evening with someone she did not know, and the more she thought of it the more he became a fantasy, a daydream like those she had as a girl newly going out to work, when every corner turned may be the one that reveals a new world, every face passed in the street may be the one that does not pass out of sight. She had thought him out of existence, so that when next Thursday came it was only rational to do what she had always done and go as usual for her evening out. It was all reassuring, customary, known. Only he was new.

Yet not exactly that. By thinking of him so constantly during the week she had made him doubly harmless, at once unreal and familiar. There seemed nothing more natural than to be sitting opposite him in the tinkling, crowded hall, eating fried plaice and chips with the tray of tea things shared between them, listening to his voice and the unselfconscious flow of anecdote and information with which he revealed himself to her.

Nothing extraordinary had ever happened to Esther in all her life until now. She had been nowhere, done nothing, loved no one but her grandfather. Once she had thought she might be in love with a young man in Hardware; but she was too quiet for him and he had lost interest almost before hers had been aroused. From Grandad she had understood that if you loved someone you did so with control, you did not give way, carry on, get into states. That was Gran's way and no one Gran loved had ever been any the happier for it. You went on quietly, doing the best you could for those you loved, asking and therefore receiving little. She used to think: One day it will happen, I can be patient. But as the weeks, months, years went by she thought: It may never happen, I must be patient. Yet all around her people married. Why? Did they love each other? What did love mean? What had been between her mother and her unknown father, between Gran and Grandad? What was between Gloria and Terry Mason, with their quarrels and the reconciliations that seemed to reconcile neither of them to anything?

Esther could not answer, for she knew nothing. All she did know was that her instinct told her there must be peace and happiness in love, self-control and quietness. And that millions of people, of whom she was one, never came across it.

'So I hope this isn't one of the nights you go back to your gran,' the young man was saying.

'Pardon? Oh no. I mean, I didn't say definitely . . .' She felt herself colouring again – really, it was ridiculous the way she went red as a beetroot whenever he asked her anything.

'Would you like to ring her up?'

'We're not on the phone.'

'Not? Well, that's probably wise – it doesn't half run up a big bill.'

'It's not that. I mean, if Gran wanted it I'd have it put in. Only we don't ever need it really – and there's one in the shop if I ever did want to get hold of her quickly. They'd always run round with a message.'

'Ah yes, the shop. I'd forgotten you were a property-owner.' He grinned at her over a plate of cakes. She took an éclair, smiling too. 'If I'm ever hard up for a job I'll come to you for a paper round. I used to do one when I was living down at my auntie's. She didn't care for it much, thought it wasn't quite the thing, you know, but I wanted the money. All I used to think about was the day when I wouldn't have to be on anyone's charity. Five bob a week I got, and saved almost every penny of it. It mounted up. I had quite a tidy little nest egg by the time I went into the Army. When my uncle died I was able to help Auntie out quite a bit till the will was all settled and that. So if you ever need a paper boy, remember yours truly.'

She laughed. 'All right. We're always needing them. They start off keen as mustard and then they start letting us down. They're a real headache.'

'How many have you got?'

'Oh – eight, nine.'

He whistled. 'Quite a big round.'

'Yes. It's very old established. My grandad started it when he came out of the war – the first war, that is. And his dad had it before him – not a newsagent-to-bacconist, Grandad turned it into that, but more of a general shop – you know, like a village shop almost. That's what he used to tell me.'

'Quite a character, your grandad.'

'Yes, he was.'

'And you're his only grandchild?'

'Yes.'

'It's a shame, isn't it, being an only. I'd have liked brothers and sisters, wouldn't you?'

'Yes. Yes, I would. I'd like to have been the eldest.'

'And look after the little ones, eh?'

'Why do you say that?'

'You're the type. One's only to look at you to see you'd be good with kids.'

She felt her blood rising once again but now not in her face alone but in her whole body, flooding her heart. It obscured her sight, muffled her hearing, so that she could only sit helplessly, conscious of nothing but the chair she sat on and the clasp of her handbag beneath her fingers.

The waitress was making out the bill.

'If we go now,' he said, 'we'll just have timed it right. The programme starts in a couple of minutes.'

He paid the bill and bought the tickets and this time Esther did not dispute. They sat in the darkness and she tried to concentrate on the screen, but all the time she was conscious of his presence beside her, although he did not even touch her arm with his. It's queer, she thought, I've been to the pictures hundreds of times and never noticed whether the seat next to me was taken or not. I go with Gran and forget she's there, go alone and might be alone for all the notice I take. But now I can't get it out of my mind that he's there, sitting next to me. It was as though all that side of her body were tinglingly alive. She was aware too of the people around her, of the clasped hands of the couple on her other side, the inclined heads of the couple in front. She felt that the whole cinema was packed with courting couples, holding hands, rubbing knees, entwining feet, kissing in the back rows, and the area between herself and Raymond Banks in which they did not touch seemed to her to sparkle like electricity.

But he did not touch her.

After the film he once again offered her some coffee and once again she refused. It was one of those mild nights that come sometimes in November, with the stars clear beyond the pink glow thrown up to them from the city, and he suggested they walk as far as the next bus stop. He came punctiliously round to walk on the kerbside, and once they were clear of the crowded corner began to talk.

'I don't care much for those gangster films, not really. Everybody shooting and bashing each other up, it's not right. I mean, you can't wonder at all these Teddy boys when that's the sort of stuff they see on the screen every week. My uncle and auntie may have been strict but at least they brought me up to know right from wrong. But young people nowadays can't hardly be expected not to be wild. That man who took the main part tonight, for instance – apart from the character he was playing, everyone knows he's a pretty nasty type himself, drinks, drugs – there was a case about him I read in the paper not long ago. And there he is, held up for a hero. It's cockeyed, if you ask me. Don't you agree?'

'Well, I don't know. I mean, I don't think people take it so serious as you do.'

He grinned. 'Meaning I'm crackers.'

'No, of course not. But the people who go to the pictures, I think they just go in and sit there and come out again.'

'You may be right. I'm sure I hope so.' They walked in silence for a moment past the shop windows full of furniture. Then he began again abruptly, 'You'll think I'm soft saying this, but it's a real privilege for me to talk to someone as sensible and – well, thoughtful as you are. No, I mean it. The ordinary run of people you meet, they're all on the surface, all loud laughter and out for a good time. But you – well, you don't say a lot but when you do, it's worthy of respect. I run up against a lot of people in my job, all sorts, rich and poor, and believe me, it's one in a hundred you ever want to see for more than ten minutes. And the women's the worst.'

'Oh surely . . .'

'Yes, the women's the worst. All they think of is grab, grab, grab, even after they're married, a lot of them. You'd be surprised.'

She had always seen him easy and smiling, and his vehemence now gave her a little shock of astonishment and pleasure. It was right for a man to feel strongly about some things, it was manly; and he must, after all, see a lot of the world which she hardly knew existed.

'We'd better cross,' she said. 'The stop's just over there.'

'Why, yes.' He took her elbow as they crossed to the other pavement, and did not immediately let it go.

'I've really enjoyed this evening,' he said quietly. 'More even than last week really, because I was able to anticipate it, if you know what I mean. I hope very much you'll meet me the same next Thursday?'

They had reached the bus stop and were facing each other, alone by the post with its rigid flag of numbers.

'I don't know . . .'

'I'll be there anyway, and I'll hope that you'll come. I can't feel we're strangers, can you?'

She met the blueness of his eyes and shook her head. He smiled, looking very young.

'Here's your bus coming. I'd like to see you home, you know, but I don't think you want me to, do you?'

Again she shook her head. The bus drew up. 'Well – till Thursday then,' he said, raising his hand in salute. She got on the bus and found a seat. Next Thursday then . . . next Thursday . . .

When Esther left home for work each morning she always felt that Gran waited through an empty day for her return. That had always been Gran's implication.

Nothing could be less true. When the door shut behind Esther and her footsteps went up the area steps and out of hearing, Gran never failed to feel a surge of pleasure, a wildness that creased her old face and made her black eyes glitter like jet. She would settle down with the *Daily Mirror*, pour out another cup of stewed, sweet tea, run her hand sensuously into the warm mound of Monty's stomach, curled already in

Esther's chair under the tablecloth, and think to herself triumphantly, 'I'm on the loose.'

She did not do very much with her freedom; she was too cautious and too old. She never wanted to get drunk or go up west or spend all her old age pension on cigarettes. But she was free in her mind, gleefully full of revolt; and even with her body she could revolt a little too, by wasting time or smoking too much or not doing the simple household jobs which Esther thought she did. She was off the leash, out of the eye of those blooming old Wilsons and could blooming well do what she liked till six o'clock and Esther's footsteps and there she was again, a lonely old woman at the end of a lonely day, and Esther would get her supper.

Gran's days were crammed full with idleness. She had not a moment to do anything but waste time. She read every line of the newspaper, even the sports pages, for she relished boxing (with those blooming great lovely men), was excited by the rivalry of football teams, and often put a shilling secretly on a horse with the newspaper-seller at the corner of the road. Only cricket failed to interest her; it was too slow and the men didn't show themselves off. Politics she never read at all.

When she had finished the paper she would take a magazine from the lopsided pile by the television and re-read the recipes and Sister Jane's advice to mothers-to-be and anything else that caught her fancy and that she could not remember having read before. That passed a lot of time.

At last she would rise, take the cups and plates out to the scullery. The rest she would leave, for what was the point of clearing it all away and then having to put it all back again? She would rattle and slop round the scullery, singing sometimes popular songs of many periods, or sometimes groaning and condoling with herself if her varicose veins were bad. Then she would go upstairs to the bedroom.

She made the bed, because Grandad had disciplined her to do so years and years ago. She'd been a great one for staying in bed then, when they were first married, and he would bring her breakfast there, and get back in with her too, very often, and be late for work. Ah, those were the days! She remembered them in all their shining colours, the tickling, the squashed pillows, George's great chest all covered with hair, the sheer feckless fun of it. She could never forget it. That had been living. But after a while he'd got more businesslike, wouldn't get back again, wouldn't bring her even her tea, made her get up and get his breakfast, make the bed, look after the house, with larks and love-making put in their proper place, nighttimes and Sundays. But he'd been a man, just the same, with his hairy chest and his big determined hands . . .

If the day were nice she'd go out for a bit. She loved looking in the shops, the surge and smell of the traffic, the roadmenders leaning with sweaty biceps on the pneumatic drill, the prim policemen, the Teddy boys lounging on the chains that guarded the crossroads, the huge breasts on the cinema posters. If it was launderette day she could spend an hour or more there, in rich conversation. She didn't make friends with the old women. She liked the lively ones, the women of forty or fifty who were young enough still to have husband trouble but old enough to have queer symptoms of queer states of health. On frying days she bought fish and chips to take home for her dinner, and sat at the uncleared table with *Woman's Hour* on, eating out of the paper. Who cared? There was no one to see and tell her not to.

Oh, they were bliss, those hours without Esther, when she was the escaping one and Esther the prisoner of work. No question then of Esther neglecting her, gallivanting off on her own and shutting Gran out as she did on those blooming Thursdays. It was Gran who gallivanted now, sailing off on a dozen voyages of imagination or remembrance, scuffling through the ragbag of her life. After dinner she'd have a laydown, the memories crowding in behind her closed eyelids; or often she would not doze but would take on the bed with her the boot-box full of photographs and souvenirs. There was a lock of Winnie's hair, soft

43

and colourless like that of a mouse. There was a lock of Grandad's hair too, in a tight ring like wire. There was one of Esther's milk teeth with a big hole in it – shocking, at that age. And there were photographs – oh my, the photographs! Each one alone was good for an afternoon's daydreaming – of what she wore and what was said and who they were and how they had felt about her and she about them.

They were nearly all theatrical, for Gran had been on the halls. She had done a skirt dance and sung a patriotic song at police concerts when she was eleven. At fifteen she had been in the chorus of the Number Two touring company of *Fancy That!* At twenty she rated eight minutes third or fourth on the programme at any provincial or suburban music hall – Victoria Vale, the Saucy Songbird. And she was saucy; not broad like Marie Lloyd (God rest her) nor suggestive like some of them now, but really saucy, flirting up her ruffled skirts, pirouetting in her calf-high buttoned boots, giving the eye to the front row stalls, a tiny, pert dynamo of a girl with her bust pushed up like two warm marshmallows and a pile of crisp black hair.

What had she been thinking of, what had possessed her, to give it all up for George Wilson? The answer, as she knew very well as she sat on the untidy bed with the litter of photographs all round her, a shrunken, ugly old woman with dyed hair, was that

George Wilson had possessed her. She could have had anybody – indeed, she had had a good many, for she had always believed that a little of what you fancy does you good. But of George Wilson there had not been a little but a lot – a blooming too much lot as it turned out, making her leave the stage, making her cook and keep accounts and make the beds, keeping her in order and letting her have only the kind of fun he thought was good for her. Yet, though she had grumbled, she had never rebelled. He had been a man, no doubt about that; no matter how it had irked her, she had never disputed that he was master. Even today the memory of him when they were young could smooth the wrinkles from her rouged old cheeks and soften into youth the bent and veined old body.

Still, she must have been mad just the same to give it all up and never dare to go back. Some of the girls she'd been on tour with had been given fur coats and silk stockings and cosy little flats in Maida Vale; true, most of them drank it away or gave it away, and now perhaps had to go charring to keep themselves alive. She didn't know, she had lost touch; Grandad had made her lose touch. And the men – lovely silky moustaches that tickled and tight-fitting jackets that showed off their waists! Not like this lot now, with their shoulders all padding and their legs like matchsticks in those soppy tight trousers.

Sometimes, if Gran were feeling bored and the past seemed too stale to nourish her for the rest of the afternoon, she would wait about for Gloria Mason on her way back from the clinic or the pictures or a ramble round Woolworth's. Gran despised Gloria, with her cross little painted face and her yellow poodle cut, but she enjoyed Gloria's symptoms and frightening her with old wives' tales of fatal labours and unnatural births. Whatever the clinic said about anything, Gran had her doubts. Gloria was so depressed by her heartburn and the loss of her figure that she would believe anything, and later on she would pour it all out to Terry. He was too soft to know what to answer; a proper mother's boy he was, in his draped jacket and drainpipe trousers; although when he wore his jeans and lumber-jacket for work you could see he was a man after all.

Gran had long ago given up hope of Esther's ever getting a man. Old Sally Sobersides, Esther was; perhaps she might get herself hitched to a widower or someone like that when she was forty or so; but what was the good of that if your cake hadn't been cut twenty years earlier? No, Esther was hopeless. Never made anything of herself, hardly wore make-up, never a touch of colour somewhere or her hair done to make the best of herself or a nice tight-fitting jumper to show off her bust. Men would never give Esther a glance; it was always the quiet, good ones that got left on the shelf. Look at that Gloria now – no more fit to be married than a she-cat, yet she'd got Terry all right, never mind how. Esther'd never do that. And although Gran despised her for all the things she was not, and was often resentful of all the things that she was, she loved Esther with the grudging, trustful love of the weak for the strong, the feckless for the prudent, surrendering herself completely into Esther's keeping as she had into Grandad's.

The Friday before Christmas week she heard Esther say, 'We'll be having a visitor for Christmas dinner, Gran.'

'What's that? Who?'

'One more won't make any difference, it's as easy cooking for three as two.' She was sitting by the table, putting on her fur boots before going off to work, for it was sleety and dark this morning. To Gran she appeared as composed as usual, a slight flush accounted for by bending down to the boots.

'We'll need to get a bigger bird, then, there's not much on a goose. Who is it, eh? Not that blooming old Miss Burroughs from business, I won't have her, all sighs and la-di-da. I'll never forget the time we had her, not in a month of Sundays.'

'Not, it's not her. It's someone I met.'

'Met? For goodness' sake, where?'

'Well, it was rather funny really. I mean, it's some time ago now.'

'Some time ago and you never told me? Well, you are a mean cat, Esther Wilson! God knows nothing much ever happens round here to be keeping things from me in that nasty underhand way.'

Esther fastened the boots and stood up, turning away from Gran's reproachful scrutiny. 'There's not much to tell. I mean, it was all so casual really. It was just we got talking a couple of times and then, well, we started meeting and now I'm telling you.' She put on her overcoat and buttoned it, still not looking at Gran.

'High time too, if you ask me. Where'd you get talking?'

'In the teashop, one Thursday.'

'Thursday!' Gran gave a grunt, and noisily finished her cup of tea. 'Well, what's she coming here for? Hasn't she got no family?'

'No. He lives in lodgings.'

'He?' Gran shrieked, setting down the cup with a bang. 'You mean it's a man?'

'Yes.' Esther tied a scarf under her chin and spoke rather quickly now. 'His name's Raymond Banks and he works for some big firm in the City that sells novelties. He's away a good deal and lives in lodgings when he's in London, and he's all on his own this Christmas, so I thought as there'd be plenty it'd be nice to ask him here, being Christmas and all alone.'

'Well, of all the blooming, sly, underhand . . .! You mean you picked up a man in a teashop?'

'Oh Gran, it wasn't like that at all!' Esther pulled on her gloves, speaking impatiently to cover her embarrassment. 'He's ever such a nice young man . . .'

'Young!'

'Well, he's thirty – and ever such nice manners and he's an orphan and all alone with no home, and I'm sorry, but he's coming to Christmas dinner.'

'My granddaughter picked up by a young man in a teashop! Months ago, and not a word said!'

'It wasn't months ago, it was the beginning of November.'

'Months ago and not a word said and he's coming to Christmas dinner! What's his name?'

'Raymond Banks.'

'And what's his job?'

'I told you – he travels for a firm. Look, I can't stop now, I'll be late. You'll like him, Gran, he's ever such a gentleman and he talks a lot, he's full of jokes. He's got ever such blue eyes.' She came round and kissed Gran's forehead. 'Bye-bye for now and I won't be home late.'

'Blue eyes!'

'Yes. Keep a good fire in the stove, it's cold today.'

She had gone.

Into the hurly-burly of Christmas Esther's news cast the last mad note. Gran adored Christmas; to her it was not Jesus but Dionysus who ruled the festival, for even the

Child Himself became to her a sensual enjoyment, a dear little baby with the animals all standing round; and behind them, row upon row of turkeys, geese, ducks; port wine, Christmas pudding with brandy sauce, stars, tinsel, glossy holly, milky mistletoe berries squashing between your fingers, coloured wrapping papers, a littered satiety of greed stung with the scent of tangerines. Into this orgasm of indulgence Esther had now dropped a man. What kind of man it did not matter, he varied according to Gran's mood. Lewis Waller sometimes, sometimes Valentino, sometimes someone long and lean in tight blue jeans with shoulders on him like Burt Lancaster. Whatever kind he was, he was a man, to carve the bird, make up the stove, kiss under the mistletoe with port tasting on the lips, bristly, full of jokes, the final, longed-for savour to the feast of Christmas.

She went about the blowy streets in a gleeful dream; and Esther too, behind her quiet façade, was in a dream, of panic and longing and astonishment. What had she done? Little by little, Thursday by Thursday, her life had opened to Raymond Banks. Now she was proposing to yield up to him Gran and her home. What would he think of them – he who was used to hotels and cars and business talk, whose uncle had been a parson? What would he think of Gran?

Decisively her fingers ran over the plump keys of the adding-machine each day in the office. Their muted chunk-chunk-chunk was comforting and familiar. She knew utterly what she was doing with them, just as she knew utterly every piece of furniture in this varnished cubby-hole high above London where she had worked for fifteen years; the old-fashioned desks upon which the sleek metal machines sat incongruously had been here longer than she had. The linoleum, which was beginning to wear under the metal feet of the chairs, had been part of a lot that had not sold well, a hot red divided by turquoise lines. She knew every bulge and gesture of Miss Burroughs' stout body, the brown cardigan, the brown skirt, the beige blouse fastened at the neck by a brooch containing a lock of her mother's hair, her National Health spectacles, her shiny, pallid face. Jacqueline she knew too, although not so well, for Jacqueline did not talk to her as Miss Burroughs did. Jacqueline was a sparrow dyed like a canary, forever hopping, chirping, sharpening her beak, dropping feathers, staring knowingly in little mirrors. As she did the filing she shook her hips, shuffled her feet in rudimentary jive, as she typed she let out little yowls of song, the bracelets on her spillikin wrists rattling. Her two little breasts stuck out beneath the shocking pink or turquoise or emerald sweaters she wore, like two little jam tarts. Her small, not awfully clean ears supported chandeliers of gilt and silver beads. She was without a care in the world.

Beyond the three of them in their familiar office was the rest of Winters' which Esther also knew. The typists' room, the stock-keeping room, the four directors' offices with their sudden carpet and curtains; the showrooms of waiting furniture, quiescent carpets, china, glass, smooth wood, the festooned jungle of soft furnishings, uncompromising hardware, the frigid stalagmites of linoleum. She knew them all, the back stairs, the lifts, the floor managers in their little cubby-holes, concealed like spiders behind their outspread wares, the packing-room, hairy with string, smelling of glue, the garage and the grey vans with WINTERS' LONDON in white scroll along the sides. She knew everyone who worked there, from Mr Winter himself, his son, his son-in-law, down through old Mr Oliver with his deaf aid, forty-four years in Soft Furnishing, to the drivers and the cleaners. And they all knew her, Miss Wilson of Invoices, quiet, dependable, pleasant. Only she now did not know herself.

She moved through the chaos of Christmas week. The streets were full of people, pushing, crackling with parcels. The shops stood open every evening until seven o'clock, their windows glittering like Christmas cards. Ceaselessly the doors swung to and fro, the cashiers stamped, tore, gave change, the lifts hummed up and down, the sales staff scurried. There was overtime and a bonus too, as well as tired feet and tempers.

No one was quite themselves round about Christmas, Esther told herself. You did funny things, things you wouldn't do at any other time. You were open, generous with a great mad openness reaching right round the world. It was all a racket, people said, whipped up by the shopkeepers; but behind the racket was a great mass faith in the possibility of hope – the ultimate hope, stretching out for ever and ever.

So she, like everyone, was a little mad, and at lunch-times ran out into the street, pushed in and out of other shops' swing doors, crashed parcels, schemed. She had not many presents to buy: Gran, Miss Burroughs, Jacqueline, Gloria Mason now she was pregnant, Cousin Em in Bangor, old Mrs Bromwich because she was so old, a ribbon for Monty. Raymond?

Yes. It was Christmas. Should it be gloves or a scarf? Not since Grandad died had she wandered between the counters of the Men's Departments. A scarf or gloves? His hands were small and square, practical, well kept. They were always warm – she knew because they shook hands now when they parted. He wore woollen gloves, which wear out. One day she would knit him some, but now she must buy. Or a scarf? He seemed to have only one, wine-coloured, creased in its fold. Blue would suit him better, a nice warm woollen one tucked round his neck. Or a tie? But people made jokes of ties chosen by women. She did not know him well enough for a tie, or what sort of ties men liked. She knew nothing, nothing . . .

But the house she knew and she concentrated on that. Swept, scrubbed, purified, it stood like an offering to the gods awaiting its garlands. Through the raucous streets of Camden Town she and Gran went for holly and mistletoe. Vociferous youths in duffle coats and pancake caps offered them fir trees trussed up like chickens. Spruce lay trampled in the gutters; barrow-boys combed their oiled hair above the blanched bosoms of turkeys, crying, 'Young turkeys from Norfolk – four and six a pound – lovely young Norfolk turkeys!' The blowy moist December dark was shattered by a hundred brilliants: silver paper and oranges, heaped nuts and the tight green nuts of Brussels sprouts built up into ramparts, sheaves of gilded teazles, crimson bullrushes, paper roses and carnations, tinsel leaves, chrysanthemums like balls of cool wool, with the golden buses rushing by and the shops lit up and opened wide to the pavements.

For it was Christmas Eve at last, the office presents given and received, the machines covered, the big building abandoned to the silence of two holy days. Now only the domestic pagan rites of evergreen and food remained to be seen to.

They bought a tree and carried it home. Usually they had only a small one but this year it was bigger.

Gently Esther cut its cords; the dark smell of forest came out of its branches as she stretched them carefully, like limbs stiffened by cramp; smoothing and soothing it, she cooled its stump, lopped like the bound foot of a Chinese woman, in earth from the backyard, decked it in jewels of tinsel and glass.

Then together she and Gran dressed the room, dripping the coloured concertina paperchains along the walls, setting out their few Christmas cards (beginning to curl already) on the mantelpiece, pricking themselves with holly. Monty came out from beneath the tablecloth to sniff and sneer and then settle on the spray of silver leaves laid for a moment on the sideboard. Gran, cigarette smoke in her eyes, her earrings sparkling, sat down to polish the best forks and spoons. As she polished she sang, thinking greedily of tomorrow, Christmas and a man. She could hear Esther moving about in the scullery, preparing supper; only baked beans and a cup of tea tonight, saving up appetite for tomorrow; then a quiet sit-down with the telly to wait for tomorrow, the goose in its tin waiting, the vegetables prepared in the saucepan waiting, the presents in their paper waiting, Gran and Esther in the garlanded room waiting.

At half past eleven St Peter's Church bell tolled softly, briefly, for the midnight service. They put on their coats, tied scarves under their chins and went out.

The wide street was empty, stretched open to the downy sky. They walked without speaking, for now Grandad was with them. The church was cold, the people filing into it with a kind of furtive jubilation, as though they met clandestinely and might be persecuted. On the altar the candles burned yellow as haloes.

They kneeled, stood, sang, kneeled again, the church rustling and coughing hollowly about them. They stepped out into the aisle and moved slowly up towards the bread and wine. Gran blew her nose, a tear hanging in either eye like the glass at her ears. She did not know if she had ever been christened, knew she had never been confirmed (what, on tour with *Fancy That!?*) but Grandad had liked her to do it, and she liked it too. Only tonight, at Christmas, not any other time. It brought her nearer to the dear little Baby lying there with the animals, nearer to the Man who had been strong and had been killed and who waited up there in heaven for her, nearer to the living, to youth, to life everlasting.

She knelt and took the Sacrament greedily, her eyes shut and the tears sparkling down her rouged old cheeks. Beside her Esther knelt, and in the great silence of Communion it was as though she stood outside a closed door and did not know who waited on the other side, listening as she listened, echoing her prayer: God, fill me.

TWO

THEY AWOKE SLOWLY, the huge vacuum of Boxing Day arched about them. In the streets, silence. In the houses all along the road, all over London, all over England, only silence. Shops, churches, factories, houses, all silent, sunk in the torpor of repletion. Only cats went about their customary business, treading softly, sitting with twitching tails; and in bedrooms children played quietly with new toys.

The day lay motionless. In the plain bedstead that had been hers from childhood Esther lay motionless also, listening to the silent street beyond the curtains. Nine o'clock struck from the church spire and she thought, I should get up. But she lay there still, curled up and warm, bereft of all energy by yesterday.

He had come. When she thought of him now it could be against the background of her own home. He had sat in the chair which had been Grandad's chair; he had carried the scuttle in from the coal cellar and made up the stove meticulously, as a bricklayer lays bricks. His coat and scarf had hung on the rack in the passage, folded against Gran's and her own. Monty had stared at him with cold eyes but stretched out his chin to Raymond's finger after a moment.

Raymond now was in the sitting-room, scullery, passages; from up here she had heard his voice, joking with Gran, when she came to tidy herself and stare desperately at her pale reflection – pale and plain and dull, yet at that moment flushed a little, with brighter eyes, younger than even a day ago. On her dressing-table lay in tissue paper the gloves he had given her, brown suede with a woollen lining. He had brought a box of chocolates for Gran. Her food had filled him, the warmth of her own home had comforted him. Together they had listened to the Queen, the cool voice addressing them both at Esther's fireside.

She lay without moving, hearing the quarter hours chime in the great space of Boxing Day. He was neat in everything, the way he made up the stove, the way he carved the bird. His hair sprang from a widow's peak into a wave, but on either side it was receding; when he was older he would go bald. His eyes were blue as the sky; she had never seen such blue eyes, forget-me-not blue, butcher's blue. He had talked and joked, kept Gran laughing, kissed Gran under the mistletoe. Gran had shrieked, the shrill sexual shriek of women on witchbacks or at music halls. He had hugged his arm round her shoulders and called her 'my new best girl' and Gran had shrieked again, the rouge, the eyes, the jetty hair all glowing. He had not kissed Esther.

He had held her hand in both his as they stood in the area doorway when it was time for him to leave. Above them the street was deserted, but from behind walls everywhere came the pulse of laughter and voices, family parties, games, dance music. He was a black shape against the whitewashed area walls and she in the shelter of the doorway was a paleness only. He held her hand in both his, her scarf folded about his neck, and he said, 'This has been like home to me today. You'll never know what that means. Thank you, Esther.' He had pressed her hand between his, looked at her long in the darkness, a dark look that she could not see but only felt, and gone away up the steps. She had stood listening to his footfalls fading briskly down the street till he was quite out of sound, quite gone. But he could never be gone now, even if she never saw him again, for she could picture him everywhere. The gloves he gave her lay on the dressing-table, his scarf would be hanging now with his coat in his characterless lodging, his look and his hands were felt still and always would be.

'Ow, he's a lovely chap!' Gran had cried when Esther came slowly back into the room. 'My, I don't know when I've enjoyed meself so much. Saucy and carrying on, yet always the gentleman with it! My word, girl, you were in luck when you picked him up!' And she had waltzed round the table, holding out her skirt in either hand, warbling 'The Blue Danube', light-footed and just a little drunk, to finish with her arms flung round Esther and a kiss on her cheek. 'It's been a lovely Christmas,' she said. 'You're ever so good to me, Etty, honest you are,' and laughing together, a little near tears, in a companionship they seldom felt, they had straightened the room, made up the stove, let Monty out, and gone to their beds.

Now in the huge silence of Boxing Day they were quiet. Gran did not really feel very well and stayed in bed for a bit, huddled up with a shawl round her shoulders and her eyes closed against the light. Esther moved about downstairs, humming softly, cleaning up and tidying away the excesses of yesterday, picturing Raymond everywhere she looked. On the top floor was absolute silence, for the Masons spent the holiday with Terry's mother.

Even when Gran came downstairs they did not talk much. They picked over the carcass of the goose (there was not much left because of Raymond, Esther thought contentedly), had a slice of Christmas cake and a cup of tea, sitting before the television. It was an overcast day and darkness came early. They sat dozily with the inexhaustible screen in front of them, and Gran nodded off and Esther dreamed as dusk filled up the room. From the street there was not quite such absolute silence now. Footsteps went by and an occasional car. The stupor of the day began to lessen, and as Esther roused herself and went to put the kettle on she felt a faint impatience with the vacant hours, a willingness to be back at work tomorrow after all. Then soon it would be Thursday again. Or, now that he had visited them, would they meet more often? Would he – did he mean . . .? Her heart felt weak, and she cut some bread and butter briskly. He was just glad to know a home, a family, that was all; glad to be taken care of. She would wish for nothing more than that, not at her age, the sort of girl she was.

They were sitting over their tea when she heard his step quite distant up the street. Why should it be his? It was anyone's. It was his. She listened, alert and disbelieving, and the footfalls stopped at the gate and came briskly down the steps. On the other side of the drawn curtain he beat a tattoo on the glass, then rang the bell. The two women stared at each other, and Esther flushed a hot uncomfortable flood over her face and neck. Seeing it, Gran said, 'My Gawd, it's him!' Esther stood up but Gran was quicker, nipping out of her chair and round the table. 'I'll open the door – you see to your face,' she hissed, and vanished. Helplessly Esther peered in the mirror over the mantelpiece, smoothed her hair and bit her lips to bring some colour in, hearing Gran outside in the passage greeting him with astonishment, and his voice saying, 'Excuse me for troubling you, Mrs Wilson, but I wondered if you two ladies would care to come to the panto this evening?'

'The panto!' gasped Gran. 'Oh my word – I'm sure I never – Etty!' she shrieked, and bounced back into the room. Raymond was behind her, smiling over her head to where Esther stood. 'D'you hear, Etty? He wants us to come to the panto! Oh my, you've took me breath away! Cool as you like – out of the blue – what will he be up to next!'

'I hope it's not too sudden for you,' he said to Esther. 'I got the idea yesterday, but I couldn't say anything till I knew I could get the seats. It's at Golders Green.'

Gran shrieked again. 'Ow, you're a deep one, Mr Banks! A real deep one! Sitting there last night and not letting on what you was up to!'

He turned his eyes away from Esther and grinned at Gran. 'How was I to know my new best girl would be the sort that likes a panto?' he asked teasingly. 'I couldn't tell till I saw you, could I? You might have been some sour old pussy with one foot in the Salvation Army and the other in the grave, eh?' He looked back at Esther. 'I hope you don't mind? You've nothing else to do?'

'No.' She had a semblance of composure now, the colour faded, her voice calm. 'No, we were just quiet. It's very kind of you.'

'It's kind of *you*.' There was an instant's pause while they looked at each other across the lit expanse of table. Then Esther moved, came forward.

'Would you like a cup of tea?'

'I wouldn't say no.'

'I'll see to it.' Gran darted round the table again. 'You go and get yourself dressed up, go along now.' She gave Esther a look of complicity and glee. 'Go on, don't stand there, I'll see to Mr Banks. It'll be a bit stewed by now. Shall I make you some fresh?'

'No, no, that'll be fine. I don't want to put you out.' As Esther left the room and went upstairs she could hear them talking, he with a mixture of banter and respect, Gran with the artlessness of a child at a party, both perfectly at home together in her home.

He sat between them in the theatre and the golden occasion buffeted them all. They were cells in the great quaking belly of the play, identities lost in the laughter

and warmth, stuffed with chocolates, singing the cho-
ruses, wiping their eyes, letting the laughter wash out
of their open mouths in a flood that washed thought
with it. In the interval they scooped ice-cream from
cartons, watching the advertisements of local shops
reflected moonlike on the asbestos curtain, scruti-
nised the programme page by page, till the orchestra
climbed back again over their instruments in the well
and the lights blossomed again at the curtain's hem.

Afterwards, still smiling, the tunes still jingling in
their heads, the jokes on their lips, still warm, they
pushed and swayed their way home under the ground,
one with all the others in that climax and catharsis,
still merged in the giant pagan body of Boxing Night.
Only when they came up into the street again, into the
cold air, did unity fall away, their footsteps ring sharply
separate. The wind crept in between neck and collar
and Gran shivered. A hand on the elbow of each, he
drew them a little closer to him.

'It's turned cold,' he said, 'snow in the air. It's times
like this I wish I still had a car.'

'Did you have a car?' asked Gran admiringly.

'You bet. That's how me and Esther first met, wasn't
it?' He pressed her elbow slightly, she could hear the
smile in his voice, and she nodded. 'Put in an advert,
to sell it, didn't I, and then asked for the loan of her
paper to check it was in all right. That's how we met.'

'Fancy,' said Gran in a refined voice. 'I've never liked to inquire.'

'Proper pick-up I suppose you'd call it.' Raymond continued, 'only no one could ever see it like that with a girl like Esther. Still, I wish I had the old car now.'

Esther said, 'Won't your firm stand you one?'

'No. They'd help me run it but they won't fork out the ready to buy it. You know how mean these firms can be. The directors can have a Rolls-Royce each, run it on the expense account, old boy – you know the form. But staff – that's a different proposition altogether. It'd save them money too if I had one – time, too. No hanging about stations, nip here, nip there . . .'

'A pity you give it up,' said Gran.

'Too right it was. But I needed the cash. Nothing naughty – I know what you're thinking.' He gave Gran's arm a little shake and she giggled. 'I wanted to help out my auntie, as a matter of fact. She'd got a bit pressed.'

'Is your auntie still alive?' Esther said in surprise.

'Oh yes, grand old girl. I don't see her much, but I keep an eye on her from afar. When I had the car I used to run up to see her every month or so. Lovely run it is too. I'd have liked you two ladies to come with me to meet her when the weather gets nicer, if I still had the car.'

Gran sighed. 'Ow, I love a nice drive in the country when the weather's nice. Freshens you up.'

'You're fresh enough already,' he teased. 'Ah well, it's no use moaning. I haven't the cash to lay out and that's that.'

'You'd think your firm would help you,' said Esther.

'You would, wouldn't you? They'd practically run it, you see – license it and all that and petrol, if I could get hold of a car in the first place. I know where I could, too, friend of mine works in a garage, often hears of a bargain. Once I'd got the car it wouldn't hardly cost any more . . .'

'It does seem a shame,' sighed Gran.

'Course, I was a fool to let it go.' He turned them deftly into their street, the wind no longer in their faces. 'But there, what can you do? Auntie hasn't anyone else to turn to, and frankly I never thought the firm would be so stingy. Seeing as they'd been glad enough to have the use of my car, I thought they'd divvy up. But oh no, they said, we can't be expected to hand out three or four hundred pounds in a lump, they said, it'd never get past the auditors.'

'Three or four hundred!' said Gran, awed.

'Well, that's what it would cost to *them*. I could get one through this chap I was telling you about for two fifty. Matter of fact, he's got one in now, proper bargain, lovely condition, one owner, a Ford Prefect. Mind you, I'd prefer something with a bit more dash, a drop-head coupé, MG, something like that. But if

I'm having a car for ladies to ride in, then I know they don't want their hair-dos blown all over the place, eh?' He squeezed Gran's arm and she giggled again. 'Oh well, it's no use talking. I haven't got two fifty now, so that's that.'

Gran glanced across him at Esther, but said nothing. Esther said nothing either. Indeed, she had hardly listened to what he was saying, only to his voice, soft and good-humoured, flowing on in the cold lamplit air; she was conscious only of his warm body, neat in its raincoat with her scarf neat at his neck, and his warm hand on her elbow, their steps matching along the pavement.

'Well, here we are, ladies – the end of a perfect day. At least, it has been for me.'

While Gran was voluble in thanks Esther stood silent. The darkness lying like a slack rope between the lampposts, the wind that gusted over the rooftops but left them in the street undisturbed, the rattle of Gran's voice needing no answer, all spread slowly out and encompassed Raymond in Esther's silence, as though she and her silence subdued the street, banished the wind, enfolded him in her unspeaking warmth. Across the sparkle of Gran's face he saw Esther suddenly, shadowed, a wisp of hair blowing over her cheek, in her plain brown coat, her new gloves on her hands, standing silent, waiting. Her look, full of words, pierced the armour of his thick blue eyes and he too was silent. Disarmed, for a moment he truly saw her.

Gran cried, shaking Esther's arm, 'Aren't you going to offer him a cup of tea?'

'I must be off,' he said. Words came back to him, jokes, smiles, weapons. He talked about beauty sleep, said something about midnight striking and glass slippers, put his arm round Gran and gave her a squeeze, shook Esther's hand.

She said, 'It's been a lovely Christmas.'

For a moment her hand lay in his; then he answered only, 'See you Thursday.' They heard his footsteps ring away on the pavement as they went slowly down the area steps.

January was cold that year. Snow blown by the east wind lay feathery on the tufted heights of Hampstead, where children, shrill and rosy, dragged out their sledges to bump over the rough grass. Skiers stood poised like penguins before the uncertain slopes and the snarl of skates sounded above the traffic past the pond. In London slush lay in brown furrows, spattering the legs, the wind blew unwaveringly from the east under an enclosing sky. Water-pipes froze and it did not seem possible that houses could ever be warm again.

It was cold in Esther's office at the top of Winters' building in spite of the heating. Miss Burroughs had chilblains and Jacqueline came to work bundled in massive sweaters, like an egg in a cosy. It was lovely to Esther to hurry from the cold office, down the raw-aired street, to the steamy rendezvous of the teashop, to clasp Raymond's warm hand, see his warm smile, settle herself in the warm room with its tinkling crockery and music, feel the warm food thaw and nourish her, as being with him thawed and nourished. On Thursdays this was still their rule: high tea and a cinema. But increasingly he dropped into the habit of coming out to Handel Street for Saturday tea and supper. He did not simply take or accept; he brought very often a cake or a pork pie or a bag of special fruit, a bunch of flowers or a magazine for Gran. He carried in the coal, mended fuses, put up a shelf over the sink, re-stained the front room floor; and while Esther was busy in the scullery or about the house, for she would let him do only what she considered properly men's jobs, he sat with Gran by the stove, listening to the remembered glees of her life. The facts dropping out like pebbles from the gold dust of her fantasies, she revealed herself and Grandad and Esther and Winifred, until there was little he did not know about the Wilsons and nothing at all about Gran.

Talking to Raymond had every advantage, as far as Gran was concerned. He was a man yet not so masculine that she could not forget it; not a jeans-and-muscle man before whom she would still, instinctively, be compelled to trail her draggled old coquetries. He was like a son or a nephew, saucy yet comfortable, and she gathered in the hours he spent in Handel Street greedily, not grudging him to Esther, for it was Esther who brought him there. Esther, who never before had caught a man, had nevertheless brought this lovely one into Gran's life and was content to let Gran have a share in him. For Esther it was enough that he was there, at home in her home. Beyond that she dared not think, with that she told herself she would be satisfied.

But Gran was not. Gran schemed and plotted through the cold dark days how to keep Raymond there forever. In the old days she knew how she would have done it – although perhaps not with Raymond, he was not what she called a passionate man; but now she must use the means nearest to her hand, and that was Esther. Trotting back from Woolworth's on a day when the ice had melted a little and she need not fear a fall, she brought Esther a lipstick and a clever one, too, not one of the bright ones she herself fancied but a gentle pink that brought colour to the whole pale face. She rummaged through the mess of powdery debris in her dressing-table drawer and found eyebrow tweezers, and with Esther laughing, refusing, made her sit down under the lamp and trimmed her eyebrows for her, leaving them thick and arched to enhance the eyes in which, half tenderly, half maliciously, Gran saw now hope and fear. She nagged Esther into doing her hair a different way, not smoothed back with combs to a roll at the neck but parted and waved a little, and had her triumph when Raymond said, 'Your hair looks nice, Esther.' With Esther's behaviour she could do nothing. She knew that, like Grandad, Esther was unalterable; and besides, she was wise enough to see that Raymond must like the way she was or he would not be here. So in all the talks she and Raymond had beside the stove she stressed the things she knew to be Esther's virtues, though half of them she despised; and praised with cunning artlessness her domesticity, her cooking, her steadfastness, her prudence. 'Me? Give it away with both hands, I would,' she said, her eyes and her earrings glinting, 'and my daughter Winnie just like me. Ran through our fingers, money did, used to make Grandad wild. That's why he left it all to Esther. Wouldn't trust me with it, he wouldn't, and I can't say I blame him, though naturally I was ever so upset at the time. Even the house is in her name, and the shop and the bit in the bank – shocking some people thought it, but I always said he knew what he was doing. Esther's a good girl, a wonderful manager, and she'd never let her granny want for anything. She's like me there, generous to a fault, and Winnie was too, poor girl, only Esther's got sense with it too, which is more than what I ever had.'

Raymond never spoke of getting a car again, except once soon after Christmas, to Gran alone. It was when the first snow was falling and the newspapers reported iced-up roads and isolated villages. 'Something to be said for not having a car,' he said and laughed. 'Give me the dear old British Railways this weather. Although now's the time to buy,' and he looked thoughtful.

'Why?' asked Gran.

'Because no one wants 'em, that's why. Come springtime and everyone's buying, but now, with all this coming down, no one gives it a thought. Same as buying a mink coat in the summer – remember?' he winked.

Gran nodded. 'Ow, I see – it'd be a good bargain now.'

'That's right. I could do it, too, if I could only raise a hundred or so. I've been saving like a good boy lately and my auntie's paid me back half what I loaned her, as a kind of New Year surprise, bless her, so I'm only short of about half what it'd cost me.'

'What a shame!' sighed Gran.

'Oh well, it's no use moaning. It can't be done now and that's that.'

He never said anything more, not ever. But Gran did, to Esther, and ended with, 'Why couldn't you lend it him, Etty?'

Esther was washing up at the sink and all Gran

could see of her was her back and head bent over the basin. Watching her warily, for she never dared talk of money to Esther, Gran saw her stand quite still and the blood sweep up her neck like a sunrise. For a moment Gran was terrified at what she had done; then Esther said in a choked voice, 'I couldn't possibly!'

Gran gained confidence. She saw that she had struck Esther and Esther would not strike her. 'Why not, Etty? I mean, you could spare it. It isn't as if it was just being paid out. You'd get it back.'

Esther began to wash the crockery again. Her voice was lower still. 'I couldn't possibly.'

'It does seem a shame, with him having half the money already and his friend at the garridge with a bargain. It's only a hundred.'

'No.'

'I never thought you was mean, Etty.'

Esther swung round and Gran flinched. The blood was still bright under Esther's skin and her eyes were passionate. 'He'd be insulted!' she cried.

'I don't see why . . .'

'If you can't see, then I can't show you. I just know. He'd feel humiliated.'

'I only thought . . .'

'Be quiet, Gran. I've said no, and there's an end.' She turned back to the sink and slowly the red left even her neck, bent under the brown hair.

It was a few weeks after this that Gran, hunched in front of television one Thursday evening, was startled out of her doze early in the evening by voices and footsteps down the area steps. She whisked her dirty cup and saucer out of sight under the table and was presentable by the time they opened the door. Through the glare of the central lamp she could not see them clearly as they stood smiling, almost giggling, in the doorway, yet she sensed about them a tension palpable as heat.

'My word, you give me a start!' she said, twisting round in the chair and peering across at them. 'You're early, aren't you?'

'Yes, we're early,' Esther said, looked at Raymond and giggled. He looked at her and giggled too, echoing, 'We are early.' He gave Esther a gentle push and she came into the room and round the table. Raymond followed, taking off his gloves. Gran saw that Esther was flushed and her eyes brilliant. Her heart began to thump like an old engine as, looking from one to the other, she waited for them to say more.

'We didn't go to the pictures, Gran,' said Esther and looked at Raymond.

'No, we didn't,' he said, looking at Esther. 'We didn't, did we?'

'No.' She turned her gaze away from him. 'Gran, Raymond and me . . .' She faltered and looked at him again.

He stepped forward, put an arm round her, and said in a firm voice, 'Gran, Esther and me's going to get married.'

'No,' whispered Gran. 'No!' Weak with joy, gratitude, relief, she shut her eyes and pressed her clasped hands against the thudding inside her chest. It beat so hard it was as if it would carry her away. 'Etty,' she whispered, 'Etty, my little sweetheart. Granny's little pet.'

'Oh Gran!' Esther left Raymond's clasp and knelt by the chair, putting her arms round her. Holding her, being held by her, Gran felt Esther's cheek against her own, felt the child and the woman yielded to her, felt herself possessed. The tears ran down between the smooth cheek and the wrinkled one, tears for mating and old age and Grandad. By their tears, wordless, the two women merged for a single moment of time and were one woman.

'Here, here, I say! All this carry-on at the thought of me for a grandson!'

They roused, separated, looked up at him smiling despite their wet eyes.

'I must say I never saw two such miserable women receiving the happy news,' he continued. 'Boo hoo hoo – I'd better be off!'

'Oh Raymond!' said Esther, laughing, and stretched out her hand. He took it and she stood up with him, pulling Gran gently after her. 'Say you're pleased, Gran.'

'Pleased! It's like a dream come true. You and Raymond . . .' You and anyone, she might have said, but best of all, since it was Etty and not herself, Etty and Raymond . . . She put her hands on his shoulders and kissed him. Her tears were drying and her voice was stronger. 'My Ray, my grandson! I can't hardly believe it.'

'That's better. That's my girl.' He put his arm round her so that he held a woman on either side. 'My goodness, I got me a proper pair of tragedy queens here. Water water everywhere and not a drop to drink . . .'

'Drink!' cried Gran. 'That's the ticket! Where's that bottle of port left over from Christmas?' She broke away from him towards the sideboard, but he drew her back.

'Here, here, don't you want to see what I gave her? Show her, Ett.' Esther held out her left hand which he took and held steady so that Gran could see the ring. It was a turquoise set in a circle of tiny brilliants, like a blue-hearted daisy. 'See, that makes it official. She can't go back on it now, can she?'

They looked at each other fondly while Gran looked at the ring. She was disappointed that it was not a diamond, something with a good sparkle to it; nevertheless, a ring was a ring. 'It's ever so unusual,' she said. 'I never seen one like that before.'

'It's old,' he said. 'I won't pretend I went out and bought it. Etty knows.'

'It was his mother's,' said Esther quietly.

'Yes.' He stood looking down at it and at the hand it lay on, resting in his.

'Well, I call that lovely,' said Gran enthusiastically. 'And the stone in the centre's just the colour of your eyes.'

'And the sparklers round it are like yours,' he replied. 'Come on now, where's that port you were talking about? I've got something to celebrate this evening, however you two girls may cry and carry on.'

They filled the glasses and standing round the table, the television screen gibbering unnoticed by the hearth, they drank.

'To my Etty and her husband-to-be,' said Gran and tossed down the wine as though it were champagne from a slipper.

'To the future Mrs Banks,' said Raymond.

The cold continued; yet for Esther the sun had risen, the world softened, widened, ripened. The wind did not scour her, the sky did not enclose her as if it were a trap, and what had been her narrow trodden path between Handel Street and Winters' became a sunlit highway full of people. She looked in her mirror and saw, not the pale reserved face she had known for thirty years, but a face that Raymond had found pleasing, still pale but now alive, the lips not closed but curving, the eyes no longer dull but really seeing. She saw the movements of her arms as she combed her hair, her body as she clothed it, and she saw the bodies of other people, young people, men and women side by side, everywhere, pairs, and she saw the bodies of children. There had been people all round her before, but she had not looked, for they had either been alone, like herself, or paired as she was not and against whom she had protected herself. She had not noticed children, for she knew none; now she saw they were little animals that would grow into men and women, she saw the characters shrill and raw in their bodies, staring out through their untrained eyes; and she saw the flawless physical beauty of babies – dirty babies, spoilt babies, babies covered in chocolate or worse – the marble eyeball, the petal skin, the fingernails, the moist red mouths; she would stop by a pram and stand there marvelling at the sheer newness of flesh and hair. It was as though until now she had wilfully blinkered herself against living humanity because she was afraid that to look at it would hurt her. She had thought she was content, a woman without much need for love, envying no one, desiring nothing; now she stared about her hungrily, amazed by the joy of possessing what she had not known she lacked.

With Raymond's ring on her finger the actual world immediately opened round her too. As she held out her hand she was aware, as she had never been before, of Miss Burroughs. Staring down at the turquoise daisy, speaking conventional words, the man who had coughed his life away on German gas in 1916 before he had even proposed to her rose up like a flame to sear Miss Burroughs, even now, even after all these years. Miss Burroughs's two sisters' pregnancies, their not altogether satisfactory husbands, their altogether unsatisfactory children, thoughtless now in their own maturity of mothers and aunt alike, the long procession of years that found Miss Burroughs now, in the Invoice Office of Winters' Stores, staring down at a ring on the finger of someone she had thought to be shipwrecked like herself on the shores of duty, contentment and religion, were illuminated to Esther's open eyes.

The news of her engagement ran beyond the Invoice Office, chattered over in the washroom by Jacqueline and carried out into the building by the juniors, as mice carry grain. Everyone looked at her differently, the older women with reserve, the younger ones with respect and curiosity. The nubile girls opened their ranks a little to let her in if she wished, to examine the ring, to ask about dates and furniture and wedding dresses; an Easter bride was nice, but May was warmer, and June was best of all. Old Mr Oliver, his deaf aid dangling, clasped her hand in both his and moistly wished her happiness, the commissionaires asked her, 'When's the happy day?', the vanmen whistled 'Here comes the bride'. The spreading circles of Esther's news reached out and touched even Mr Winters himself, for she was a senior employee and would have been pensionable had she stayed on. He sat in a room of mahogany and turkey carpet behind the rolltop desk his father, who had started the store, had used, a long sallow old man like a stick of bamboo, his knobbly fingertips touching, regarding her sadly.

'We shall be sorry to lose you, Miss Wilson,' he said. 'You're certain you won't stay on, hm? Not just for a time, hm? A great many married ladies do so now, you know. Or perhaps half-time, hm? Until you settle down?' and he looked at her as though hopeful that marriage would disappoint.

Young Mr Winters also said, 'Sorry to lose you, Miss Wilson,' but continued, 'and who the devil's going to take over from you I don't know.' He sat behind a desk shaped like a huge pale caramel, the most contemporary of all the contemporary furniture in the shop, set in the centre of a black carpet against acid yellow curtains and a screen of silver Venetian blinds. He tapped his teeth with a cigarette holder and swung in his desk chair, which was shaped like half an egg. 'Can't shift Miss Burroughs. She knows her own job, besides she's too old. And that little girl you've got – Jennifer, Georgie, what's her name?'

'Jacqueline.'

'Jacqueline. She's no good, she's too young.'

'She knows the work though, sir. She can use the machine.'

'Can she use her head?'

'Well . . .' Esther considered. 'I think she could. She's never had to, but I think if I trained her . . .'

'Do that and see if it works. Let me know in a couple of weeks how she's shaping. When are you leaving us?'

'In a month.'

'Let's hope the weather's a bit better for you by then.' He smiled. 'Ah well, you girls will do it. You'll furnish your home from Winters', I hope.'

Esther smiled too. 'We shan't need very much, sir,' she said. 'We're going to live where I am now. It's my own house, you see.'

He raised his eyebrows. 'A woman of property?'

'Well—' She flushed a little. 'It's not really like that. It was my grandad's, you see, and I've got my old Gran to look after, and there's room . . .'

'Very sensible, very nice. Wish my grandad had left me house property instead of this dear old brontosaurus, the family business. Staff, premises, overheads, and toil – my head never stops aching.' He shot her a shrewd look and laughed, tapping his teeth. 'Still, as they say, it's a proud tradition. You'll let me know if there's anything you want – saucepans or lamps or something – so that Winters' can wish you well.'

She left him thoughtfully, touched by the firm's regard for her, surprised by the glimpse he had given her through a chink in Winters' huge façade. Seeing only the business they did, as mirrored in the invoices she handled, she had never considered the difficulties: costs, wages, upkeep, stock, if you stopped to think of it, and staff getting more and more difficult to get – and keep; and the other stores getting bigger and bigger, swallowing each other up like pythons did . . . Here was another opening prospect for her to stare at, another world revealed by her union with Raymond.

And beyond that, the lives of half a dozen people were altered by the change in hers: Miss Burroughs, who would have to get used to someone new in their office; Jacqueline, the veneer peeled off her unsuspected hard little business brain; the junior, still sloshing teacups, who would step up to take Jacqueline's place; the new one they would get in from the Labour Exchange to replace her; and all their families, better off by that much pride and wages gained; and their boyfriends and perhaps their view of life – all changed in some small or greater way because Raymond and Esther loved each other.

Love. A short word, a word to evade. One was 'fond' of people, one thought they were 'smashing' or 'lovely' or 'very nice'. Even Raymond had not said he loved her, that hazed evening when, in the back seat on top of the bus going home, he had asked her to marry him. He had said, 'I'm ever so fond of you, Esther,' and she had said nothing. He had held her hand tightly, his other arm along the seat at her back, and had continued, 'D'you think you and me . . .? Could you and me make a go of it, Esther?' She had made a small questioning noise and he had said, 'Yes, I mean it. Will you marry me, Esther?' And she had answered, 'Are you sure?'

'Never was more sure of anything. You do care for me a little bit, don't you?' The blood came up in her face, suffocating her. 'Because I'm ever so fond of you, Esther, and I think we could make a go of it. What do you say?'

She had hung her head so that he should not see the tears spilling over, had squeezed his hand and nodded jerkily. But he had seen the tears. Relinquishing her hand he had turned her face to his and looked at it, his eyes blazingly blue. 'Don't cry,' he said. That was all. They had sat hand in hand in silence as the bus jolted on; it was only when they dismounted at the corner of Handel Street that the exhilaration they had brought in to Gran that evening had seized them.

'Love' was not a word one used. Even to herself Esther was shy of it. She did not think: I love Raymond. Her thoughts were huge, luminous, the pearl formed round the tiny grit of getting him his favourite chop for supper, mending his clothes, seeing the way his mouth twisted upwards when he was chaffing Gran. She did not think: I am in love, when she saw children, or the first cold snowdrops, heard Cho-Cho-San's fare-well over the television, smelt the frosty woolly scent of Raymond's overcoat as she held close to his arm, hurrying home together. She did not think at all but only felt; felt herself to be both the source and the initiate of the richness of the world, to be Gran and Gloria equally with herself.

Gloria was not well. Her legs were swollen and brownish circles came under her eyes. The clinic said her blood pressure was high and sent her into hospital three weeks ahead of time. Furious and frightened, she was taken there in a taxi by Terry, a bedraggled little balloon of life and death. Gran watched her go with pleasurable apprehension and waited for Terry's solitary return. He was as insensible from shock as a young bullock that has just been corralled and branded, and followed Gran dumbly into her kitchen, sitting with his knees spread, sipping the tea, staring at her from under his crest of hair, uncomprehending and forlorn. Without Gloria, without his mother, he was as helpless as a fledgling pushed from the nest. His big hands with their dirty knuckles, his big feet in their crêpe-soled shoes, seemed like the appendages of a man stuck on to an orphan boy, and Gran was moved to substitute for her forebodings a stream of comfort. 'She'll be all right, dear, don't you fret. Right as rain she'll be once them doctors get working on her. Why, I've seen girls with legs swelled up, you wouldn't believe it, like elephants they were and all with the carrying. My word, if it was you men as had the pain maybe you'd think twice about the pleasure, but there you are, that's human nature, and you'll see, all's well that ends well, dear, and as soon as she holds her little bundle of love in her arms it'll all be over and forgotten. Drink your tea, dear, it'll make you feel better.' When Esther returned from work that evening she found him watching the television, his hands limp, waiting for seven o'clock when he could go back to the hospital.

At any time Esther would have offered to keep his part of the house straight for him while Gloria was away, but in her new openness she did it eagerly. She washed again the breakfast dishes which Terry thought he had already washed, rinsed out tea-cloths, dusted round Gloria's collection of plaster animals won at fairs or bought on holidays. True, as she did so she noticed with a landlord's eye the dirty marks on the wallpaper, the scratched floorboards, the cigarette burn on the dressing-table, the curtains turning grey under their rings. Gloria was not a corner-cleaner; but there, thought the new Esther, she had been pregnant and sick ever since she moved in here, why should she be as house-proud as a sterile spinster? Other things had been filling her mind and body; she was young and she was living. Esther gathered up the socks and underclothes which Terry had stuffed into a pillow-case, and gave them to Gran to take with their own washing to the launderette; and as she flung back to air the bedclothes which Terry pulled into place each morning before he went to work, almost sensing still the warmth rising from the mattress, the rumpled sheets, the indented pillow, where all night had lain the unclothed body of a man, she would often fall into a kind of dream, a trance-like premonition of the intimacy of married life, of bedclothes and pants and hair brushes and dishes in a sink, from which she would waken only at Gran's screech up the staircase, 'Etty! You'll be late!'

They did not see much of Terry after that first evening, for he drove a greengrocers' van all day and went to the hospital every visiting hour. Afterwards he did not come home but, now that Gloria's hand was off him, went to the pub where he and his mates had drunk their quick ones near the bus turnround when he had been a driver and Gloria a clippie before they were married. The weekends, after visiting hours, he stayed at his mother's in Plumstead. It was strange, but when he was away Esther felt the emptiness of the rooms above her. She and Gran, Terry and Gloria had always kept themselves to themselves; save for the handing over of the rent each week there had seldom been contact between them. Often for days Esther had forgotten they were living there, reminded only, and then vexedly, by sounds of tears, angry words, the radio turned too high or peculiar creaking sounds from the bedroom above her own; but now she missed them, felt the lack of living bodies breathing in the rooms upstairs, was glad to hear Terry's returning steps late at night, not always steady, or to invite him to a cup of tea on Sunday evenings when he came back from Plumstead. She asked with genuine concern how Gloria was, looked forward with genuine affection to her return with the baby. She bought a woolly rug with a lamb worked on it from Winters' Carpet Department and took it up one Sunday afternoon to lay beside the cot. Raymond was with her.

'There,' she said, 'that looks a bit more cosy.'

Raymond was looking round. 'They don't take much care of the place, do they?' he remarked.

'Well, she went off in such a hurry.' She ran her hand along the rungs of the cot; it was painted blue, with heart-shaped spaces cut out of head and footboards and rabbits wreathed with rosebuds painted between them. 'It's sweet, isn't it? They've got everything new for the baby.'

'You know what, Ett?' He stood in the middle of the room, hands in his pockets. It was cold up here and their breath showed in the still air. 'If you was to furnish these two rooms as bedsits and let them separate, you'd make twice as much.'

'I suppose I would.'

'Of course you would. Put in a couple of gas-rings, scrap the cooker, turn the kitchen into a bedsit as well – that'd be three to let. How much do the Masons pay?'

'Two pounds ten.'

'Whew!' He raised his eyes to the ceiling in disgust. 'You could get pretty well that for each of these rooms alone. You're giving it away.'

She was laughing. 'Why shouldn't I give it away? I don't want it.'

'You could make double.'

'You are an old miser, you are! I don't want to make double. The rooms don't cost me anything, what the Masons pay me is almost all profit.'

'But there's income tax and dilapidations . . .'

'Oh, that! I'd have to take care of the place anyway. After all, I wouldn't want the rain coming in through the roof whether these rooms were let or not, would I?'

'You could make double,' he repeated. 'I don't like to see you being done.'

'I'm not being done, silly. I don't want to make anything out of people.' She came to him and put her hand through his arm. 'The fact that I'm lucky enough to have somewhere to live doesn't mean I don't feel sorry for people who haven't. Suppose it was us, Ray, starting off together with nowhere to live but in other people's furniture and having to pay through the nose for it. It's hard on young people nowadays. How can they save?'

He put his hand over hers. 'You're soft, that's what you are.'

She stood for a moment lost in the comfort of being beside him, with her arm through his. Although the room was cold she did not feel it. She felt nothing but Raymond.

'This used to be my room when Grandad was alive,' she said, 'and the room I have now was my mother's. It's funny to think back to those days, me a little girl and the whole house belonging to us, and now here it is split up, with a different family in it and a baby coming and everything.'

'You're going to regret that baby – howling all night, prams in the hall . . .'

'Oh Raymond!' She laughed again, shaking his arm gently. 'Don't you like babies?'

'Some.'

'Haven't you ever looked at them? I've been looking at them lately. They're – surprising, somehow. I mean, till you look at them you don't pay attention and then suddenly you look and you see them – I don't know, I can't explain.'

'You're never one to explain much, are you?' he said indulgently.

'I used to talk to Grandad – but then, he used to listen. It's no good talking to Gran, she never lets you get a word in edgeways. You're sweet with her, Ray, the way you let her talk.'

'She's as good as a play.'

'Poor Gran. She finds life dull now.'

'Just you wait till you've got that baby bawling its head off.'

'Raymond!'

'You'll be sorry you didn't take my advice and have two nice quiet business girls, nice and cosy with their gas-rings.'

'Brr, it's cold! Maybe I ought to leave an oil stove up here, with Terry out so much.'

'And pay for it yourself, I suppose?'

'Well – no, not the paraffin. I'm not that soft, Ray. After all, I do run the shop, let alone my own job.'

'The shop,' he said thoughtfully. 'I must have a look at that shop one day.'

'It's not much to see. Mr Grover sees to it all, I only just look at the books.'

'When?'

'Once a month.'

'You never told me.'

'I never thought of it.' She moved away to the window and looked out. A grey light lay over everything and the grey yards lay in a row of double segments like the sections of a honeycomb, side by side, back-to-back. There was nothing to see but a monochrome of grey pails and dustbins, black earth, black coal tips, the mottled grey and black of slush half frozen in corners, black trees that in the unimaginable spring would blossom with lilac and may, the grey and black skeletons of plants shivering in the twi-light; and beyond, over the wall and at the end of the opposite gardens, grey brick houses under purple tiles, smoke hardly greyer than the sky drifting from their chimneys above the black squares of windows. Here and there a window was lit, showing a bedroom or a kitchen with a woman moving about in it. 'I used to look out of here when I was little. It was more of a slum then – that's the back of Fox Street over there. People never used to draw their curtains then, not like they do now. I suppose the blackout got them into the habit. You could see right in, see all sorts of things going on. And in the summer when the windows were open you could hear the most terrible rows – there was one house in particular, that one across there, where the woman used to throw things at her husband and shout and carry on. I used to get into bed and pull the clothes over my head when that started.'

He stood beside her and put his arm round her shoulders. 'Poor little girl.'

'We never had any rows in our house, so of course I thought it awful. Sometimes Gran'd cry and carry on but never when Grandad was there, and sometimes she and my mother would go on at each other, but it was just to pass the time. And Mother wasn't here much. I used to lie in bed up here and listen to her practising with the piano in the front room, singing scales and bits of songs. She had a lovely voice.'

'Was she pretty?'

'You've seen her photo downstairs. I don't remember her really, only her singing.'

'Still, you've always had your home and your grandad and gran. You've always known where you were – not like some.'

She turned to him, touched by the hardness in his voice. 'I've been lucky,' she said. 'Luckiest of all now.' She put her arms round him and kissed his cheek. It was firm and warm under her lips, faintly pricked with bristles. Her lips were drawn to his flesh in little gentle kisses, feeling out the bone under the skin, the modelling of lips and nostril, receiving his breath as he stood passive within her arms, her mouth pulled to his without volition, kindling from its own warmth. Warmth seemed to reach out and fasten her mouth to his, reaching out and through and down, plumbing her with its slow pressure, infinite, unreal. She was not, as she had been before, Esther gently kissing Raymond; she was Esther drawn to the source of the long trance-like dreams that came upon her sometimes by the bed. Her kiss transfixed her in a limbo she had not known before, lonely, profound. She hung there on his mouth, and then he moved, put his arm round her, pressed her lips with his own, lightly, and the source was gone. The bleak furnishings of someone else's home surrounded them, it was dusk in here and almost dark outside. She shivered.

'Gran'll be wanting her tea,' she said. 'We'd better go down.'

They were being married on the 27th of March and Esther left Winters' two weeks before. It was quite an upheaval. First of all on her last afternoon she had to shake old Mr Winters' hand in the rich gloom of his office. 'Ah, Miss Wilson, leaving us after all,' he sighed. 'Don't forget – if you ever want to come back call and see me, hm? Call and see me.'

Then Mr Ian came into the Invoice room, the staff from the other offices crowding through the door behind him. Miss Burroughs got to her feet and Jacqueline spun round on her metal chair in front of the adding machine, two tiny baskets of breadfruit tinkling at her ears. Diane, the new junior, shuffled the teacups out of sight behind the filing baskets, upsetting them and letting a trail of tea seep out over the invoices. Mr Ian perched himself on the edge of Miss Burroughs' desk and said, 'Well, Miss Wilson, we've come to see you off. It's a sad day when a trusted member of the staff leaves us but no doubt, like Sydney Carton, it is a far far better thing that you're going to do than you have ever done before.' The older staff laughed quietly, the younger ones looked blank. 'Anyway, we all hope so. We shall miss you. Most of you know,' and he looked over his shoulder at the others, 'that Miss Wilson came to us when she was sixteen, starting as a junior, running round with the teacups like this young lady here . . .' he nodded unexpectedly at Diane, who blushed, 'and has become one of the most trusted and well-liked members of the staff.' 'Hear, hear!' and the Head Clerk of Dispatch clapped his hands diffidently. 'We're sorry to see her go,' said Mr Ian, 'but we quite understand that in spite of being an all-purpose store, there are some things even Winters' cannot provide.' A faint tremor crept among his listeners – slightly risqué . . .? But Mr Ian went carelessly on, 'So off you go, Miss Wilson, to a very happy, very full new life, with the good wishes of us all – and just to make sure that you always keep the whip hand in your new life, here's just the job to do it.' He stood up and handed Esther an electric mixer. Everyone applauded. She took it nervously and made a lame reply. She had not expected everyone. She had not expected Miss Burroughs to cry a little, or Jacqueline to kiss her. She had not expected that, before Mr Ian had arrived with the firm's present, the office staff would present her with a tablecloth and napkins. She had not expected to feel panic as she closed the emptied drawers of her desk for the last time, packed up her soap and nail-brush, slipped the last small manila pay envelope, thick and chinking, into her handbag. Nor had she expected to feel, as she went through the emptying offices, down the empty stairs, as though she were leaving the only home she had ever known, which was not true, for an alien and frightening land, which was not true either, for it was, she knew, the promised land.

THREE

GLORIA HAD A DAUGHTER, after a long labour with a breech presentation. Terry came blundering down the steps to tell them, stammering, red with joy, then collapsed by the dining table, his face puckered up like a baby's, wiping the tears away with the back of his hand. Gran threw her arms around him and gave him a kiss, rocking him awkwardly to and fro as a child rocks a teddy bear that is as big as herself. He sat craggily within her clasp, sniffing and smiling sheepishly, while Esther got him a cup of tea. Then he went out to telephone his mother and came back very late, stumbling, singing a little. Lying awake Esther heard his shoes drop to the floor over her head and the springs of the bed, when he threw himself down on it, groaning; then snores. She smiled in the darkness, imagining the heavy boy's body flung untidily among the bedclothes, imagining Gloria, sleek and empty now, asleep in the darkened ward and the baby asleep in its crib.

The baby lay squeezed up with sleep under its rigid coverings in the cot beside Gloria's bed when Esther visited her, and the two women looked down at it in silence for a moment, Esther with the attention all her seeing had now, Gloria leaning sideways on her elbow in the bed with an impersonal expression.

'She's not much to look at, is she?' she said.

'She's sweet.'

'She's yellow 'cause she's got jaundice. Born with it. They are sometimes, nurse says.'

'Poor little thing.'

'It doesn't matter. I mean, they're not ill with it or anything.'

'She's got red hair.'

'Yes. That's a surprise, that is. You wouldn't believe the chaffing I've had to put up with, what with Terry being so dark.' A shadow of gratification crept into her face and she put up a hand to touch her own yellow curls. 'I don't know where she got it from, I'm sure.'

'Somewhere back in the family, I expect, one side or the other. I've heard it often jumps like that.'

'I suppose so.' Gloria lay back on her pillows and Esther sat down. The square, light ward was humming with the voices of its visitors, clustered on either side of each bed like sucker-fish to the sides of their hosts.

'I've brought you some grapes.'

'That's ever so kind of you.' She sent a furtive look along the ward towards the Sister's office. 'I'll have to ask nurse if I'm allowed, though. They're ever so strict, you can't hardly have anything tasty, because of the milk or something.' She giggled. 'Imagine!'

'Do they treat you nicely?'

'Well – some of them are all right. But if they once get their knife into you . . . That woman two beds along on the other side, the one with the ribbon in her hair, well, the other evening she wanted a bed-pan and she kept on asking and the nurse said, "You'll have to wait, Mrs Jowett, you've only just had one." Well, I mean! And they're always coming round after you for something, temperatures or pills or seeing you've drunk enough. You wouldn't believe the amount they make you drink, gallons and gallons. That's because of the milk, too. And I daren't move because of the stitches – I split, you see, and they had to give me three stitches and I've got ever such a sore tail. I tell you, having a baby's no picnic. If they was to tell you the half of what you have to go through, you'd think twice, believe me.'

'Still, it's worth it now,' said Esther gently.

Gloria glanced at the baby curiously. 'Oh yes, it's worth it now,' she repeated. 'I mean, there it is, over and done with. Like you and business. You've given it up now, Terry says.' She looked at Esther with attention for the first time. 'When's the happy day?'

'The twenty-seventh.'

'My goodness, only another week! Are you having a white wedding?'

'No, it's only quiet. But it's in church, St Peter's in Fox Street. Raymond – my fiancé – he didn't want to be married in church at first, he wanted it to be more private, at the Registry Office you know. He said he didn't want a lot of people hanging about outside the church and staring at us when we came out.'

'Ooh, that's the best part! There was ever such a lot of people when me and Terry was married. Of course, it was a slap-up affair – four bridesmaids and a matron of honour . . .'

'Well, me and Gran persuaded him in the end. I wouldn't feel right if it wasn't done in a church.'

'What are you wearing?' She sat forward and clasped her knees – stitches, milk, forgotten.

'Well, it's only very quiet, you see. I'm wearing blue – a kind of a light blue costume and a little hat with blue and grey feathers on it, and navy-blue gloves and shoes. And pink and white carnations. And Gran's wearing a kind of a peacock-blue dress with a navy coat over it and a hat to match.'

'No bridesmaids?'

'No, because it's only quiet, you see. Gran was all for getting Cousin Em up from Bangor and asking Mrs Bromwich next door and people from business, but Raymond and me decided we'd keep it quiet. You see, he's an orphan and he hasn't got anyone, only his auntie in Scarborough, and she wrote and said she wasn't well enough to come down for it, so we're just having Gran and Mr and Mrs Grover from the shop and Miss Burroughs and Jacqueline from business – and you and Terry, if you'll be home again and would like.'

'You bet! I can't wait to get into some glad rags again after all these months of flipping smocks.'

'Then we shall just go back home and have a quiet celebration and then me and Raymond's going to Torquay for a week.'

'Oh, doesn't it sound lovely!' Gloria leaned back on her pillows again. 'The church and the flowers and the honeymoon and all . . . and then bang, before you know where you are, you're flat on your fanny in the maternity ward with people nagging at you to drink up your Lucozade! Honest, if I'd known then what I know now – but no, they don't tell you till you're caught and then it's too late. D'you know, there was a woman come in after me – you can't see her now, her bed's farther along this side – and she was nearly forty-eight hours having hers? Forty-eight hours! Imagine! My goodness, mine was bad enough – it started in the evening just after supper – they make you have supper at six o'clock here, would you believe it? – and it went on all night and all the next day till four o'clock in the afternoon.' She was well away on relished reminiscence, reliving the drama and the indignity, her eyes half on the clock that measured out the visiting-hour, half on the traffic of the ward. The baby slept motionless in its wrappings and the nurses, crisp as cabbages, whisked by on their black nylon legs. Esther sat, hardly hearing Gloria's drama, looking at the tiny skull with its fuzz of ginger hair, and at the mothers ranged triumphant in their beds, fleshy and fresh. The smell of warmed-up food, ether and flowers filled an air which seemed not of the ordinary world at all; the bedside lockers with their jug and tumbler, dishes of fruit, and magazines, the ear-phones spread like moths against the wall above each bed, the coverlets bleached with cleanliness, the stilt legs of the bedsteads rising from the floor like the legs of wading birds, all existed only in a special world, the doorway into which was marriage.

'. . . and when they said it was a little girl I nearly burst out crying,' Gloria was concluding, 'after all that performance!'

'What will you call her?'

'Well, Terry's mother wants Jennifer and his grandma wants Mary, but I rather fancy Marylyn – except maybe it's got a bit common.'

'She's sweet.' But it was not sweet that the baby was. Rather it was awe-inspiring, as some ancient relic of fertility inspires awe. The core of man lay there in the crib, its character concealed within its pygmy skull, tenacious, secret, immutable save by death. Esther could not imagine this little creature being human any more than, when she had looked at Grandad dead, she had been able to remember him alive; their primeval form removed them from humanity.

At the end of the ward a handbell was vigorously rung. 'Uh-huh,' said Gloria, 'there it goes. End of the programme.' She hitched herself up irritably in the bed.

'Well, it's been lovely,' Esther said. 'Gran can't hardly wait to hear what she's like. I had a job stopping her coming with me, but I thought you'd have other visitors perhaps.'

'Not on a Wednesday,' said Gloria resentfully. 'Terry's mum only comes over on Sunday and of course any of my friends who might be interested are all at business, bar the weekend. Of course Terry comes regular, but there's a special half-hour every evening for husbands – you ought to see some of them! You wouldn't believe it!'

Esther got up, lingering at the cradleside. 'Terry's so proud. He's like a cat without a tail with you away.'

Gloria smiled. 'Perhaps he'll value me more now he's had to do without,' she said smugly. 'It's been ever so nice to see you.'

The handbell was rung again and in twos and threes the visitors began to drain from the bedsides.

'You'll let us know when you're coming home,' said Esther. 'I'd like to see everything's nice – and the wedding and all.'

'You bet!' said Gloria. 'You won't see me for dust getting out of this place!'

Esther had imagined she would be idle in the two weeks after she left Winters', for without the framework of going to the office, working, coming home, she could not conceive of a day being filled. That had been the routine of her life for fifteen years – more, if she counted schooling – and to be without it had seemed to promise unending, frightening leisure.

Yet the more time she had the more things crowded into it. There was the house to clean from top to bottom, a jubilant marriage cleansing; there were her own and Gran's wedding clothes to buy or make; the rearrangement of her bedroom to plan. The first week of her leisure Raymond was with her every day and they went to Winters' together to choose a second bed, a wardrobe and a chest of drawers for him. Everyone welcomed her; as they made their choice people from other departments popped down to shake her hand and congratulate Raymond. She was rosy with pleasure and the excitement of buying. She felt springs and opened drawers and cupboards gleefully, while Raymond stood smiling by.

But when they left he did not smile. He was silent as they went into a coffee bar, and silent as they sat at the narrow shelf, warming their hands round the cups. Her pleasure faded and she asked, 'What's wrong, dear?'

He was staring down at the mug of coffee. 'I feel a bit ashamed,' he said.

She felt a dart of fear. 'Ashamed, Ray? Ashamed of what?'

'Ashamed that it's all your money you're spending.'

'Is that all! Why, whatever difference does it make?'

'It makes a difference to me. You going out and buying furniture for me – it's not right.'

'Of course it's right.' She laid her hand on his. 'What does it matter who pays – it's for *our* home.'

He still kept his eyes away from her, down on the cup. 'It's not right,' he repeated. 'I feel – humiliated somehow.'

'Oh Ray, how could you? Not between us.'

'Women don't understand. Men feel these things. And it isn't as if I'm not able to, just that I can't at the moment.'

'I know, dear.'

'Those flipping directors of mine! If they'd only get a move on! They know I've got a bonus coming, I know I've got a bonus coming, but not until the proper date, oh no, might be a precedent or something. I don't want to hang on for it till April 5th, I want it now.'

'Well, you know how business is, Ray. They have to keep to what's customary.'

'That's all right for others but not for me. Think how I feel sitting here and letting you do all the buying! There's things I'd like to get you – pretty things, for your dressing-table maybe, or a nightie, things for Gran – a hundred things I could get if I had the money now.'

She laughed. 'It's a good job you haven't got it then,' she said. 'It wouldn't last long.'

'I'm not joking, Ett.' His voice was level and his eyes, looking at her now, were hard as china. 'I feel it.'

'There's no need.' Despite herself, she was sobered by his tone.

'For me there's need. I can't stand not having the money. Give it to me and let me buy the things.'

'But Ray – why?'

'Because it's right. The man should have the money.'

'But if I give it to you, what difference would it make? I mean, it'd still be . . .' She faltered.

He smiled wryly. 'You mean it'd still be yours.'

'No I don't, dear, I don't. It's ours now, not mine, just as when you get the bonus, it'll be ours.'

'I'll pay you back when I get the bonus.'

'Don't Ray, please.' She put her hand on his arm, turning away her head. 'I can't bear talk like this between us. It's like we were different people.'

'There are things I want to get you.'

'I wouldn't want them, got like that. All I want is what we've got together. That's how I think of it.'

'Well, I don't.'

'Please, dear. Don't talk about it anymore.'

He gave her a long look, his hand still grasping the mug. At last, slowly, he covered with his own her hand with the turquoise daisy on it that lay upon his arm, and managed a tight smile. 'OK, Ett. I didn't mean to upset you.'

'I'm not upset. It's just that I can't bear talking about money. It spoils things.'

'I know. I'm sorry. Forget it. It's just that I want so much to buy you things it drives me crazy not to be able to lay my hands on it. Say you understand, dear. Here's me earning good money and getting married and moving into a lovely home and all, and none of it's mine. Oh, I know it's shared, dear, and I feel that, too, in the way you mean. But it's not the same, not to a man. I want to be able to do something big, buy two dozen bottles of champagne for the wedding, a mink coat for Gran . . .'

He was making her laugh, her hand safe and warm now in his; but as she laughed she studied his dear, loved face, the flexible lips, the moulding of his cheek, savouring them, as he talked on, with love in which there was a small new seed of sadness. Not grief, but the tenderest pity that deepened love. She saw with clear eyes, as he justified and excused, that he loved money, deeply, obsessively, and the knowledge seemed to her quaint and sad, growing from a past of which, although he told her much, she knew so little. It was an astonishment to her to find how little love was based on knowledge; no matter how many words had flowed between them she knew as little of him still as he of her. There were flaws in each like hidden chasms, strengths never to be known till put to trial. Each day, perhaps, they would learn something new, as she had now, and the knowledge would deepen love; she would understand more, see him more wisely, more nearly as he was.

He was urging her. 'Say you understand, dear.'

'Yes.'

'If you was to pass the couple of hundred pounds you must be running into over to me, Etty, then I'd feel more like the man of the family, see? I know it wouldn't be different really, but it'd *feel* different. I could get those little surprises – and then when my bonus comes in I'd pay it back to you.'

'I wouldn't want that.'

'It wouldn't even be like a loan, really, more like just changing who happens to handle it.' His eyes were blazing and candid, like those of a child pleading for an ice-cream.

She said gently, 'You've got enough for paying the cars and the church and your new suit and Torquay and all, haven't you?'

'Of course. I'm not a pauper. I've got some in the bank, you know that, Ett – but not enough to lay out the way we both want to.'

'I don't have to pay Winters' now – they'll send in the bill in a month or so and even then it won't be as much as you think, not with the discount. They're a good firm like that. And my dress and Gran's are all seen to and none of your business – my goodness, the groom's not supposed to know anything about that side of it all! – and the food for after, Gran and me are doing anyway. So there's really nothing we need any money for, not yet, not till the bills start coming in. And by then you'll have your bonus and can be as bossy as you like, if you want to.'

They looked at each other deeply for a moment, he trying her strength, she steady and smiling.

'You won't, then!' he said abruptly.

'There's no need, dear. It'd just be silly.'

'OK.' He looked away.

'You're not cross?'

He smiled. 'Course not. It's just a thing I'm funny about – you'll find plenty more.'

'I don't mind.'

He pushed the empty mug away impatiently along the plastic ledge. 'Would you like another coffee?'

'Would you?'

'No. Let's get weaving.' He slid off the stool and went ahead of her to the cash desk. When she joined him he took her arm and pressed it close to him, his voice tenderly warm again, and they got a bus and went home.

He left London two days later, as she had known he must. She knew that his firm liked him out on the road the first three days of each week and back to report to them on Fridays. They had given him her first week off so that they could make the wedding arrangements together, and would give him a second week for the honeymoon; but there was a customer, a big one, up in the Midlands who placed a regular order every middle of the month with whoever reached him first with the best offer, and Raymond had to go.

Esther did not mind much, for there were, in this last week of maidenhood, so many things to do and so much to savour that would never be hers again – at least, she corrected herself, not wholly hers. She found it hard to imagine her room being her own no longer, or that she would never more be sole arbitress of what went on in her life and Gran's. The only married lives she had any knowledge of were Gran and Grandad's and there Gran had always been the subservient one. Was that the pattern, the husband taking over everything, the wife resting on him? She did not know. She could not imagine it quite like that with her and Raymond; in any case he would be away half of every week, and she would still have the shop.

She had never been able to explain the shop to herself. She took no part in running it, she did not need it, it would have been simple to sell it after Grandad's death and add the money to the nest-egg that he had left to protect her and Gran. She seldom visited the shop save when, once a month, she fetched the books, leaving the management entirely to Mr Grover, who had been Grandad's assistant there after the war and who now ran it with his wife as though it were his own. Yet she knew to a shilling how much it had gained or lost each month, and the knowledge that it was there gave her a satisfaction that nothing else did, a sense of security and achievement, all the stronger for being in a way secret. The shop was hidden beneath the surface of her ordinary life and even with Raymond she had so far kept it so. She had not volunteered to take him to see it, and now, when the time for her monthly audit had come round, he was not here.

The little window was full of its customary greeting cards, envelopes and pots of ink, show cards for cigarettes, and a board of advertisements in various handwritings. As she pushed open the door a bell whirred beneath the mat, sounding in the parlour behind the counter. The smell, familiar since childhood, of newsprint and paraffin greeted her, for the weather was still cold and an oil stove straddled the linoleum; she had warmed her hands over its breathing flower ever since she could remember. Every evening when she was a little girl she had come in to see Grandad on her way back from school, and once a week he had given her comics, smelling of ink still, from the coloured sheaves that covered the counter like a harvested field; and on birthdays and festivals he and she together had chosen cards for Gran and Cousin Em and Cousin Em's son Rodney who was lost in the *Repulse* and, for a year or two, Esther's mother Winnie. With the war the habit was broken, for she was evacuated; and afterwards Grandad had been there less and less. Mr Grover had taken over, small, pink, hardly less bald then than he was now, for his pale hair seemed to have been too lightly rooted in his skull to survive the months of sweating inside a tank under the sun of Libya. He had joined up sandy and come back pink, and Mrs Grover had cried when he first took his cap off. Now they lived in their cave of newsprint and tobacco like a pair of mice, inquisitive and tame; but shrewd mice, running the business well, stocking new lines, cherishing their regulars, advising Esther when they felt it right, but regarding her always as proprietor. They loved the shop and they loved their wares; Mrs Grover read all the women's magazines and cut out the recipes and the crochet patterns, and Mr Grover kept a scrapbook of odd happenings and police court cases and the reports of every Test Match.

Mrs Grover wrapped up the ledger in a newspaper for Esther to carry home, for it would have been embarrassing for all if she had gone through it in their presence. 'There,' she said, 'I hope that's handy enough.' Esther took the parcel, thanking her. Mrs Grover's eyes, bright with feminine questions she would never ask, searched Esther's face. 'We're ever so looking forward to the happy day,' she said. 'Let's hope the weather turns warmer by then, one can't look one's best in the cold.'

Her husband said, 'I had enough heat to last me a lifetime when I was in the desert.'

'Well, we could do with a bit of it now,' said his wife. 'All the bridesmaids shivering and the church cold and all.'

'No bridesmaids,' said Esther. 'It's just a quiet affair.'

'I wonder,' said Mr Grover, gazing at her with a face at once expressionless and urgent, like a goldfish in a bowl. 'Shall we have the pleasure of meeting your husband-to-be before the wedding day?'

'No, he's away for his firm.'

'He's a traveller, then?'

'Well, sort of. He's away half the week – novelties . . .'

'Ah.' A look passed between husband and wife, then Mr Grover said awkwardly, 'We were wondering if perhaps when you're married Mr Banks will be taking an interest in the business.'

'Oh no,' Esther said, 'not at all.'

Mr Grover smiled jauntily. 'Gentlemen do, you know. Kind of an outside interest at first and then it gets a kind of hold on them.'

'Not Raymond.' She said it firmly, then, considering, repeated it. 'Not Raymond. He's got his own business, you see, travelling about. He wouldn't be interested in the shop, no more than just casually.'

'We were wondering, Mrs Grover and me,' he said, and the uncertainty of his tone caught Esther's ear. She realised suddenly what they were asking and why, sensed with a pang of guilt the weeks of uncertainty, hours of discussion that lay behind Mr Grover's words. Ever since the news of her engagement, which Gran had brought them proudly like a dog bearing a bone, they had worried over what it would mean to their future, and she in her selfishness had not thought to reassure them.

'Of course he won't take an interest,' she said, more firmly still. 'That isn't his line at all. I'll rely on you just as I've always done to look after the shop. You know I've always done that, Mr Grover, ever since Grandad had to give up.'

'It's been a good many years,' he said vaguely, but his face grew pinker and his eyes were no longer urgent. 'Mrs Grover and me feel about the business as if it was our own.'

'I know. I'm ever so grateful.'

'It's for us to be grateful,' broke in Mrs Grover. 'Somehow right from the start we always felt as if this was our home.' She stopped and they all looked away from each other in an impasse of embarrassment. 'Of course you'll be having your own home to see to now, cooking and mending . . .' Mrs Grover suggested; but Esther had always had that, as they all knew. It was having a man in it that would make all the difference.

Gloria and Terry too were unsettled by the marriage. Gloria and the baby came home two days before it, Gloria blooming but tearful, the baby a motionless cocoon of wool. The place in the hall where they had thought the pram could be kept was occupied by packing cases from Winters' containing wedding presents and a large trunk initialled R.B. Esther and Gran were out – deliberately, for Esther knew she could not restrain Gran from the baby and wanted Gloria to have peace for her homecoming.

They put the baby in an armchair and Terry lit the gas fire. Despite the anemones Terry had put in a vase and the new rug by the cot, the rooms seemed hostile to Gloria. Her breasts were drawing, for it was nearly four o'clock, and no one now would bring her tea or supper or see to the baby, and her legs were weak after the stairs. She began to cry, for it was not at all as she had pictured her return: radiant, with a cooing baby boy, and the neighbours and Miss Wilson crowding round to see and old Mrs Wilson saying she'd never seen such a lovely baby and Terry proudly smiling, carrying them both away up to their little nest and there taking her in his arms and kissing her like he couldn't wait . . . Instead her breasts hurt and the doctor had said they must wait at least six weeks, and the room was cold and Terry nervous of touching her and the baby was a girl and lay there as if she were dead and there was no one who cared about Gloria and her baby, she was over and done with, now it was all Esther and the wedding . . .

The baby cried in the night and Terry got up and brought her to the bed and Gloria fed her, mother and baby half asleep in their primitive intercourse.

The wind was brought up and Gloria fast asleep again while Terry changed the baby's napkin, balancing her gingerly across his pyjamad thighs, marvelling at her folded female pinkness. The baby stared up at him with eyes blue as space or stared round, craning its non-existent neck at the meaningless objects she had never seen before and then back at this huge face bent over her. He lay awake a long time afterwards, listening to her clucking gently to herself, hardly aware of Gloria. Through the maze of emotions in which he was lost one thought reared itself: If she's going to cry in the middle of every night we'll soon have Mr What's-his-name downstairs complaining; and to Terry it seemed that he himself had never been newly married, not ever, not even long ago, had never even been a schoolboy safe and snug at home with Mum and everything done for him, never . . . and he fell asleep at last, an old man and a father.

Next day was better. He brought Gloria her breakfast in bed and put the baby beside her before going off to work. Presently Esther came up with the milk and the *Daily Mirror*, and then Gran came. 'Ow, bless her!' she cried when the baby stared at her. 'Ow, the little darling!' when Gloria put her in her arms. She jigged gently up and down, took a turn or two about the floor, talking and singing to the baby, her gnarled hands spread in the immemorial gesture of protection over the warm woolly bundle, nestling her to the ageless comfort of the breast. Raptly she listened to all that Gloria had to tell, the pains, the waters, the stitches, the Lucozade, what the nurses had done, what the Sister had said, the Caesarian across the ward, the twins two beds up; and when she said anything Gloria did not listen but simply talked on, for Gloria knew it all herself now, she had nothing to fear from Gran any more.

When Gloria paused Gran said, 'You must bring baby to the church tomorrow, bless her. That is, if you're strong enough.'

'Of course I'm strong enough. I wouldn't miss *that* event for the world,' and a tiny shaft of malice shot out and clashed with the tiny shaft from Gran.

'Well, you don't want to overdo it, dear,' said Gran. 'Make haste slowly, that's what the doctor told me after I had my Win. After all, you've had those blooming stitches and everything.' Her eyes glinted speculatively. 'You could do yourself an injury being in too much of a hurry, you know, you must make that Terry of yours be a good boy.'

Gloria flushed with rage and prudery and Gran returned to praising the baby. Presently she left, with injunctions to call her if Gloria felt queer, and Gloria sat on in bed with tears running down her cheeks and splashing on to the cheeks of her baby who now, clutched for comfort in her mother's arms, had withdrawn herself in sleep once more.

Still, Gloria felt better presently and got up to try on the clothes she had not worn since she was pregnant, searching for something for tomorrow.

Raymond returned that afternoon. Hanging fresh curtains at the front room window Esther saw a taxi draw up and Raymond jump out, looking quickly up and down the street in the way he always had, drawing a suitcase from the taxi. She knocked on the window and he looked up, raising his hand in salute. When she opened the front door he slung the suitcase into the passage and kissed her.

'Well?' he said. 'Missed me? Think I wasn't going to show up?'

Smiling, loving, re-seeing every contour of his face, she shook her head.

'Well, you're wrong, see? Nearly didn't get here. Ran down a smashing new customer yesterday, had to stay longer, missed the last train, got on the first this morning, went straight to the office and wow, are they pleased with yours truly!'

He released her, picked up the case and carried it into the front room. From downstairs Gran called, 'Etty? Who's that?'

'It's me, you gorgeous creature,' he called. A shriek came from below. 'We'll be right with you – just give us a minute.' He took Esther's hand and drew her into the room. 'Let her wait a sec, I've got something for you.' He lifted the case onto the table and snapped the fasteners open. She watched, entranced by his presence and the excitement he seemed to contain, like the engine throbbing in a car. 'Shut your eyes,' he said.

She did so and felt something laid about her shoulders. It was a fur cape.

'Ray! Whatever . . .!'

'Like it?' His eyes were a blazing blue and his normally pale skin flushed. He stood with his hands thrust into his pockets as though forcing them to be still. 'It suits you a treat.'

Her hands and eyes savoured its softness. 'Oh Raymond! However much did it . . .?'

He cut her short. 'It's the groom's present to the bride. I wasn't going to have you shivering on your wedding day.'

'Oh it's lovely – so soft and warm. Oh Ray, you shouldn't have.'

'Why not?' He surveyed her with unaccustomed arrogance. 'A man has the right to give presents to his wife, hasn't he? I told you I wanted to, and I had a bit of luck unexpected. I got a smashing big order, a new one, as well as the old one I went up for. I landed 'em both. And the firm was so pleased they give me the bonus, smash out like that, and a bit over. "Good work, Banks," they said and coughed up the lolly. So

I cashed it and did some shopping and here I am. I've got something for Gran too.' Out of his pocket he brought a case and opened it. On the velvet lay a sparkling lizard with emerald eyes. 'Pretty, eh? Just her style. It's marcasite but I think the eyes are real.'

'It's lovely, Ray. You shouldn't have spent so much.'

'I like to have nice things.'

'Oh dearest, it's like a dream!' She hurried to the mantelpiece and looked in the mirror there, turning and craning to see herself all ways. 'It'll just go lovely over my costume – and it's so soft!' She raised one flap of it and smoothed it against her cheek. 'It even smells nice . . .'

'They keep them with scented things hung in them, anti-moth things. It suits you a treat. I wanted you to have something nice. It's just right for Mrs Raymond Banks.'

Laughing, she came to him and put her arms round him. 'Did you get anything for yourself, you bad boy?'

'A few shirts, nylons. And a wedding tie.'

'Oh dearest, I'm so pleased! That the firm appreciate you and show it like this, and just before tomorrow too – after we were complaining.'

'It's the least they could do.'

Her arms round him, she drew back her head and looked at him, colour in her pale skin, her hair dishevelled, the cape slipping askew over the jersey and apron she was wearing, her lips and her eyes defenceless with love. 'Oh Ray, I'm so proud of you! I know you're going to do great things. I'll always love you, Ray.'

He frowned, making a sharp gesture as though to silence her. Then his face softened and he took her by the shoulders, looking not in her eyes but at her gentle mouth and stubborn chin. He kissed her lightly. 'Suits me,' he said, 'if that's how you want it.'

FOUR

A WEEK had never been so long for Gran as was that of Esther's honeymoon. She had never known such solitude, never felt old age so keenly, never before found her memories sting rather than solace. There was nothing to get up for in the morning, no point in tidying the house; she could not be bothered to cook, subsisting on fish and chips from the High Street, beans on toast and tea at the ABC, once a meat pie and a rhum baba soaked, apparently, in brilliantine at a milk bar, but the clientele there seemed so young and cruel, with their curled hair, string ties and narrow skirts or trousers, that they frightened her and she never went again.

She was lost, adrift in a limbo of belonging to no one. Bitterly she mourned the friends she had dropped when she married, regretted that, snug in Grandad and Esther's care as a baby in its cot, receiving everything, responsible for nothing, she had never bothered to be sociable among her neighbours. She did not even know on what nights the old age pensioners met, and she was too proud to ask. Nor was Gloria any company, for she had kept herself and her baby out of sight upstairs and when Gran ventured to visit her had been pettish and unwelcoming. Gran heard the radio sometimes and the baby crying; once she heard Gloria sobbing and thought, 'Serve you right, my girl; life isn't all roses even when you're young.' There were no roses at all when you were old and had no being. Only for an hour or so did she exist, in the launderette among the sporty housewives, bragging of Esther's wedding, showing the lizard; but she could not go there more than once, there was not enough washing. She went to the cinema two, three times, but the love scenes reminded her of Etty and Raymond and the seats all around her were full of canoodling couples in the evening, in the afternoon of lost old people like herself, dozing off, sitting long in the warmth, not understanding the noises and pictures that battered at them from the screen: marines in Okinawa, Rita Hayworth in a nightclub, men kicked in the belly, men with guns in their hands, busts from Italy and Things from Outer Space, Xs and Us and As and next week's programme with this week's flavour and the news bringing you floods in the USA and Stirling Moss and the Queen Mother . . . The old people sat like cobwebs in the darkness, clutching their bags, slopping the tea (4*d*. a cup from the attendant) in its saucer, bemused, bewildered, not all there, but at least among people and warm.

It gave her the hump; she was all there all right, she knew what nearly everything was about and she was frightened by the old people around her who were her own age; and then there was the coming out after, the let-down, hungry, with no one to go home to, only Monty and he most likely would be out already. She could go and sit in a public house, and once she did; the company was robust there and conversation easy – so easy that she did not go again, for she knew that Esther would not like it nor Grandad; she could flout their approval only when she was happy.

One afternoon in despair she called on old Mrs Bromwich next door. She put on her wedding clothes and the lizard brooch and took the wedding photographs to show.

Old Mrs Bromwich went through them silently, holding them in her lumpy freckled hands that shook a little, peering at them through thick spectacles. 'Not in white,' she observed.

'Etty didn't want white, she didn't want to be showy,' said Gran. Her own hands were freckled and the veins swelled up on them too but they did not shake.

'I like a white wedding,' said Mrs Bromwich. Her teeth did not fit very well and looked too white inside her pale old lips.

'Young people don't want to be bothered with all that nowadays,' said Gran. 'Modern, up to the minute, that's what my Etty's Raymond is.'

'It's not the same without white,' said Mrs Bromwich. She laid the pictures down on a lap which could never have been legs and Gran snatched them from her.

'See that lovely fur cape she's wearing?' she said and jabbed at it in the print. 'Raymond gave her that.'

'Them short things don't keep your parts warm,' said Mrs Bromwich and began to cough, carefully, like someone walking on a tightrope.

Gran came away.

There was always the television, and with a cup of tea and Monty and the stove built up the evenings were not so bad, for by then another day was behind her and she was a day nearer belonging to Esther again. Often she thought of Esther and wondered what she was doing; she had never been to Torquay, not even with *Fancy That!*, and imagined it all palms and sunshine like where Princess Grace lived now. She imagined them strolling along the promenade, Raymond in his nylon shirts and Esther carrying her fur, taking tea and listening to the band, going for bus rides perhaps, sitting in deck chairs and watching the people pass. But she could not follow them too far in her mind, for there was some veto there which forbade utterly the concept of Esther in bed with Raymond. They were married and that was lovely, on their honeymoon and that was lovely too; soon they would be home again, living here with her as man and wife, and that would be lovely, a dream come true; but she, with her bawdiness and gusto, her larky youth and her fulfilment with Grandad, could not bring herself to admit of Raymond doing *that* with Esther. A block came down in her imagination, a prudery so profound that it stunned. So she followed Ray and Esther along the promenade, perhaps for a trip in a speedboat, perhaps to a concert on the pier – was there a pier in Torquay? – and dozed her way back to her own honeymoon and the disciplined rich years of her marriage, to wake with a start to the stove burned down to ash and the TV screen empty, Monty sitting testily by the closed door waiting to be let out, and no one to put a hot bottle in her bed except herself.

Grudgingly the days succeeded one another and at last came the weekend of their return. She polished all the brass and silver, cutting up a pair of bloomers especially for new cloths to make a good shine; she scrubbed the kitchen floor, getting down on her knees with her skirt kilted up, rubbing and panting till she had used up all her breath and had to go and lie down. On Saturday she went out to the market and bought a chicken, daffodils and narcissi. She stuffed the chicken, not very well, for she had forgotten, under Esther's care, how to cook the way Grandad liked, and put the flowers in Esther's room – in Esther and Raymond's room. All week the door had stayed shut, she had not even been in to dust, as though the room, like her thoughts, were forbidden. Now she stood in it timidly, the white flowers with their staring eyes quivering in her hand. Instead of one bed there were two, new, glacial. A new chest of drawers stood beside the mantelpiece, with nothing on it yet but a clean white runner; and a space had been cleared in Esther's wardrobe where presently Raymond's suits would hang.

When Sunday tea-time approached, the hour they were expected back, Gran could not sit still. She had rouged and powdered herself, put on her best black dress with the serpent in green sequins down one side on a kind of panel, and Raymond's lizard by the neck, squeezed on her now too tight best shoes with the diamanté buckles. The table was set with the new best cloth, with three kinds of cake and scones and a jar of bloater paste.

It was as if she too were new, dressed in her finery like someone receiving a queen, or perhaps she herself was a queen. Certainly the couple she awaited would be as grand and strange as the Queen and the Duke of Edinburgh, and she herself as grand and strange to herself in her sparkling tight clothing, surrounded by all her best. She hungered to see them, search their faces, to read their happiness or perhaps disappointment, for in her new grand personality she thought she could enjoy, mischievously, a little disappointment, a little anticlimax to Love's Young Dream, while all the time her old lost self clamoured for reunion, to be enclosed once more in the happiness of which she demanded a greedy part.

She heard the taxi and darted halfway across the room, then paused irresolutely, for she did not know to which door this new couple would come. Esther had always used the area, but now . . .? Her heart began to heave and she put her hand against it, feeling dizzy and bewildered. Tears came into her eyes and she felt a stab of anger at being betrayed like this when she had meant to be all vigour and sparkle and now stood here like a watery old hen not knowing which way to go. Then she heard footsteps coming down the stairs – they had used the front door, then – and Esther was there, home again, with her arms round her.

She had not changed a bit. She was no different. Nothing had happened to her, no magic, no seal was set on her. She sat across the table pouring tea, quiet and competent as always, wearing, it was true, new clothes and with a seaside freshness on her skin, but nothing else that Gran could see, no loosening, no signs of love.

All the week's longing turned sour in Gran. These were not the lovebirds she had envisaged. It was not for this staid unromantic couple that she had wandered in limbo for a week, gone neglected and hungry, stuffed a chicken and bought flowers. They owed her something for that week, owed her their absorption, passion, foolishness – anything that showed them to be what she herself had wished on them. They should be moony, larky, holding hands, flushed, giggly, anything but ready to tell her of a charabanc trip to Dartmoor and tea in the Palm Lounge, anything that would repay her for her exclusion from what they had, that could compensate her even a fraction for being past forever the full tide of living.

Deliberately she sucked her tea noisily and set the cup down on her plate. Deliberately she cut cake with a bloatery knife and crumbled it over the teacloth. Deliberately she lit a cigarette while they were still eating and blew the smoke over the table, towards Esther not Raymond. She saw Esther look at her sharply, and deliberately she sucked her teeth and wobbled them up and down and said, 'Those blooming carraway seeds get under me denture.'

She saw a look pass between Esther and Raymond, a look of utter communion and consent, of utter exclusion, and rage rose up in her throat and nearly choked her. 'Proper stick-in-the-muds you seem to've been,' she cried. 'Didn't you never go dancing? Didn't you go on the pier? Ain't there a Butlins?'

'It's not that sort of place,' said Esther. 'It's quiet.'

'Select,' said Raymond, 'only a nice class of person goes there.'

'Dead and alive, if you ask me. Wouldn't surprise me if you was both wheeled about in bath chairs. My goodness, didn't you have any laughs, go in the pubs, have some drinks, do Knees-up-Mother-Brown on the prom?'

'That's silly, Gran,' said Esther gently.

'Silly, is it? Not half so silly as acting half dead on your honeymoon!'

'Me and Esther enjoyed ourselves. We walked on the front and listened to the music. We went in a speedboat one day, didn't we, Ett? If it was a bit blowy we sat in the Sun Lounge of the hotel and watched the people go by. And we went to the pictures.'

'Is that all you did?' cried Gran, and the rage forced tears out of her eyes. 'Doesn't hardly seem worth going all that way for, does it? Might as well have stopped at home with me!'

'Now, Gran!' Esther pushed back her chair and came round the table. To Raymond she said, 'She's upset.'

Gran pushed her away. Her face was puckered and the tears ran down and into the corners of her mouth. 'I'm not upset! I'm blooming fed up with the pair of you! Leaving me all alone – I've not had a decent meal – carrying on like you'd been married for years – not even a white wedding . . .'

'I'll take her upstairs,' said Esther. She put her arm round Gran and half lifted her to her feet. Sobbing and whimpering, Gran allowed herself to be bowed to Esther's shoulder. From his seat Raymond watched them noncommittally and when they were gone leaned forward and cut himself another piece of cake. 'Might never have been on your honeymoon,' he heard Gran wail as she was helped upstairs.

But Gran was wrong.

Perhaps it was because Esther had always spent her days in an office that she had not noticed the seasons. Now, going about the house, to the shops, even for a walk sometimes, nature seemed to burgeon while she watched. Spring had already begun in Torquay, where violets had been out and pods of blossom clung on the trees, but even in London green things were springing and although an east wind blew for Easter it blew out of a sky growing steadily lighter. The inexorability of the year's progress amazed Esther; though there was hail one day and they still needed the stove and Gran had her hot bottle, yet all the while the days lengthened, the buds burst, the birds sang rapturously among the stretching leaves. She had not seen it before; before it had always been winter and then had become summer, the stove and no stove, jackets instead of a winter coat. Now as she did her housework she looked out of the windows at the sky and the changing light and listened to the birds. The whole world seemed expanding and growing buoyant like a balloon.

Soon after Easter the Masons' baby was christened. It had to be done over in Plumstead, safe in the camp of Terry's mother, and Gran and Raymond and Esther made the long bus journey across London to be present.

Terry's mother was like a horse-hair sofa, massive, tightly upholstered, glossy. She dominated. It was her voice that led the responses round the font, she who appeared to have called the baby into being. Her two daughters ran at her direction here and there among the guests who sat round the walls of the sitting-room afterwards, an audience before the glowing stage of the tea table, but she kept Terry beside her. The daughters took after Mr Mason, small and wily, but Terry was hers. She claimed him as she claimed the baby. Gloria, buttoned tightly into a yellow costume, was no more than another guest; she stood in a corner with Mr Mason and one of her brothers-in-law, talking vivaciously and smacking away the hands of a young nephew who kept clutching at her skirt. There were three children, all under six, and they ran and squirmed among the grown-ups, jogging elbows, dripping ice-cream, jealous of the baby in its carry-cot in the next room and of the jollification going on above their heads.

'And now,' cried Mrs Mason, quelling conversation by the slightest raising of her voice, 'if you'll all have your glasses ready – Doreen!' She glanced at one of her daughters, who began to take round a tray of glasses. 'Mr Mason will fill them so that we can all drink a very hearty health to my latest little darling.' Everyone took a glass; Mr Mason came to each and poured out a little champagne. ('My word,' whispered Gran. 'Slap up!') Mrs Mason drew them all to their feet by her eye. 'To my little Kim,' she said. 'She's not my first grandchild and I don't suppose she'll be the last' (laughter and cries of 'That's the spirit!'), 'but she's my own newest blessed little sweetheart. Long life and happiness to her!'

'Long life, happiness, hear hear!' said everyone, sipping their wine, and one young man cried, 'Up guards and at 'em!' and was slapped by his giggling wife. 'Where's Gloria?' said Terry. He went and put his arm round her, taking the attention of the room with him, and under the encouragement and laughter of his friends he and Gloria drank from one glass and he kissed her, clumsily but with ardour, and everyone laughed again and applauded. The champagne did not last long and Doreen came round with cider. Under the nods and nudging of Mr Mason the men began to cluster round him in a corner where he poured them whisky. The sexes began to separate and Esther and Raymond found themselves with Gloria. Terry had joined the men, being slapped on the back and urged to drink, watched proudly by his mother. Gloria also watched him; her voice and her laugh were high.

'It's ever so nice to see you,' she said as though they had not met for weeks. 'I do hope you're enjoying yourselves. Sorry the champagne didn't last long, but of course we've had no say in this affair, Terry and me, it's all been laid on by Her Grace there. Oh well, eat, drink and be merry, I say.' She drank down the remains of her champagne and someone filled her glass again with cider. She turned herself on Raymond. 'I'm ever so glad you could come, Mr Banks. You being away so much, it's lucky we picked a day you could make it. It wouldn't have seemed right for Mrs Banks to have come on her own somehow, not being so newly wed.'

'I'm always home weekends,' said Raymond. Well-brushed, serene, with none of the jovial grossness that was beginning to sweat on some of the men, he stood beside Esther with his hands neatly behind his back.

Gloria coquetted. 'Well I know, but you travellers are such rolling stones you can never be certain, can you? I'm sure I'd never have a minute's peace if I was married to a traveller, wondering what he was up to, you hear such stories!' She giggled into her cider, lowering her eyelids in a provocative manner, then opening eyes wide again. 'Don't you get nervous, Mrs Banks, letting him go off on his own every week? I always say you can't trust men no further than you can see them.'

There was no answer Esther could make to this save a noncommittal murmur; she did not know how far you could trust men but it would never cross her mind not to trust Raymond.

'The things they got up to when I was on the buses,' continued Gloria. 'Honest, it'd make your hair stand on end, married men and all. It taught me a thing or two, I can tell you. Some of them couldn't hardly keep their hands to themselves. I made up my mind I wouldn't let Terry go on with the buses after I had to leave, not after I'd seen what went on. Keep him under my eyes, that's what I said I'd do, and no nonsense about going off on shifts at all hours. That's why I think you're ever so brave, Mrs Banks, with your hubby going off every week. I suppose you never know when he'll be called away on some big deal or something – or then, of course, you might be taking Mrs Banks away for a weekend somewhere. Go while you can, that's what I say, for once you start a family you're tied hand and foot. At least, that's what people are always telling me, but I don't mean to let Kim interfere with my life like some women do.'

All the men save Raymond were now huddled, guffawing, in the corner with the whisky. Gloria did not look their way but drank some more cider. 'I mean, I don't intend to stop having a good time and buying clothes and taking a pride in myself just because I've got a baby. I mean, you don't have to look like something the cat brought in, do you?' She sent a sultry look at Raymond, drawing in her stomach and pressing her breasts out in their tight yellow jacket to demonstrate how little maternity had weathered her. 'I don't believe in letting yourself go like some women do, getting fat and just living for the baby. After all, there's more in life than just having babies, isn't there? I mean, I got rights as well as the baby and I don't see why the wife's always the one to suffer, do you? Of course, I'll look after her and all that, I mean that's only right, isn't it, but I'm not like some women, stick at home all the time and never have any fun. I mean, stuck there all day with the baby I'd go crackers, and I've told Terry, I've always made it plain I might want to go back to work one day. After all, there's always places you can leave them in, isn't there?'

'Yes,' said Raymond. His voice was so utterly without expression that Esther glanced at him. His face was without expression too, but his eyes were blazingly blue, the blue she had seen only once or twice before that seemed to have a fire behind it, of excitement or rage or – hatred? He was perfectly still, but behind his back the hands clasped one another as though locked together and in amazement she perceived that he was petrified with anger, blind and numb to everything but what he saw with that blue stare.

She touched his arm. 'It's time we were going, dear.' He turned the stare on her too so that for an instant she was afraid; not for herself but for him, for the terrible solitude in which his rage locked him behind that opacity. 'Ray,' she said, 'we'll go.'

'Oh don't go yet,' cried Gloria, 'it's early yet. They'll keep it up till all hours, I expect, singing and carrying on. It's lucky babies sleep sound, isn't it, for the boys don't half get noisy when they start beating it up and Her Grace there likes to see Terry enjoying himself. Why don't you stay and make a real night of it? I'm sure Mrs Wilson'd like to.'

'No, we must go,' said Esther. She hardly heard Gloria anymore, her attention was entirely concentrated on releasing Raymond from this strange rigor of emotion. She laid her hand on his arm, a gentle steady pressure, and said again in a low voice, 'Ray, we'll go now.' Slowly his arm relaxed under her fingers, the blaze left his eyes; sight came back to them. 'Right you are, dear,' he said. 'I'll get Gran.'

It was Raymond's custom to get to bed first and lie quietly while Esther undressed and did her face and hair. She had learned that this was a time when he was silent, lying on his back with his wrists crossed behind his head, staring up at the ceiling. She would go about her own affairs very much as she had usually done, for this had always been her only hour of true privacy from Gran. She used it still for small personal tasks, withdrawn in her own pursuits as he in his own thoughts. Yet how strange it still was to her to be busy in her own room while there stood a second bed with Raymond lying in it!

She was undressed and washed and was pinning up her hair when Raymond said, 'Etty.'

'Yes, dear?'

'I've just about had the Masons.'

She put in the last hairpin, then came slowly to his bed and sat down on it. While her intelligence was busy on how to answer him, her eyes dwelt lovingly as always on the texture and contours of his face. She looked away so that she might not be lulled by looking, and said, 'What made you take against Gloria so?'

'Me? When?'

'When we were talking.'

'I don't remember . . .'

'Yes you do, dear.' Their eyes met and a faint flush crept up his cheeks.

'She made me mad.'

'She's only young.'

'She'll be the same when she's ninety. Not a thought in her head except her own silly self, yapping on about men as if she was the Queen of Sheba.'

'She's ever so pretty, Ray, I expect the men do run after her.'

'Pretty!' He moved his head impatiently. 'Duck her in the pond and see if she's pretty. Then you'd see the curls and the colour all run, yes and her vital statistics too, I shouldn't wonder. Sticking out like that they're bound to be falsies.'

'Raymond!' It was Esther who blushed now.

'You saw her, didn't you? Right under your nose, shameless, pushing herself out at me, fluttering her eyelids, giving me the old come on. It's not the men behave like tomcats, it's women like her. They're no better than tarts for all they act so airy-fairy!'

'I think she was upset. She's jealous of Terry's mother.'

'There's another of them! Man-eaters, cannibals! She can't get what she wants from her husband so she's fastened on to her son. See the way she looked at him? She'd eat him up if she could. She can't bear another woman should have him, no, nor the baby neither. Self, self, that's all women ever think of – I know, I've had some!'

He stopped abruptly. Then he said more quietly, 'I don't want her in the house, Ett.'

She looked down at her hands, trying not to tremble at the passion of his unexpected words. 'She's not like that when she's here. She's not like that at all really, I'm sure. She was only showing off.'

'I don't want her in the house.'

She began to pleat the sash of her dressing-gown. 'We can't just tell them to go, Ray. They've been good tenants. I've never had to complain.'

'There's the baby.'

'I couldn't put them out because of the baby. Where would they go? Landlords are awful about children and it's not right.'

'You could let those rooms separate to business girls and make double the money.'

'But I can't turn the Masons out, dear.'

They stared at each other in an impasse. He did not move, but after a moment she reached out and laid her hand on his chest. She could feel his heart beating. 'She's upset you, I know, but you needn't ever see her if you don't want to. After all, you're away half the week and they're over at Plumstead most weekends.' He said nothing. 'There's no real harm in her. I expect some men like to be teased like that. She wasn't to know you're not the sort. She's only young.'

'You're soft, Etty. You don't know nothing.' His voice was hard. 'You think everyone's nice and kind and don't mean no harm to anyone. I tell you people are rotten, rotten and selfish right through. All they're out for is to see they're all right, that's the way people are and that's the way you've got to be to get along. Look out for Number One. And women is the worst. A woman wants something and it don't matter what's in the way, she's got to have it. They'll hand you a line about love and romance and sacrificing themselves, but what they really mean is they want what you can give them and they want it fast. They don't care about nothing else, they'll lie and cheat – all they want's a good time, their sort of good time.'

'That's not true, Ray. Gloria . . .'

'Yes, Gloria! Little Gloria with her tight skirts and her bubble curls and her chase-me-Charlie eyes. She's not thinking about her husband or kid, she's just thinking about herself. She's had her fun and she's got the kid but she won't let that interfere with her getting more fun, just whenever she wants. Terry, the baby, they won't matter – that's what made me mad, the way she spoke of the kid. Why the hell do they have them if they don't want to be bothered with them?

Why bring them into the world and then say I'm sorry, I can't be bothered, I want a good time? I'll tell you why – because women are animals, that's why. They think of nothing else but men, men, men, morning, noon and night. That's the only thing they want. That's why I don't want your precious Gloria here, chasing off after her good time when she's tired of Terry and never mind what happens to the kid. I don't want that kind of bitch in the house. Animals they are, animals on heat!'

She began to shiver. She could not speak or move or think, only sit there with the ague shaking her. His monstrous words echoed in a huge solitude; she could find no cause for them, no meaning within the Raymond she thought she knew. She felt a great loneliness gathering at her back. Everything seemed terribly still, the furniture standing, the curtains hanging, the light burning, herself sitting looking at her cold clasped hands. She could think of nothing to say, for Raymond had gone beyond the bounds of her knowledge. Once again he was lost in a wilderness and she lacked the clue to follow him; she could only sit motionless, with the ugly words re-echoing and with them a snatch of senseless tune – 'Ten tiny fingers, ten tiny toes, two tiny faces each with a turned-up nose . . .' The pert little tune jingled over and over in the desert and the shivering swept her.

From a great distance she heard him say, 'You're cold.'

She could shake her head. 'Here, get in.' He folded back the bedclothes and numbly she rose and got in beside him, half sitting up, still in the dressing-gown. He put his arm round her, feeling her hands. 'You're frozen. I'm sorry, Ett.'

The faint warmth of a smile touched her lips but she could still say nothing. He bent his head so that all she could see was the fair hair smoothed back to the small loved peak at his nape. In a low voice he said again, 'I'm sorry, Ett.'

The shivering was slowly ceasing. She was able to turn her hand so that it clasped his. She laid her cheek on his hair and the warmth seeped through to her, but she could still say nothing. The warmth of his hand and of his arm about her, the smooth warmth of his hair, brought love throbbing through her like blood returning to a frozen limb. She kissed his temple, saying nothing.

In a low voice, face still hidden, he said, 'I'm sorry, Ett. I didn't mean to sound off like that. It's just – the way she spoke.' She kissed him again. 'My mother – it wasn't like I told you. She run off when I was a kid. That's why when Gloria talked like that – I couldn't stand it.'

'Your mother did?'

'Yes, when I was a kid. I've never told no one. That's why I'm a bit funny about it, see, good-time girls and all that. I know what it means in misery.'

'Why didn't you tell me?'

'I've never told no one. I never meant to tell you only somehow – I don't like upsetting you. My mother went off, see? She went off and left me when I was only a little kid. She didn't give a damn.'

'But Ray, neither did mine.'

'You had a home.'

'But no mother. She didn't care about me, she was never here. All she wanted was a gay time, like you said, poor mother. That's how she had me.'

'Wasn't she married?' He stared at her, intelligence blazing back into his eyes. 'Gran never told me that.'

'She's ashamed of it.'

'You!' He still stared at her as though seeing someone he had never recognised before. 'So your mum wasn't married! Didn't you mind?'

'What's the good of minding?'

'Didn't it make you hate her?'

'Why should it? She couldn't help it, I suppose.'

'Did she live with the fellow?'

'I don't know. On tour, perhaps. He was a singer like her.'

'You never knew him?'

'No. I suppose he was married already. No one ever said. Grandad told me a little when I was ten, but not that.' She remembered that solemn talk. It had been a Sunday, Gran upstairs having a sleep after lunch and Grandad in his dark suit and stiff Sunday collar had talked to her, standing with his back to the stove while she, also in Sunday dress, sat listening. His face had got red but his voice had been steady and gone on to the end. She had been impressed by his manner and embarrassed by his embarrassment, but it was only later on that what he said meant anything to her. 'It's right you should know who your parents were,' Grandad had said, 'that's everyone's right, be they saint or sinner.'

'Who was he?' asked Raymond.

'His name was Rudolph Belmont – his stage name, that is. I don't know what it was really. They were both in the chorus.'

'And you never saw him?'

'No. I hardly ever saw Mother. Sometimes she'd come rushing back if the company had a week out or a London booking, but she never stayed.'

'What was she like?'

'I can't remember.' The photograph on the mantelpiece downstairs, Grandad talking, a soprano voice rising through the house sometimes to a slapdash accompaniment, a smell of roses, a memory of curls . . .

'She was gay and pretty. She brought me a Pierrot doll once – Gran's got it somewhere. It upset Gran when she died.'

'A car smash, wasn't it?'

'No. That's what Gran says, but really she was just knocked down by a bus in Manchester. There was a whole lot of them running across the road to the theatre, Grandad told me, and she just didn't look. It was like her, I think.'

'And your father?'

'I don't know. They gave out he'd gone to Australia – I don't think Mother had seen him for years.'

'Still,' he said, 'you weren't left on your own. You had your grandad and your gran.'

'And you had your uncle and auntie.'

'Yes, that's right. We wasn't both quite thrown on the rubbish heap like something nobody wanted.'

She held his hand tightly. 'So we're together, Ray. We're both the same.'

'Yes. It's funny, that.' They lay together in silence, too wearied by their admissions to talk any more. When at last she made a move to leave him he let her go. She slipped out of the dressing-gown and turned off the light, sliding into her own cold bed in a darkness bright only where a sword of moonlight came between the curtains. She heard him sigh and rustle down under the bedclothes. 'I'm sorry, Ett,' he said again, drowsily.

'Sleep well, dearest,' she answered – sleep well, sleep well . . .

She slept so soon and so deeply that he was beside her, in her bed, before she woke. It was full daylight, which she knew must mean it was after seven o'clock, and soon indeed she heard the bell of St Peter's sound briefly for early service. That was the only sound, for it was Sunday and a counterpane of quiet seemed to lie over the streets. Raymond snuggled down beside her, putting his arm across her body and kissing her cheek, whispering 'Good morning' in a way she always found disarming – it disarmed her of practical thought, shyness, sleep, of everything save love. She said nothing but turned so that her head was on his shoulder.

'Ett,' he said, kissing her hair, 'you know what we told each other last night? Ett, I never told anyone that before. It was my secret, see? I never told anyone.'

'It doesn't matter,' she murmured.

'No, I know it doesn't matter. It's just that I never have, see? I've been kind of funny about it, as if it wasn't my secret, more of a sacred trust, see, not to let my dad down in front of everyone somehow.'

'But he died?'

'Yes, I know he died, and while he was alive my mother was just like I said to him, nursed him, looked after him wonderful. It was after he passed away she changed – trying to forget maybe, I don't know, trying to mend a broken heart. She changed. She wasn't the kind of mother I wanted any more. And finally she run out.'

Esther said nothing, stroking his arm.

'Only I never told no one, see, you're the very first person I ever let it out to. And I don't want you to tell anyone, Ett – not anyone.'

She smiled. 'Who would I tell, dear?'

'I don't know, but I want you to promise. It's not just my secret, see, it's hers and my dad's and – and Auntie's. Auntie'd be upset if she knew I'd told you. You know how clergymen are, they're ever so strait-laced, and it took Auntie a long time to get over the shock when Mother went off. So promise me, Ett.'

'As if I would . . .'

'Promise,' he insisted.

'I promise.'

'That's a good girl,' he said and kissed her again.

It was queer, she thought drowsily, that they should both have the same secret – or nearly the same; and that one confidence should have drawn forth the other so that still they were equal, paired. Her knowledge of her parentage had always held her back, had built up her reserve as perhaps Grandad had intended it should. 'You have to be careful,' he had said. 'You have to remember one can't play fast and loose in this life. As ye reap so shall ye sow, Esther,' and he would smile and stroke her hair as he said it as though to rob the words of sternness. She had remembered it; and Raymond too had remembered, only with him the knowledge had come out a different way, in bitterness. It had taught him not to trust anyone, she thought, only himself and the money that gave him confidence. Money would be father and mother to him, she could see that; could see too why fury had possessed him over poor little Gloria. Now that she knew its causes Esther was not afraid of that rage anymore. She would watch for it, deflect it, make him secure by her love and knowledge and shared shames. From the beginning she had loved – with her eyes, with her touch, with her cautious heart; now bit by bit she was knowing too. To know, deeply; and no matter what it was you found, only to love more steadily: was that what marriage was? She was learning, learning . . . and then a terror struck her. She raised her head a little.

'Ray?'

'Mm?'

'You won't think the less of me because I'm – because my mother wasn't . . .?' She could not utter the words, fear closed her throat, for people did feel strongly about these things, that was why Gran had always kept it dark; people did blame the children and perhaps Ray . . . What did she flatter herself she knew of Ray?

She heard his voice scornful above her. 'Think the less of you because your mum was a fool? What do you take me for?' His arm tightened over her. 'The whole lousy world's not worth sixpence. Except you, Ett. You're all right.'

She felt a surge of feeling come from him, as though a door had suddenly been opened wide on a warm room and the warmth enveloped her. He lifted her face and pressed his mouth on hers, sliding downwards in the bed so that their bodies matched. She took his warmth and his decision more easily than ever before. There seemed hardly any strangeness left.

He went at tea-time. Occasionally he stayed till Monday morning but usually he preferred to catch an early evening train that would bring him to his destination in time for a night's rest. He was cheerful all day but a little withdrawn, as though embarrassed by what had been between them earlier, both the confidences and the intercourse. He was not a passionate man – at least Esther, judging by what Gran told her of admirers she had resisted, supposed he was not. She had understood from Gran that men were ravening beasts, up to anything at all times; from the chatter in the Ladies' at Winters' too she had gathered that sex was seldom from their minds and indeed that both men and women passed their nubile years in a state of fever. That Raymond was not like that she had known from their first meeting: he had always been respectful, polite, and later when they were engaged, gentle. There had been for her none of the tussles, the slapping away of hands that seemed to occupy so much of the courting time of the girls at Winters', and this was one of the many reasons why she loved him. No one had ever made love to her; Mrs Bromwich's grandson had held her hand and kissed her twice after a social, and once when she was new at Winters' the young man in Hardware had made a grab at her in the goods' lift; but beyond that not only had she not met many men but she avoided those she did, not in fact but by retiring into the reserve and caution Grandad had advised. She could not have loved Raymond if he had frightened her.

She did not know what other men were like. She knew only that Raymond was gentle, quiet, courteous, embarking on her body only when the time seemed proper for it, when she was able to ignore the strangeness of the act and see it only as the ultimate expression of her love for him. This morning – and she found herself remembering it – there had seemed a joy in it she had not known before. They had joined together without courtesy on his side or awkwardness on hers. Yes, she thought of it through the day and after he had gone. She thought of it, smiling. That he had retired into himself a little was a sign that he thought of it too, that he too recognised that this had been union, not merely a gesture required of him by contract.

So he went and she was left with Gran and the empty house. It was very empty without him and the days dragged. She missed the company at Winters' and the routine of going to work. She had not yet established a similar routine at home, and she found Gran's company all day less enjoyable than that of the people at the store. She was homesick for the store, and as she did not wish to visit it yet, lest they guessed her return to be a kind of haunting, she asked Miss Burroughs to supper. Miss Burroughs replied that she would prefer to come to tea, as she was away from work with an attack of bronchitis and did not want to be out late in the night air. So she came that Tuesday.

They used the front sitting-room, a fire burning glumly in the unaccustomed grate. 'We ought to use this room more often,' Raymond had said a week or two ago. 'You and me can sit up here and leave Gran all cosy downstairs with the telly, eh?' Esther had assented, but thoughtfully. The telly would be no compensation to Gran for being excluded; the sitting-room must be brought into use little by little. So they sat now in the plump chairs, drinking from the best tea-cups, Gran wearing her lizard and Miss Burroughs an immense cardigan with a silk square over her shoulders against the draught, which Esther had to admit to herself was keen. If this room were to be used something would have to be done about that draught before next winter.

Miss Burroughs appeared unshaken by her illness, although her cheeks were a little flushed and the sound of her breathing filled the silences, as does the ticking of a clock once one begins to notice it. It was as if the machinery of Miss Burroughs were beginning to show. She had 'taken' bronchitis, she was convinced, because of Jacqueline's insistence that the office window should be opened. 'She *smokes*, Miss Wilson – oh excuse me, I should say Mrs Banks, of course, but really I've thought of you so long as Miss Wilson . . .'

'Why not call her Esther?' said Gran. 'You've known her long enough.'

'Oh well – thank you – this habit of Christian names, all the juniors do it now but when Miss – Esther joined Winters' I'm glad to say we still kept our formal business approach. I'm afraid it will take quite a little time for me to get used to calling you anything new. Of course I call Jacqueline Jacqueline because I always have, but I don't care for it and it's my belief that if we were more formal she wouldn't defy me the way she does.'

'Go on!' said Gran.

'Yes she does, Mrs Wilson.' The flush was bright now. 'She *smokes* at elevenses and again at tea, and then she opens the window to let the smoke out, because you remember Mr Winters really doesn't allow smoking, especially from the girls, and it's right behind where I sit, if you remember, and she leans over my machine fanning the smoke out and there I have to sit. And this has been going on ever since you left, Miss – Esther, and all through that bitter weather we had, so naturally I had to pay for it.'

'What a shame,' murmured Esther. 'I'm sure she can't realise . . .'

'She *should* realise,' said Miss Burroughs. 'I'm not one to speak, but if she had any consideration for other people she would sense my disapproval and discomfort. Well, now that I've been laid low perhaps she will.' Her breathing sounded loudly and she accepted another cup of tea.

'Does she do the work properly?' asked Esther.

'Well yes, she does, I'm bound to say. There's nothing wrong with her little grey cells, as Monsieur Poirot calls them. It's just that she's like all young people nowadays, bone selfish.'

'And Diane?'

'Well *there*, Miss – Esther, there we have a surprise! Diane turns out to be a *femme fatale*. Honey to the bears, it's really surprising. It's not as though she were pretty – and she really doesn't appear to lead them on in any way at all. I suppose there's just something about her, something friendly and soft . . .' She mused for a moment, then lowered her voice. 'Do you know, I think even Mr Ian . . . oh, nothing wrong, of course, but he does come into our room just a little more often than he used to. Perhaps it's my imagination, but it's really very surprising – honey to the bears.'

'My Win was like that,' said Gran.

'Well,' said Miss Burroughs, 'I have to smile. For she's ever such a nice child with it all. Not like Jacqueline. Jacqueline's sharp.'

'How long have you been off?'

'Just on the fortnight. I'm going up to my sister's in Scarborough on Friday for a few days to get some sea air into my poor old chest.'

'Scarborough's where Ray's auntie lives,' said Esther. 'I wonder if your sister knows her?'

'Eileen knows nearly everyone, Bernard being in the bank. What is her name?'

'Well – Banks, I suppose.' Esther laughed. 'Isn't that silly, d'you know I don't really know? I don't know if she was his father's sister or her husband was his brother – they were relations of his father, I do know that. I've never actually had occasion to use the name, she's always just been Raymond's auntie. Her husband's dead, you see. He was a clergyman.'

'It's the same as me with your married name,' said Miss Burroughs. 'When I go back on Monday and say I've seen you, I know I shall say Miss Wilson.'

'But it's silly, I ought to know. I'll ask him on Thursday when he comes home and send you a postcard.'

'Do, and I might call and tell her I've seen you. It would be quite an adventure – have you never met?'

'No, we never have. She wrote when we were first engaged – such a nice letter, it was – and of course I've seen her photograph.'

'And she sent Etty ever such a lovely brush and comb set for a wedding present,' said Gran. 'Ivory it is with initials all written in the backs, two brushes and a mirror and a clothes brush all in this lovely ivory. Show it to her, Etty, when she's putting her hat on.'

The hint was accepted and Miss Burroughs rose to go. The visit had been looked forward to, enjoyed, and now was over. Miss Burroughs had liked Esther. When Esther came to Winters', not very different than she was now except that she was then sixteen, Miss Burroughs had still been a young woman; young, that is, as years went now, in her forties. It had still been possible that something more might be round the corner for Miss Burroughs, while for Esther, of course, the whole of her life was to come, by which was meant marriage. Well, it had come to her, but to Miss Burroughs nothing had come but the years and the certainty of a pension, the slow accumulation of savings in her bank, more weight, more slowness, more – yes, content. She did not want anything more now. She and Esther had set the tone of their office, worked amicably together, respected each other; she had expected Esther to develop as she herself had done and that the structure of their department would be unchanged even after Miss Burroughs' retirement, for by then Esther would have become Miss Burroughs. With Esther's marriage something basic had altered for Constance Burroughs; it was a confirmation that things might happen to other people, even people she had thought safe, but for her nothing would happen. It was, perhaps, the end of hope, but also the beginning of contentment. She did not want to be changed now; she wanted only what she had: a furnished room, a safe job, a pension. She went away from Handel Street serene, full of goodwill, touched a little with pity. For Miss Wilson – Esther – there must be a host of new problems, anxieties, experiences. For Constance Burroughs there were, mercifully, none.

Certainly there were new problems for Esther and one of them was money. Before she married she had been in the habit of living on her salary, banking the Masons' rent; the revenue from the shop was banked automatically by the Grovers. When they came back from their honeymoon Raymond had given her fifteen pounds and said, 'See how you go with that, Ett.' It had run out three weeks later while he was away and she had put the Masons' rent into the housekeeping. She had done this ever since, for Raymond had not raised the matter again and she, able to manage on her own, had not raised it either. She shrank from talking about money with Raymond; she knew his touchiness on the subject and knew also that, despite the bonus, Torquay and the presents and the general expenses of the wedding must have run him down. She knew too that his earnings were not constant; he was sure of a minimum but, to be comfortable, he was dependent on commissions and these fluctuated. She had never asked for details. Sometimes she had read controversies in the papers, 'Should a Wife have her Husband's Paypacket?', from which it was plain that thousands of women never knew how much their husbands earned and were dependent on their charity for every pound. Men were funny about their earnings: she could not remember Grandad ever mentioning money or the shop to her, he had held that these were masculine affairs; and after all she did not need to ask for housekeeping money because she could always use the Masons' rent and, if necessary, the takings from the shop.

But it was a problem, just the same, at the back of her mind – should she mention it and if so, how much should she ask for? Should she, even, ask for any? Would it not be more tactful to go on using the Masons' rent and let Ray pay his money, whatever it was, direct into the bank? She did not know how married people handled these things and it was no good asking Gran, who had never been trusted to do more than buy the food in all her life.

Nevertheless, knowing Raymond, she felt he would not want his wife to be subsidising his house for him; had he not several times said to her, 'A man ought to have the money'?

'Money? Why of course, Ett.' It was Friday; he had come back the day before as usual and as usual they had gone out together to the pictures, for they still kept up the ritual of 'their Thursdays'. Pleasure at his return had sent her problem to the back of her mind but now, when Gran had gone upstairs for her afternoon sleep, it seemed a good time to talk to him.

He reached into his breast pocket and took out his wallet. 'How much do you want?'

'Well . . .' She began to redden and flounder. 'It seems so awful asking – it's only the housekeeping – but I can easily manage, dear . . .'

'Don't be soft.' He smiled. 'I ought to have thought of it myself. I reckon we're neither of us much cop at knowing the ropes of this sort of thing, eh? How much d'you need – a fiver, ten?'

'Oh no – not for the week – five will be plenty. Unless we do it for the fortnight – or perhaps monthly? I don't know what's best.'

'Weekly's best for me,' he said and opened the wallet. He felt in it and brought out a couple of pounds, looking up at her ruefully. 'The only thing is, that's all I've got. I draw my money the end of the month, see, and I've run myself down a bit because – well frankly, dear, I paid out a packet not long ago and I've been trying to go as short as I can so as to get some lolly back in the bank again. I don't like having no lolly in the bank. So I've been cutting things as fine as I could and these two quid is all I've got on me till next week.'

'It doesn't matter, Ray. It doesn't matter a bit. It was just that I thought I ought to mention it. I can easily manage . . .'

'No, no.' He replaced the wallet and stretched across to pat her hand. 'We've got to have everything cut and dried like a respectable old married couple. We can't none of us live on air. You tell me what you want and I'll try and provide it as of the end of this month.'

'Well, if it's by the week – five pounds would be plenty. I mean, I could put by out of that for the gas and the coal and so on. Or if that's too much, then three and I can do the rest from the Masons like I have been doing. It's just you must tell me the way you want me to do it.'

'The Masons' rent, eh? How much is that? Two pound ten?'

'Two seventeen six now.'

He shook his head. 'You could get double that if you was to let the rooms single. Still, we won't argue that again. Two seventeen six? Maybe it'd be best if you did use that towards the coal and things. Then I'd just give you the two or three odd quid and put the rest safely back in the bank, eh? What d'you think about that?'

'I think that would do well, dear. There's no sense in your paying a lot out when I've got the Masons' money coming in. This way's much more sensible and fair.'

'You don't mind using your money?'

'Of course not. It's the same as if I was earning. If I was still at business I wouldn't be letting you pay all the house, it wouldn't be fair. This way the house pays for itself almost, I can do my share.'

'That's a thing I've been thinking about,' he said slowly. He took her hand where it lay on the table and began to fold the fingers gently to and fro. 'Sharing things. I've been giving it some thought, Ett, since the weekend when we both shared – well, we shared our secrets, didn't we?' She nodded, pressing his hand. 'And it seems to me we ought to go on, share everything, see – secrets and living and everything. So I went to my bank and I got them to make out a letter, see, a sort of form entitling you to draw on my account, making it into a joint account, so that if anything happened to me or anything, you could draw on it, see, and I'd know you were all right.'

She felt the colour come up in her cheeks again. 'Don't say things like that, dear.'

'Well, we have to get things straight. I'd want to know you'd be all right.'

'You know I'd never . . .'

'You might need to. Anyway, it's right you should be able to. Share and share alike, eh? Isn't that it?'

She nodded, gripping his hand. Her mind was for an instant adrift at the terror of losing him, the husband, the loved one, longed for and despaired of, bestowed at last, held safe in the heart and the home, impossible now to be lost. With his other hand he felt in his breast pocket again and drew out a paper. It bore the printed heading of a bank. He smoothed it out and gave it to her; she read the instruction that the bank should accept her signature for withdrawals on the account of Raymond Cavendish Banks. 'You sign it there,' he said, 'where it says Specimen of Signature, and then I'll post it off and you can draw on it when you like.'

'I don't want to. It's not necessary . . .'

'You do it,' he said gently. 'Here – do it now.' He disengaged his hand to find and give her the Biro from his waistcoat. Unwillingly she took it, read through the words again, and signed her name. He took the paper from her and signed also. 'There,' he said. 'Share and share alike.'

'Then I ought to have a joint account too,' she said, 'if it's to be share and share.' He smiled her away. 'No, but I ought, Ray. After all, it's only fair. Something might happen to me just as much as you. Of course it's fair.'

'Nonsense.'

'It's not nonsense, dear, it's only right. I'll go to the bank tomorrow morning and get the form.' Activity drove the emotion from her mind and made her practical. She drew the paper towards her again and studied it. 'I'll get the same kind of form exactly and you can sign it and then we'll be even. We'll go round together in the morning. It's no good arguing.' She smiled at him tenderly, rising and beginning to stack the after-lunch cups and saucers. 'It's only just round the corner, not more than ten minutes' walk. Where's yours, I didn't notice?'

He folded the paper and put it back in his pocket. 'Birmingham.'

'Birmingham? That's a funny place for it to be.'

'Not really. You know I'm through Birmingham most weeks in the month, it's my sort of headquarters. I don't want to go up and down to London with a lot of cash on me so I've got my account up there. It's handy.'

'Yes, I suppose it is.' She put the crockery on a tray and carried it out to the scullery. Coming back to fold away the cloth she said, 'Miss Burroughs was here to tea. Talking of Birmingham reminded me.'

'What, of Miss Burroughs?'

'No, Scarborough.'

He laughed. 'Go on, I'm giddy!'

'No, honest, Ray, she's going to Scarborough. She's been ill.'

'She has?' He was standing with his back to the unlit stove, hands in pockets, teasing her.

'She's going to stay with her sister in Scarborough and I promised to send her a postcard giving your auntie's name. I felt ever such a fool not knowing it. She's just Raymond's auntie, I had to say, and she gave me ever such a look as though she was thinking I must be getting soft, not knowing whether it was Banks or what.'

His voice was still light. 'What's she want to know for?'

'Never mind her wanting to know, I want to know!' She folded the tablecloth deftly and laid it away in the sideboard. 'Her sister's husband works in a bank there and she says she'll most likely know her. We thought it would be nice if she called, gave her our news.'

'Her sister wouldn't know Auntie.'

'She might, dear. It's not all that big a place.'

'Yes it is. It's a very big place. Besides, Auntie lives just outside it, not really in Scarborough at all. She doesn't go out much.'

'Oh. Still, she might like a visitor.'

'I don't think she would, Ett, not someone she didn't know. She leads such a quiet life, see, and she's getting old and frail, you know how old people hate surprises.'

'Like Gran does?' she mocked.

He smiled dutifully. 'OK, like Gran does. I don't think she'd want to see Miss Burroughs.'

'Well all right, dear, then I won't write. It probably wouldn't have caught her anyway, I think she goes tomorrow – or is it today? I just thought it might be nice, give Miss Burroughs something of her own to do. I think she feels a bit out of it among all her sister's friends and children and in-laws.' She set a vase of daffodils on the table and pushed the chairs in neatly. 'All the same, what is Auntie's name?'

'Cavendish. Mrs Cavendish.'

'Like your second name?'

'That's right. She was my dad's sister, see, and she married a Reverend Cavendish.'

'And they gave you their name? That was nice.'

'Yes. He christened me. And Auntie used to tell me how I put out my little tongue and tried to lick the holy water when it ran down my nose.'

They laughed together and Esther went to do the washing-up. Presently they would go out into the High Street for the shopping and he would buy the four or five magazines in which he indulged himself each weekend. He was a great reader of digests and do-it-yourself manuals. 'They teach you something,' he would say. 'You learn something you didn't know before – never know when it may come in handy.'

His hobby, Esther often thought, was information. When he found anything new or strange in the newspapers he would read it out: 'Listen to this,' he would say. 'This beats all getout,' and they would listen and Gran would say, 'Fancy!' He would never miss one of the quiz programmes on television and if he knew an answer which the panel did not he was as pleased as a baby; his face seemed to fill out, his eyes sparkle and his whole body relaxed in a casual I-just-happen-to-know attitude which Esther found touching and Gran admired as she had admired Grandad when he used to talk about the war or politics. Raymond never talked politics; they filled him with the same contempt as multi-married film stars. 'It's got nothing to do with us, each lot's as bad as the other,' he would say. 'They're all rotten, the whole pack of them.' Gran thought he was wonderful. With a man in the house who knew so much there was no need for her to use her head at all. She was sorry he was so down on elopements and breach of promise cases and divorce, but she could read those for herself, whereas the things Ray read out she never would ever have looked at. 'Doesn't he know a lot!' she whispered to Esther when Raymond described how atomic energy was created. 'That's because I read a lot, Gran. I keep my eyes open. You never know what won't come in useful one day.'

He went to the bank next morning with Esther. He had never been before and was impressed by the deference shown her; she was obviously a well-known and respected customer. They were put in a little room, all blotting-paper and mahogany, and attended by a sub-manager who presently produced the authorisation. Esther signed twice, checking it through before she did so, then handed the pen to Raymond. He took off his glove. 'Where do I sign?' he asked naïvely.

'Here, sir, just below Mrs Banks.'

He took up the pen and started to write, then paused. '*Two* signatures?' he said.

'Yes, just the two,' the sub-manager smiled.

'I only had the one on mine. Just the one signature, that's all that's needed.'

'No, dear, you signed it too, I remember,' said Esther.

'I signed the authorisation. I didn't sign a Specimen of Signature. Only one signature's needed.'

'That is so in certain cases,' the sub-manager said. 'If I may say so, it's less customary than might be expected between married people.' He smiled a little, cynically. 'The more usual form is that both signatures are required for withdrawals from a joint account. Of course, in cases of serious illness or death, prolonged absence abroad of one or the other party . . .'

'We didn't need both signatures on mine,' repeated Raymond. He stood with the pen in his hand, looking from Esther to the sub-manager, a slight flush in his cheeks.

'We usually advise it,' said the sub-manager. 'In certain cases it does provide a safeguard . . .'

'We don't need no safeguard,' Raymond broke in. 'It's a joint account, see. Share and share. I trust her, she trusts me. I haven't asked for a double signature on mine. I trust her.'

'Ray – please, dear . . .'

'We always advise . . .'

'It's a joint account. She can draw on it or I can draw on it. That's what I've done.'

'Ray, listen.' She laid her hand on his arm, gazing into his blazing eyes as though trying to draw the fire out of them. 'Don't get upset, dear. It's just a formality . . .'

'Formality!'

'It is, dear. I didn't explain to them how it was to be, you heard me, I just told them we wanted to make it so's you could draw on it too.'

'I don't want to draw on it.'

'I know, dear – the whole thing's just a formality really, isn't it, like me drawing on yours? I never would, you know that, it was just your silly old idea and thought for me.' The sub-manager turned away tactfully and rearranged the set of the blotter on the table. 'It doesn't make any difference how we sign it, if that's the way they do it here.'

'If you trusted me, my signature'd be enough.'

'Ray!' She flushed and felt tears stinging up in her eyes. 'That's cruel.'

'I'm sorry.' He looked across at the elaborately pre-occupied figure of the sub-manager. From beyond the glass-panelled door a cushiony murmur of adding machines and typewriters sounded mutedly, shot through with an occasional bell. The air seemed ripe with polished wood, smooth-running drawers, plumply swinging doors, the slither of coins into copper shovels, the fat presence of money. Over the frosted glass the tops of heads could be seen passing to and fro, and on the outside wall, between the sun-shiney windows, a clock and a calendar recorded the passing of time. He managed to smile. 'It's just – it upset me, that's all.'

Esther turned to the sub-manager. 'Could we have it altered?'

'Well . . .' He sounded somewhat embarrassed. 'We don't usually advise it. In the case of a substantial account, you see – unless it is really urgently desired for some reason?'

She turned back to Raymond. 'I don't really see that it matters, dear. I mean, I'm always here if you wanted to draw on it. And perhaps in a way – you see, it's not really as if it was all my own money. It's what Grandad left, you see, half of it anyway, for me to look after Gran.'

'Wouldn't I look after Gran?'

'Of course, dear. It's just that in a kind of way I wouldn't feel right, not having nothing to do with it. Together, yes. Unless you're really dead set on it.'

'If, as I gather, the matter is merely a formality,' said the sub-manager, 'the point becomes rather an academic one. It is the bank's practice, as I said, to advise the double signature. It does act as a check and as a safeguard against one party drawing in excess of the other, for instance, as it might be if the wife has bought a new hat or the husband been unlucky on the Derby!' He laughed appreciatively and Esther smiled.

'Nothing like that would happen,' she said. 'I do think perhaps it's best, dear. And if you want we can get your bank to alter yours so that we both have to sign that too. Then we'll be square again.' She looked at him inquiringly, her hand still on his arm. The blaze had gone from his eyes and his face had a sulky look. She knew he was trying to cover his outburst in front of the sub-manager.

'Very well.' He drew his arm away and picked up the pen. 'It's nothing to me,' he said as he wrote his name. 'It's of no importance. It just upset me, that's all.'

The velvety blotting-paper pressed, the smooth paper was folded; the oiled hinges swung back the varnished door, the warm breath of money reached them. The double door with its shining brass was drawn open from its padded junction; they were smiled out into the gusty street again. On the wall the clock recorded that ten more minutes of eternity had passed.

FIVE

GRAN SAT in the saloon bar of the Dick Whittington, face to face with a small gin and lime. It was just past noon. Save for a man in the striped trousers of a floor-walker she was alone – alone but for the gin and lime. It stood starkly, almost belligerently, on the glass-topped table in front of her, its greeny-yellow transparence erect on its stem. She stared at it, and it seemed to stare back at her.

It was Wednesday and she was supposed to be at the launderette. She had left the washing tumbling unwatched in the machine and had come sneaking along to the Dick Whittington, not on impulse, not because she felt cold or poorly, but deliberately, with forethought. Instead of the old felt hat she wore every day to the shops she had put on the one she had bought for the Masons' baby's christening; and under her coat, which in the warmth of the bar parlour she had thrown back, she wore the lizard. She had sneaked out of the house when Esther was upstairs polishing the bedrooms so that her hat should not be remarked; although the chances were, she had thought resentfully as she scuttled along the pavement, half expecting to hear Esther's voice at her back, that Esther wouldn't have noticed. That was part of the reason why she was here, alone, spruced up and intimidated by this glass demanding in front of her.

The bar was very contemporary. The chairs were of mock bamboo, upholstered in a design of continental sauce bottles in plastic basket weave; the same material topped the tables under their glass. The neon sign 'BAR PARLOUR – SNACKS – TELEVISION' was obscured from inside by a forest of rubber plants and a descending curtain of tradescantia which wept greenly from its withering roots as it hung from wicker wine-bottles under the fluorescent lighting. The bar was faced with bamboo also, posters of bullfights and St Tropez hung behind, a hidden record-player itched out calypsos and the horn-palmed clapping of Andalusian gypsies, and from the handles of the beer machines one expected explosive milk to froth. The floor was linoleumed in a kind of mock gorgonzola.

A real up-to-the-minute place, thought Gran, avoiding the eye of her gin and lime. Nothing dead-and-alive about this. You wouldn't catch any of the old cats round our way coming in here, not likely. A nice bright class of customer you'd get here, people right on the spot, car salesmen and perhaps even actresses. At the moment, of course, it was quiet; it was early yet. She could safely leave her washing for half an hour or so, and by then she would have seen a bit of life. That's all she wanted, a bit of life.

The thought emboldened her to pick up the glass and take a sip from it. Sticky and sweet, nine parts lime to one of gin, it was delicious. She took another and set the glass back on the table. Humbled, it no longer stared at her.

All she wanted was a bit of life. She was sick of playing gooseberry. Ray was lovely, a fine chap, full of jokes and a real gentleman, you couldn't wish for a better grandson-in-law. When he was with her she felt twenty years younger. The things he knew, it would surprise you! And ready every Saturday afternoon to take them out to tea in the High Street or for a bus ride up west. There was nothing wrong with Ray – except that he was Esther's.

Even when they were all together it was the two of them and her. It hadn't been like that before they were married, then they had all been jolly together. Of course, once you'd been to bed together it was different (she could say that to herself now, meaning only the bedroom with its two beds and shared clothing and Ray's shaving things on the washstand, nothing more – she still could not go further than that). It was only to be expected; but she had not expected it, had not expected to be excluded even when they all sat together round the telly or played three-handed whist after tea. She had not expected Esther not to belong to her anymore.

It was only to be expected. But not from Esther, who had thought so little of boys that she hadn't even had the sense to use lipstick till Gran had told her to. She kept her face smooth and quiet now just as she always had, but Gran knew where her thoughts were. She was sensible and busy and dependable as always, but still Gran knew. Only the surface of Esther belonged to her now; and no matter what they said to her or gave her or took her to, the inexorable door would close upon the two of them and there was only one of her. It was only to be expected; but she had not.

At least when Raymond was home it was lively, but when he was away Gran sometimes felt like screaming. Although she wanted Esther's full attention she did not want her full attendance. She longed for the lazy, slatternly hours that had been hers after Esther had gone to business, when she had been free and on the loose, safe in the knowledge of exactly when Esther would return. The cups of tea and cigarettes, the rummaging and dozing, the blissful liberty . . .! Now there was always something being done somewhere about the house or, if not, Esther sitting, her hands busy with sewing or knitting but her mind concerned only with Raymond's return. Both of them felt a boredom and impatience they had not known when their lives were emptier.

So Gran had planned this escapade and now sat in the Dick Whittington's bamboo jungle. She felt rather hot, not only from the fineness of the day, for spring had come with a sudden surrender of blueness and softness, but from gin and guilt. Whatever would they think if they knew she was here, Esther and Grandad? She had tried it once before, during Esther's honeymoon, and been frightened off by her conscience. Yet the breach had been opened then, the thunderbolts dared; and this place was ever so much nicer class, really artistic, not one of those common places where often and often she'd gone in her youth after the show with some of the girls and the men, for oysters and stout and a good old singsong . . . This was not that sort of place at all, she assured herself primly, taking another sip.

She sat and little by little the place filled up, and they were the kind of people she had expected: stout men in black homburgs ordering whisky, hatless young men made pale by the virility of their moustaches, handsome women in little black suits, the veins showing too clearly through too thin nylons, a girl or two with identical tumbled hair, identical polonecked sweaters, identical black rimmed eyes. Half of them knew each other and even those who did not seemed all of one kind, one world, glittering, thin, modern as the décor surrounding them, strange to Gran but fascinating because they were lively. If these people with their marble eyes intimidated her they cheered her too, for they were not the company that old ones kept, you wouldn't find old Mrs Bromwich here or that prim and proper couple the Grovers or that Mrs Mason, Terry's mother. This was a place for those who were young, and she was in it.

Nobody spoke to her, of course, but she did not mind. The talk whirred and clattered about her like the traffic outside and the footsteps clapping by on the pavement: and when she knew the washing must be more than done she rose regretfully and left, a jaunty shapeless little figure with glittering earrings whom nobody noticed.

As she clasped the damp bundle, her lips still sticky from the gin, she thought: I'll go again. I'll get in the habit. It can't hurt me. What the eye don't see the heart don't grieve over. Where's the harm? Then they'll get to know me there. They're not the only people in the world, Etty and Ray. I hope Etty don't smell it on me breath . . .

When Gran got home Esther was cooking the liver for lunch. Dumping the laundry down on the sideboard, Gran complained hypocritically, 'Past one o'clock and the table not laid!' and without taking off her coat began to rattle about with knives and forks, putting Esther in the wrong to conceal her own guilt. Monty was weaving in and out among legs of furniture and humans, tingling on the tiptoes of lust, for the smell of liver drove him mad. 'I did think you'd have dinner ready – mind out, you silly cat! I might have saved meself some breath, hurrying home with that heavy great bundle and it's turned ever so warm too. I was sure you'd have it on the table and be sitting there blooming old-fashioned . . .'

As though she had not heard her, Esther said, 'Ray won't be back this weekend.'

'Won't be back? Oh, do give over, Monty!'

'No, I've had a card. He's going to Scotland and it's too far to come home and then go back again. I suppose his firm wouldn't pay the fare. So he won't be back.' She bent her head.

'Well I never! Scotland. What a let-down!' Gran stared at the knives in her hand, forgetting what she had meant to do with them. The whole shape and structure of the week was demolished, her escapade forgotten. There was nothing to look forward to. 'He might have warned us.'

'I suppose he didn't know.'

'Well I never. Scotland.'

The liver spat as Esther turned it and Monty reared up against the back of her legs, his front paws limp with supplication.

'Well,' Gran started again to lay the knives in their places, 'we shall have to make the best of it on our own. It won't be the first time, after all.' Indeed, now her first disappointment was over she felt some satisfaction. At least Etty'd be with her all the time like in the old days – if she wasn't moping, that is. 'Just you and me on our own, without a blooming man . . . You can give me a home perm, Ett, like you promised and never did. It's not the end of the world.'

Esther did not answer but wiped her cheeks with the back of her hand. With amazement Gran saw that tears were running down her face, renewing themselves like a spring welling out of the earth. 'Why, Etty!' she cried. 'Etty sweetheart! My word, this isn't like you!' She threw down the knives and ran to enfold Esther, although Esther was taller than she was. 'Why, girl, it's only a week! He'll soon be back again. Think if he was away in the Forces!' But Esther still wept, passively, in Gran's arms and Gran's own eyes began to water. They stood by the gas stove crying together while the frying-pan sizzled and Monty still paced up and down against their oblivious legs.

'This isn't like you, Etty, this isn't like my girl at all,' sniffed Gran. 'I never knew you carry on like this, crying and all,' and a shaft of satisfaction shot through the pity, for Etty's tears righted a balance somewhere; it was only just that the young should weep sometimes when by being young they had so much to be glad of.

With the fork in her free hand, her eyes blurred with tears, Esther turned the liver again, for even this undisciplined grief could not shake her from her routine functioning. She tried to laugh. 'We're a fine pair,' she said.

'You set me off.' She released Esther and felt for a handkerchief. 'Carrying on like this ... I can't remember when I last saw you cry, not since you was a little girl.'

'There was nothing to cry about.' It was true. She looked back over the years behind her, the trodden path of a corn-grinding donkey, holding nothing to alarm or surprise – or gladden or despair. Safe, comfortable, known narrow path on which no tears were shed. She had thought she was happy enough – until she met Raymond; and with her realisation of what happiness could be had come fear, the terror of loss. She had been safer before, but only half alive.

They pulled themselves together and afterwards in the spring sunshine they went into Regent's Park. The flowerbeds were cushions of colour and the birds sang above the cries of the children too small to be in school who ran about on the grass, chasing the sparrows that lurked besides the seats in the hope of crumbs. The rowing-boats jerked inexpertly over the shining surface of the lake and on the banks ducks shook their tails while their ducklings fussed among the reeds. Gran and Esther had tea at a kiosk and there was something good on telly that night, and for Gran, by the time she went to bed, it had been a lovely day; but Esther cried into her pillow, her back turned against the emptiness of the other bed.

They organised their weekend somehow, slipping back, but with a conscious effort on Esther's part, to their routine before Raymond. It was pleasant in a way, uneventful and empty. It was odd that someone so newly a stranger in their framework of years should be so missed, but everything that Esther did now without him seemed unreal, even the things he had never shared. I must pretend, she told herself, that these are the days at the beginning of the week, when he is always away. I will pretend that today is Monday and not Saturday and that is why I am frying skate which Gran likes but Ray does not, and I will pretend that his bed is always empty on this night but will be full again in five days' time – four days' time if you count today as gone already. I will pretend that it is normal for Terry and Gloria to go out this evening, as they do every Saturday (but this must be Monday), and I will listen in case Kim cries, but not listen when they return upstairs, trying to be quiet in the noisy way of people who have been to the pub; and I will not listen but be asleep before they start to quarrel or to bounce the springs above our room, Ray's and my room . . .

But she was not deceived; and with detachment she observed herself alone in the great desert of his absence, and she thought, this misery must be love.

They went to church on Sunday, for otherwise the day gaped unbearably before them and there would be nothing to give it shape. Gran loved it, loved getting dressed unexpectedly in her best clothes and hurrying out towards the bell, clean and holy and eager. One with many all of one purpose, rising and kneeling, thinking and chanting in unison, she felt the strength of the multitude buttress and bear her up so that as they came away, shaking the vicar's hand as if he knew them, standing in the sunlight outside the porch to put on their gloves, clean and holy and assuaged, Gran said, 'Why don't we come more often? It does you good,' and Esther, calmed by the discipline of ordered hopes, said, 'Yes, we must.'

They had lunch and Gran slept and Esther wrote to Raymond, a letter telling nothing save the snippets of news she could muster out of the empty days, and then there was tea and the telly and supper time; and Raymond came back.

Smiling under their amazement, still amidst their flurry of places to be laid and extra chips fried, quiet under Gran's flood of welcome and question and surmise, he sat in the chair that was now his chair, tickling Monty's chin under the tablecloth, his face serene, his eyes clear and blue. 'I got fed up with where I was,' was all he said. 'I'd rather be here.'

SIX

EVEN THE WEATHER was pleasant those next few weeks. The trees stood in their clean leaves and in every garden and backyard swags of laburnum and lilac illumined the grey London brick and the smell of May blossom twisted the nostrils, its petals drifting along the pavements like confetti. Sooty buildings seemed pearly, the red buses and pillar-boxes were like flags along the streets, and the mild air bewildered early tourists who had expected rain and even snow. Only pigeons the colour of rain clouds scudded across the sky; if it rained it rained at night so that the city was newly rinsed each morning to a limpid elegance that made it seem as beautiful as anywhere in the world. Even the ugly streets were beautiful in that light, their variations of grey and black and dirty red washed into harmony, their purple slates gleaming; and everywhere, glimpsed or soon sighted, in yards or squares or parks or cemeteries, the trees in their living green.

People were mild too, sitting on benches in the public gardens or beside their open windows, with no dust yet to dry their mouths or rain to beat in against the curtains. Raymond was affectionate, Esther happy, Gran spry, hugging to herself her secret visits to the Dick Whittington where now several regulars accepted her as regular. It was all very genteel. Even the women in black suits and the men in black homburgs, though they drank double whiskies and laughed loudly at saucy stories (Gran had overheard them), did it in a classy sort of way, nothing common about it, and no one was shabby. Right up-to-the-minute smart people they were, from Mr Robinson, the turf accountant, to Deidre Moore with her casual hair style, who modelled, it was said, for one of the wholesale dress firms – 'the rag trade' she called it, and so did Mrs Jesmond, who owned Sheelagh Modes in the High Street. You got a different sort at lunchtime than you did in the evenings, of course; Gran never came in the evenings but Mr Phelps, who sometimes brought his Guinness to her table, told her that. Mr Phelps was not quite one with the double whiskies at the bar, any more than she was. He sat from 12.15 to 12.30, swallowing a large

Guinness in three measured gulps, on civil terms but not conversing. He owned a shop which sold nothing but luggage, and a smell of leather hung pleasantly about him. He was a silent man with pouches under his eyes, and as Gran got used to him she began to speculate as to what caused them – sleeplessness or a bad liver or family troubles? She did not like to ask, but after a week or two a sympathy seemed to establish itself between them. He did not always bring his glass to her table, but began to do so fairly frequently; he knew almost everyone by sight and between gulps and silences would emit small pellets of information, which would occupy Gran's thoughts for a great part of the rest of her day. Now that she had the people at the Dick Whittington to keep her busy she no longer minded quite so much that Ray and Esther were together and she on her own. She was not on her own now, she had Mr Phelps and the Dick Whittington, a delicious secret treasure, like a rude book read under the bedclothes.

She did not go every day, of course. For one thing she could not afford it, for another she could not often escape Esther's company; but every washing day she was there and once or twice during the rest of the week if she could make some excuse to slip out of the house for half an hour. On one such morning, just as she had her hand on the swing door, she saw Gloria.

'Why hullo, Mrs Wilson,' said Gloria. 'Fancy meeting you!' Over the hood of the perambulator she observed Gran's new hat, decent coat and the hand quickly withdrawn from the saloon bar door.

Gran went red but was gracious. 'Good morning, Gloria. Taking your little darling out for some air? Ooh, isn't she a pet!' She peered into the pram. It was a superb vehicle, glossy and sprung like a coach, and in it the baby lay in a swaddled perfection of muslin and wool and satin. Her hair was covered by a frilled bonnet, her hands in angora mittens waved vaguely over a mauve satin coverlet edged with lace. The immaculate hood was half raised to protect her from the sunlight, and she stared up without much interest at the new face looming round its edge. 'My, don't you keep her lovely!'

'Well, thanks,' said Gloria. 'It's ever such a lot of work.'

Gran studied Gloria while making cooing noises to the baby. She had rather lost interest in the Masons since the christening and now noticed for the first time that Gloria was letting herself go. Her hair needed cutting and was showing dark at the roots and she had not bothered to renew her lipstick. She wore a thick cardigan that had stretched in the wash and her hands on the gleaming handlebars were coarse. Altogether she looked a proper sight, thought Gran, pity and satisfaction mixed agreeably. On impulse she said, 'Let's pop in and have one.'

'In the pub?' Gloria stared.

'Come on. Let's be devils.'

A little colour came into Gloria's face. 'I don't think I ought.'

'Rubbish, girl. Do you good. I'll treat you.'

'Well . . .' She glanced round, doubtful but already won. 'Can I leave the pram?'

'Well, you can't take it inside, dear. Push it up against the window.'

'Supposing someone sees?'

'What if they do? There's no harm in it.'

Gloria following, Gran pushed open the door and walked jauntily in. The bar was not very full, and the barman and Mr Robinson nodded to her and said good morning. Mr Phelps had not yet arrived.

'What'll you have, dear?' asked Gran, splendidly.

Half an hour later they came out again. Gloria's eyes were bright, she had pushed her hair into a kind of order and the gin had reddened her cheeks and lips. She was talking endlessly, tirelessly, as perhaps one talks on a psychiatrist's couch. Gran did nothing but click her tongue and say 'Well I never!', but her eyes were bright too and enjoyment shone from her. They walked to the corner of the street together, then halted.

'Well,' said Gran. They looked at each other with complicity.

'I must get home.' Gloria turned the pram. 'Thanks ever so much, Mrs Wilson. That was a real treat.'

'Does you good to get out and about. You don't want to be stuck in all day by yourself, a girl your age.'

'Too right I don't! Well, cheery-bye. See you again sometime, maybe?'

'I shouldn't wonder,' said Gran and tucking her handbag under her arm she scuttled away.

When Gloria got back she put the baby down in the cot and went straight to the dressing-table. She leaned forward until her nose almost touched the mirror, turning this way and that, stretching her mouth, seeking under the daylight for every line, blemish and pore. From the cot the baby gave two speculative grunts, then after a moment began to whimper. Gloria did not notice, but found from the rubble of toilet things in the drawer two side combs with which she fastened the hair back from her ears; searched again and chose the brightest of the lipstick stubs and smeared her lips with it. The baby began to wail.

'Oh my God!' cried Gloria under her breath. She went and peered within its clothing. 'Oh my God!' she said again and tears came into her eyes. As she went about the noisome routine, lifting the baby like a chicken by her joined ankles, the tears splashed down, making the child blink. What was the use of trying to keep your hands nice when they had to do this sort of thing? What was the use of wearing anything but old clothes when there was never a waking moment of the baby's life when one end or the other might not spoil a decent dress? What was the good of all the brave things she had said about not letting the baby interfere with her life?

It was hopeless. She was trapped, as much by an unsuspected quirk in her own character as by the little creature on her lap, for gradually, rebelliously over the months she had discovered that she would rather die than give Mrs Mason the satisfaction of saying Gloria was a bad mother. That was what it came to. She knew very well how little Terry's mother had expected of her, and she would rather die than enable her to say 'I told you so.' Gloria's baby was going to be the most beautifully kept in all north London or south London either. But she could not do everything; she was not a natural housewife and she had sacrificed herself in her determination to spite Mrs Mason. She had bursts of energy when she did her hair and her nails and put on her stiletto-heeled sandals to wheel the pram into the park, but they could not last. It was too difficult, too exhausting. The baby and the boredom of being tied within the walls of the flat or to the handlebars of the perambulator were too strong for her. She was not equipped to resist the housework, the mess, the loneliness – for except at the clinic she knew no other young mothers, and although conversation was warm and often intimate there, it did not lead to companionship; at the gate the prams separated like a fleet dispersing, there was no tradition of calling at each other's homes. The girls Gloria had known when she was free were mostly still free and working during the daytime. Of course, there was Esther; but she had always been uneasy with Esther, half in awe, half scornful. The scorn could not hold now, for Esther had got herself a husband; and although Gloria knew that on points the possession of a baby put her ahead, she could not really feel that it did. She saw Esther going about the house, neat and serene, better-looking than she used to be, and it made Gloria feel inferior. Just you wait till you've got a kid, she said to herself spitefully; but she surmised that when Esther did, she would continue neat, serene and rosy.

To Terry it was all a mystery. He adored the baby, she was like the magical pink dolls in tinsel skirts that perched on the top of Christmas trees, except that he had made her. Holding her, he would scrutinise her perfections, smiling and making idiot noises to her, while she stared and answered him with bubbles or little cries, sometimes even regurgitated milk which he would wipe from her chin tenderly. He loved to hold her up close to his face so that she could beat at it with her hands, the miniature nails so sharp, or tug his hair. He could watch her senseless movements endlessly; and when she lay asleep would lean over her cot, straining to hear the breath that reassured him she was not dead.

He could not understand how Gloria could be insensible to this enchantment. 'You wouldn't be so stuck on her if you had to clean her bottom,' said Gloria crossly; but he did and he was. He knew that the child had come from Gloria's flesh, but more and more he felt her to have been merely the container which had held his creation, as a pot contains the flowering bulb. He had planted it and now he marvelled at it, while Gloria held aloof, with her hair uncared for and any old thing on her back.

Had Gloria reverted to her old, cross, pretty self he would not have minded. Mum had always said she was too flighty to be the wife for him, but he had married her like that and liked what he was getting. Even if she had been a bad mother he would have understood; but that she should be a good one, depriving herself and fading yet resentful, he could not comprehend. She seemed to stand apart from him, sneering, and he was on his own with his tiny wonderful creation. 'The first but not the last,' Mum had said at the christening, and when she had kissed him afterwards she had whispered, 'Terry – my boy!' in a way that made him tingle, draw himself up and flex his muscles, as if it was a challenge somehow, to prove that he wasn't only Mum's son but a man, potent, capable of getting kids.

Magic and pride mingled in Terry's head and he longed to test himself again, to call forth another miracle from his own flesh; but Gloria baulked. She fell asleep at once and was unwilling to wake in the morning; her back ached or she had washing to do or it was time Kim went out for her airing. And on Saturday nights when, secure in Sunday's long morning, they came back from their one evening out, she was tense and demanding, as though she sensed that he was only using her and was resisting, suspicious, closed. Now that she no longer resembled the Gloria he had married he would not really have felt much desire for her, save that he was young and healthy and urged on by the longing to repeat his miracle.

He took to coming home late from the shop – he had missed Kim's bath-time anyway and could not see her awake till ten o'clock. 'There was a lorry load of potatoes came up from Norfolk late,' he would say, or 'Some crates of oranges was mouldy and I had to take them back to the wholesalers.' Sometimes they quarrelled over it; but more often Gloria just looked at him with hard eyes and said nothing at all, so that for company he was forced to go to the baby, to talk to, and love, her. Him and his little fairy doll, he thought – that's what she'll be when she's bigger, Mum had said so.

And Gloria, banging his tepid supper down on the table, had smelt the beer on his breath. The day would have been so long, so echoing with silence, that an hour or two more made no difference to her, she was past caring. Let him drool over the baby, let him boast about it to his mum, let him go out boozing to the pubs, she was too tired to care – so long as he did not interpose between her and her sleep, her longed-for, oblivious, drugging sleep in which only sometimes now did she dream that she was Gloria, who had desired Terry.

For a week or two after their escapade at the Dick Whittington she and Gran hardly met, except occasionally in the hall, when they exchanged good mornings but looked at each other like conspirators. Then one morning at launderette time, when Gran was sipping her gin and lime and waiting for Mr Phelps to say something, Gloria came in. She had done her hair and made up her face, although the clothes were still those of a working housewife. She came straight over to Gran and said, 'Morning, Mrs Wilson, mind if I join you?'

Gran was slightly put out, for Gloria spoke loudly and had a pugnacious air about her; besides, she enjoyed her companionship with Mr Phelps and did not wish to share it. However, she introduced them and Gloria went to the bar to get a drink. 'The young lady who lodges in our house,' Gran said quickly to Mr Phelps, 'her and her husband, but it's my belief things isn't quite so good with them since the baby came.'

'Ah.' Mr Phelps nodded. 'Just like my sister's Maurice.'

'Is it?' asked Gran eagerly, but Gloria returned.

'I couldn't stick it a minute longer,' she said, sitting down on the stool facing them. 'Something's upset Kim and it's been nothing but dirty nappies since early this morning. If you'll excuse me, Mr Phelps,' she smiled for a moment. Mr Phelps waved his hand in acquiescence. 'Have you children of your own?' asked Gloria. 'If you have you'll know what I mean.'

Gran was shocked by so direct a question; for weeks she had been fishing and caught only scraps of information, yet now he answered meekly, 'Not of my own I haven't, but plenty of nephews and nieces. Always in trouble.'

'Don't tell me that!' cried Gloria. 'I keep thinking once she gets older things'll be easier. Well, I felt I'd go crackers if I stayed in a minute longer, so here I am. Cheers!' She drank.

'Happy days,' said Mr Phelps.

'I don't usually come in a pub without my husband. We used to know ever such a nice bunch of people over at the Queen of Sheba, a real happy crowd. But once you've got a baby you're not so free as you were.'

'They're a very nice class of person comes here,' said Gran with dignity. 'That lady with the fur, she's Madame Sheelagh in the High Street, and her friend's in the same business, isn't that right?'

Mr Phelps nodded. 'They're mostly a quiet type here,' he said.

'Well, when all's said and done that's nicest, isn't it?' said Gloria. 'I mean, specially in the daytime. I mean, it wouldn't be nice to come to a rowdy sort of a place on your own, and leaving the pram outside and all. I feel quite naughty as it is.' She giggled.

'Does you good to get out,' said Gran. 'After all, your Terry's out all day, getting about and seeing people. That's what my grandson-in-law says. I see plenty of people during the week, Gran, he says, I don't want to see no more when I'm at home, he says, but you and Ett. He thinks the world of his home, Raymond does.'

'He's the quiet type all right,' said Gloria, looking into her glass. 'Same as Mrs Banks.'

'They suit each other,' said Gran defensively. She looked to see if Gloria was getting at her but Gloria sat impassively, twiddling her glass. Her downcast eyes gave her face a sullen look.

'I'm different,' she said. 'I go crackers if I don't see some life. Day in, day out the same old routine. They don't tell you that when you get married. And come the evening I'm too tired to go out, what with the washing and cleaning and all.'

'You ought to go out to business,' said Gran. 'Get yourself a job.'

'What, with the baby?'

'Put her in one of them day nurseries. That's what a lot of them do. Or get a part-time job, mornings only. There's plenty going, I'll be bound.'

'I'd still have the baby.'

'Etty'd look after the baby – you ask her. Just for the mornings, it'd give her something to do.'

'Hasn't she got enough?'

'She makes work,' said Gran sourly. 'It's not the same as when she went to business every day. She's always busy with something now, gives me the hump – except when Raymond's at home. Then nothing's done but what he wants. Mind you, he's no trouble. Not like some men. But she wouldn't want to mind the baby when he's at home, I don't think he'd care for it.'

'Then it wouldn't be any use.'

'We could work it so Raymond didn't know.' Gran's eyes sparkled again, partly with the pleasure of planning Gloria's rebellion, partly at the thought of having an infant in her arms again – and the infant would more often be in her arms than in the pram, too! 'I could look after her when he was home. She wouldn't be no trouble, the little darling. I could take her for walks . . .' It would get her out of the house more often too, for a glimpse of her friends here and Mr Phelps. 'And I could give her her dinner if you was late and leave the washing for when you came home. We could manage lovely.'

'Well, I don't know. I never thought of it, not going out to business now I've the baby . . . I don't know if Terry'd stand for it.'

'Pooh!' said Gran, and her earrings twinkled. 'Long as you're there when he comes home at night, what's it to him? It's just what you need, dear, take you out of those blooming four walls.'

Esther was easily persuaded, not so much because she wanted the baby, for she was nervous of her igno-rance of children, but because she was sorry for the Masons. She had regarded Gloria more carefully since Raymond's outburst and had seen with relief, but also compassion, how Gloria's brave words had come to nothing and her prettiness grown drab. She herself was so lucky, living in her own home in perfect hap-piness with the perfect husband; it could not be easy for two young people living on sufferance in someone else's house, with a baby and everything to be learned. So she said yes, she would mind Kim if Gloria went to work, she and Gran between them; and Gloria got a job in Woolworth's.

At first Terry did not know what to make of it. He banged the table and strode about the room, shouting that people would think he didn't earn enough to keep her, his masculinity outraged in obedience to all the traditions of marriage that his mother had taught him. Gloria screamed back, then burst into tears, bowing her head into her hands and rocking to and fro on a chair. She looked so childish and piteous that his anger drained away, and kneeling down he comforted her, awkwardly, for it was a long time since she had asked for comfort. Holding her, wiping her face with his handkerchief, a spring of sweetness flooded him; it was like in the old days before Kim came, before Gloria was pregnant, even before they were married, when there was nothing between them but the physical awareness that led, he supposed, to their getting married; a sort of mixed-up excitement and enjoyment and rightness of being together, because they were both young and liked the same good times, and that was why you got married . . . he supposed.

She braced herself away from his shoulder. 'You can't stop me!' she cried. 'I'm going crackers here! I shall do as I like.'

'OK,' he said gently. He stayed on his knees, his hands passive in his lap, looking at her blotched face and the hair wet against her cheeks. 'You do what you want.'

She stared at him, sniffing noisily. 'Honest?'

'Honest.'

The passion went out of her. She blew her nose. 'It's what everyone does now, Terry. It's not for the money.'

'OK.' He smiled, and suddenly she smiled too, the first true smile they had exchanged for weeks. She pushed back her hair and wiped her face, then got up. 'Only Kim's got to be looked after proper,' he said.

'D'you think I wouldn't?' Sharpness returned, but the old wilful sharpness, without spite. 'I'll be back every day dinner-time and she's in her pram all morning anyway. They won't have nothing to do for her.'

Nor, really, did they. Gloria brought her down each morning, and if it were fine and a day on which Raymond was away, she was put in her carry-cot on two chairs in the backyard where the morning sun reached her and she could be watched from the kitchen window. When Raymond was at home she went in her pram on the pavement by the front steps. She was no trouble. She watched the clouds passing and the celluloid rattle dangling from the hood or her own hands moving spasmodically; and then slept.

It was curiously soothing to look out over the sink and see the hands waving above the rim of the cot and hear sometimes the small squeals and croonings with which she tried out her voice. It was like having a pet to watch, like Monty when he was a kitten. Unless she cried Esther did not go to her, but Gran kept darting in and out to look, to tickle, to talk baby-talk, to offer the child her finger to hold and exclaim with pride if she did so. Unerringly the baby would draw it towards her mouth, and from the kitchen Esther would call uneasily, 'Gran, don't let her suck it. It might be dirty.'

'Go on, a nice suck of my finger won't hurt her, will it, you little sweetheart?' cried Gran indignantly; but withdrew her finger all the same.

Best of all Gran liked the days when Raymond was at home, for then, without a word being said, she would put on her hat and go quietly down the steps and set off with the pram for a walk. Oddly, she never took it to the Dick Whittington, although that had been one of her motives in offering to mind the child at all. Somehow, she felt, it would not be proper for *her* to leave the pram outside the saloon bar doors; if Kim's own mother chose to do it, that was different. Instead she walked slowly along the pavements, looking in the shops or at the flowers in the park, if she got so far, wondering if people took her for the baby's granny. It was strange how the years fled away at the grip of her hands on the handle; nearly thirty years since Esther was out of a pram, nearer fifty with Win. She was an old woman, yet her fingers remembered, her arms manoeuvred round corners, up and down kerbs, carefully, so as not to bounce the little creature asleep there. Sometimes, if the morning were really warm, she would sit for a while on a seat just inside the park gates and think about Win as a baby. As a little girl it was Esther she remembered, but Win was a baby, pink and curly and laughing, cuddled in her arms, smelling of milk, sucking her mother's fingers, pulling her father's moustache – warm, pink, pretty, beautiful Win-baby that had nearly split her in two to have and Grandad had said she mustn't have no more. 'I won't expose you to it,' he had said; fancy that, a funny way to put it and to remember after so long. 'I won't expose you to it, Vicky,' and he never had, not having another, that is. There was plenty of loving but never only the one, Win, the baby, cuddled up and sucking her mummy's finger . . .

She would have liked Mr Phelps to see her with the pram and one day she walked past his shop with it, pausing at the doorway as though examining the bags and satchels hung on its lintels but really looking inside. Every inch of wall was obscured by luggage of various kinds, suitcases stacked shelf upon shelf, shopping bags, handbags, briefcases hanging like bats, trunks ranked on the floor, purses, comb-cases, shoe-horns, wallets packed in trays on the counter, behind which sat, not Mr Phelps but a large, dark, mournful woman. Her glance met Gran's through the doorway and hurriedly Gran moved on. Was that Mrs Phelps? She knew nothing about her, not even if there was one, come to that – he mentioned his wife's sister and his various nephews and nieces but she couldn't remember his ever having said, 'Me and Mrs Phelps went to the pictures', or 'Mrs Phelps said to me this morning'. It was aggravating but she couldn't help liking him for it; she didn't like a man who was always blabbing about his wife when he was with another lady.

So, although in theory it was Esther who was looking after the Masons' baby, in practice it was Gran. Esther was relieved, for she had a guilty conscience; she knew Raymond would not like her doing Gloria a favour and she had therefore kept it from him. It was not difficult. He did not come home before Thursday evening and always reported to his office on Friday morning; it was easy enough for Gran to slip off with the pram without his noticing that both were absent together. It was a new experience to Esther to have something to hide; it flustered her and she wished she had not agreed, then reproved herself, for what real reason could there be for refusing this small help to the Masons? No one could possibly object, not when they considered it quietly; but she did not want to put it to the test.

Therefore when, one Saturday morning, Raymond came into the kitchen while she was peeling the potatoes for lunch and said, 'Where's Gran got to?' her heart gave a leap and she had to bend her head to hide the guilt that coloured her cheeks.

'Why – she's gone out for a little, I think.'

'It's a good thing she toddles off on her own a bit more these days,' he said, 'more independent.'

'She likes to get out in the sunshine.'

He stood looking out at the yard, whistling under his breath and jingling coins in his pocket. 'Those lobelias make a nice show.'

'Yes.'

'We ought to get some ramblers up on the end wall, fix 'em on a trellis. I like ramblers.'

'I know you do, dear.' She smiled, first at him then out at the yard, neat and flowering with the quickly blooming annuals she had planted now that she had so much time at home. The yard was so small it did not take much to make it pretty and it gave her pleasure to deck it out as she decked out everything now for Raymond.

'Ett,' he said, 'I've been thinking.'

'Mm?'

'A funny thing happened to me this week – leastways, it wasn't really so funny. It might have been serious.'

A tiny thud of fear stirred her heart, sensitive now to the least breath of loss.

'I was up in Newcastle, see, and I'd been kept a bit late by a customer – couldn't make up his mind, wanted special terms, you know the sort of thing – and when I got away I was tired and fed up so I thought I'd go to the pictures. So I went and had a cup of tea across the way from the cinema and while I was there I saw in the local paper someone had left lying there that the film was just going to start, so I gulped down my tea, grabbed my case and ran out – and I got knocked down by a motorbike.'

'Ray!' Her hands fell into the dirty water with the potatoes and she stared at him aghast.

He turned to face her, leaning on the corner of the table. 'Now hold on, old girl, hold on. No bones broken or nothing. This motorbike came round the corner sudden, see, and I ran out sudden and it was just getting dark and there we were. I went flying, but luckily I landed on a dear old biddy with a shopping bag – knocked her for six up against the shop window but she wasn't hurt and she broke my fall. Nothing worse than a shaking up and a few scratches.'

'Oh Ray – you might have been killed!'

'Well, I might. And that's what set me thinking. I think I ought to make a will, Ett.'

'Oh Ray!'

'Now don't keep on saying "Oh Ray" like that.' He smiled at her. 'There's nothing wrong in making a will.

Everyone ought to, it's common sense. I made one myself when I was in the Forces but when I met you I tore it up. Whatever came off between you and me, I knew that old will wasn't going to be needed no more.'

'I don't like thinking . . .'

'Of course not, but it ought to be done just the same. Haven't you got a will?'

'Well – yes I have. I made it when Grandad died because of the house and the shop and Gran, you see. The lawyer said I ought.'

'Well then . . . And as I was lying tucked up in my lonely couch in Newcastle that evening, feeling a bit bruised and shaky and sorry for myself, I said, "Now you might have had it this evening, Raymond Banks, you might have suffered a fatal accident, my lad, and then where'd your Esther be?" I said. So I drew up a will and if you think it's OK, I'll get it done properly by the lawyer who handles my firm's business.' He reached into his breast pocket and drew out a folded paper. 'Course, it's only a draft. They have to put it all legal, see, so there can't be any argument.' He held it out to her.

She recoiled, shaking her head. 'I don't want to see it.'

'You ought to.'

'I don't want to.'

'Well . . .' He drew it back and looked at it thoughtfully. 'I'd just as soon you didn't, really, in a way, because I want something personal put in about you and me and – well, I'd just as soon you didn't read it yet.'

She began to peel another potato, paring it too thickly because her eyes were blurred. 'You're upsetting me, Ray.'

'I don't want to do that.' He put the paper away, repeating gently, 'I don't want to do that, Ett. It's just – these things have to be done. No need to get upset. I'll tell you what I've put in . . .'

'No, don't.'

'It's only right you should know, dear. You must know what to expect. It's for you first, of course, but after that, if she's still alive, it's for Gran. There's not much chance of that but still, one has to cover everything. Mind you, I'm talking as if it was millions. It's not. It's only a hundred or two and some Savings Certificates and fifty pounds in Premium Bonds. But whatever it is, it ought to be settled properly.'

She lifted her head and looked at him, her face blanched but firm. 'Then I'll make one too. I'm not going to have you talk about dying and leaving me. I'll make one too and then we'll – we'll be even.'

He did not answer for a moment. 'You've got to think of Gran.'

'I will. I'll make it the same as you do – you first and then Gran. Perhaps I'll make a bit special for Gran anyway, the shop perhaps, that was specially Grandad's, you wouldn't mind that?'

'What do you take me for?'

'It'd be right, I think, although I know there's no need. I know you'd look after Gran.'

'I'd look after Gran,' he agreed gently.

She began peeling again, her voice steady. 'So let's have no more talk about it, Ray. If you feel it's right, that's what we'll do, but I don't want to talk about it ever again, only just get it done and forget it.'

'OK,' he said. His voice was very soft. She put down the knife with a clatter and stood motionless with her back to him. In a whisper she said, 'You might have been killed, Ray. I might never have seen you again.'

'All's well that ends well.'

She took up the knife again and went on with her job, 'You might have gone out of this house last Sunday and never come back again.'

'Don't say that, dear. You don't want to upset yourself.'

'No, I know. But somehow I can't help it. I think I never knew what it was to be afraid till I was happy.'

He stared at her and for an instant the blaze flared up behind his eyes; then with a brusque movement he pressed her shoulder with his hand. 'That's silly talk,' he said and went out of the room.

SEVEN

EVER SINCE the fine weather had come Gran had been thinking about their summer holiday. The year had always been marked by the pendulum swing Christmas–seaside, Christmas–seaside, the great birthday and the great fruition. There was always her day's outing with the old age pensioners to Ramsgate every August (she couldn't be bothered with their socials and jumble-sales and all, silly old cats, but she never missed an outing) and then the fortnight at the beginning of September when she and Esther went on holiday. Left to herself, Esther would always have gone to Bexhill; but Gran liked new places, and places where there was plenty to do if it rained, and so they had sampled towns as far east as Clacton and as far west as

Llandudno. Gran loved it all, from the cleaning of her white canvas shoes that she never wore any other time to the sitting bundled up in raincoats in the shelters when the rain came beating down, all of it, salty and scoured, nourished on fish and chips on the front and beetroot salad for high tea in the boarding house. If there were sands it was as much as she could do not to scamper along them as the dogs did; and certainly if there were not many people by she would hold up her skirts and paddle, her gnarled feet wriggling into the sand, facing the waves with eyes half shut and mouth a little open, surrendered to the sea.

But now Etty was married what would happen? What would they decide, how dispose of her without first asking what she wanted? Would they send her off, but where? And if not alone, with what dreary collection of old bags, outlawed like herself by the young, dumped, exiled? Or would they take her with them and if so, where? A quiet place with nothing to do, select, and bed at quarter past nine and always the two of them and only the one of her? Or would they, after the expense of the honeymoon, not go at all and the purifying rite of the sea be unperformed, if this year then, somehow, not ever again.

She dared not mention it but stayed as still as a mouse in a corner. And then one Friday at the supper table Ray said casually, 'What d'you think of Eastbourne, Gran?'

She glanced at Esther, as she had got into the habit of doing now when Raymond asked her something, as though to see how Esther wanted her to answer, before saying cautiously, 'It's a nice place.'

'Not too quiet?'

She could see he was smiling. 'You're teasing, Ray. I know you, you bad boy! Eastbourne's a nice place – we went there once, didn't we Etty, and that woman kept the boarding house was a medium, you know, talking to spirits and all, give me the creeps. You can take a lovely lot of bus rides from Eastbourne.'

'Me and Ett reckon we'll go there.'

'You and Ett . . .?'

'Yes. First two weeks in July, before the crowds get going. That be OK with you?'

'With me? If you say so . . .' She seemed to dwindle down in her chair, looking from one to the other, for she did not at all know what he meant, whether they alone or the three of them . . .

Esther broke in gently, 'Don't tease her, dear. Would you like to come to Eastbourne, Gran?'

'Me?' Vigour flowed into her, the salty wind, the pebbles, the spray . . . 'Ow, that'd be lovely! It's a lovely place, Eastbourne. When did you say, July? My word, it don't give us much time.'

'Why, what are you going to do, buy a trousseau?'

'Don't be saucy, Raymond Banks. It's all very well

for you men, a tennis shirt and a pair of plimsolls and you're all set up for a holiday. Me and Etty used to go in September.'

'Well, me and Etty's going in July, so you can please yourself.'

'July's nice too,' she said hurriedly. 'You can get rain any time, I always say. Have you booked any rooms?'

'I'll see to that,' he said. 'No spiritualists neither.'

'It's a nice place, Eastbourne. It's got like sort of three promenades, hasn't it, Etty, one on top of the other? And Brighton's not more than an hour's bus ride, all along the top of the cliffs, lovely. And that big shop, what's it called, in all them big seaside towns – Billy's, Bertie's – Bobby's, that's it. That's there, isn't it? And Beachy Head . . . oh my, up on the cliffs there on a fine day, lovely!'

She was delighted. Eastbourne! Stony and scoured, and those lovely gardens at the back with the tennis-courts and the Lifeboat Museum and the nice-class roads with trees that led up to the downs, and was it there they had the floral clock? No, it wasn't – or was it? Never mind – Eastbourne! Her toes curled in anticipation of the astringent sea.

Esther was not so pleased. They had had quite a discussion about it, low-voiced in their room while Raymond lay in bed with his arms crossed behind his head and Esther did her hair. She had not mentioned a holiday to him, for she did not know if he could yet afford one, and since the business of the joint account, she was unwilling to talk of money with him again; but she had thought that although they might not have a holiday this year, Gran should have one; perhaps with Cousin Em, perhaps at some holiday camp or club, for after all Gran was entitled to her share of Grandad's income and had besides been saving up her old age pension as she always did for this. Gran should go and she and Raymond would remain, alone, just the two of them, alone for the first time in their own house, blessedly alone . . .

When he told her they could go away she was pleased nevertheless; it would be more of a change and do them good, and immediately she had envisaged them at Bexhill, the two of them, sitting on the beach in the sun, Raymond perhaps asleep beside her, his body spread to the sun, innocent and familiar and loved. For Gran was not going to be with them. With shame but ruthlessly Esther wanted that. The thought of Raymond and herself alone at home had opened a door on longing that surprised her. It wasn't much to want, just a fortnight to themselves. Gran could not grudge it; and even if she did (and Esther knew she would) Gran had more than her share of them all the year round. Surely sometimes they were entitled to be just by themselves?

But – 'I thought we'd try Eastbourne,' Ray had said. 'Gran'll like that.'

'Gran? Yes, she would, but . . .'

'Plenty going on and not too crowded in July. You always get the sunshine in Eastbourne, too, something to do with the bay, the bad weather sort of jumps over it, see, you're in a kind of a pocket.'

'I'd thought perhaps somewhere smaller . . .'

'Well, not with Gran. She'd be round our necks all day. In a place like Eastbourne there's plenty for her to do while we go off on our own sometimes. That's what I reckoned.'

'I thought . . . I wondered . . .' She flushed, for she knew her thoughts had been betrayals. 'I wondered if this time we could go away on our own?'

'What, without Gran?'

'Yes.'

'And do what with her? Leave her here on her own again?'

'No, I wouldn't do that. I thought – perhaps she could go to Cousin Em – or somewhere . . .'

He paused before replying in a sober voice, 'She wouldn't like that, Ett.'

'Well, not at first. Not the idea of it. But if we found somewhere nice for her . . . It can't be much fun for her being with us all the time.'

'It is, you know. She'd be ever so cut up, Ett.'

'Well, suppose she is? I mean, she can't always . . . Couldn't we, Ray?'

'It never crossed my mind.'

'We've never been on our own, dear, not since the honeymoon. Married people need to be on their own sometimes. Couldn't we?'

Again he paused, frowning at the ceiling; but then he said, 'I don't think we could. Not in decency. I really don't think we could.'

'If we sent her somewhere she'd enjoy, if we didn't even go away ourselves . . .?'

'She'd feel it terribly, Ett. I just don't think we can do it. I don't think I can and I'm sure you can't, not when you think what it would mean to her.'

'But just the once? She can't go on and on like a child that has to be taken care of . . .'

'That's what she is, though, isn't it? I mean, that's how you've always seen her, isn't it?'

'Yes, but . . .'

'Besides, what would people think?'

'What people?'

'Why – everyone, the Masons, the old girl next door. It wouldn't look nice, sending her off on her own like we didn't want anyone with us.'

'We don't – do we, Ray? Not all the time.'

'No, dear, we don't. But we're stuck with Gran and we have to accept it. She's our responsibility. It won't be for always, poor old girl.'

So they went to Eastbourne.

'Shinglenook' was really no more than a red brick villa set in a garden hardly bigger than itself, but it called itself a Guest House and had divided its four large bedrooms into eight which, with two box-rooms, made it more than pay its way. A sofa had been put into the hall, which turned that into a lounge as well as the front sitting-room – although it would be hard indeed to lounge on any of the monolithic furniture that challenged the visitor with its unyielding laps and arms gaping like jaws. There was a hoarse radio in one corner under a pile of antique *Everybody's*, but the television set was kept shut up in the back kitchen with its proprietors, the Swains. There were five Swains, including a teenage son and daughter and Mrs Swain's aunt, and during the season they seemed all to live in the back kitchen, sleeping no guest knew where. When autumn faded and the last visitor had gone the Swains came out of the kitchen and ran over the house, joyful and expanded, five people living in a ten-bedroomed house with crockery for twenty and a fridge the size of a cupboard and the television set luxuriously out to view in the drawing-room. Winter was a time of easeful refreshment for the Swains and they did not mind serving their seven months in the back kitchen for it.

The aunt and Mrs Swain did the cooking, could have done it in their sleep so unalterable was the course of roast meat, cold meat, cottage pie, ham and salad, braised beef, fish cakes and mixed grill (one cutlet only). As at most seaside towns, fish was seldom included; indeed, you might not have been by the sea at all, for the house was in a dip behind taller buildings and from none of its windows could you get a glimpse of it. Only the salty air, the pebbles arranged in a mosaic in the front garden which gave the house its name, and the gulls told you where you were; at first light the gulls would begin to scream and wheel, and sometimes they perched on the garage roof near Gran's window so that their malevolent chuckles mingled with her dreams and she woke with her heart thumping, wondering who it was.

The people who stayed at Shinglenook were quiet, middle-aged, small tradesmen, senior artisans, clerks. There were no young people, there was nothing lively about it at all, and yet Gran liked it. It was good class, she felt, and the beds were comfortable; it was a luxury to have running water in her bedroom, even if the basin was small and the water hot only in the mornings, and she very much enjoyed changing into a dress for supper each evening. If Raymond and Esther went out for a stroll before bedtime, she did not mind or wish to accompany them; the strong air made her sleepy and besides, she was content to sit in the lounge in a genteel fashion, chatting to the other ladies or watching a game of whist if one were started. Being on holiday with Raymond was a more dignified affair than she and Esther on their own. Alone there had always been the chance of Esther meeting 'someone' – a holiday romance, perhaps even for Gran, getting into conversation in the shelters, you never knew. But now they were established, a family; nothing exciting was likely to happen to them now, except their due of respect; it was too cold to paddle.

They took the bus to Brighton; they visited Lewes and stared at the prison; they took the coach to Arundel and stared at the castle; they took the bus to Beachy Head and stared down in awe at the lighthouse finger below. The turf was smooth, starred with tiny yellow flowers, and the cliff swelled up and up to where, at its peak, the ruins of a mansion stood eerily, shattered as an old skull, the wind blowing through the empty eyes.

'My word, isn't it creepy!' said Gran as, Esther's hand beneath her elbow, she panted up the slope. 'Was it the war?'

'Us, not them.' Ray stood with his back to the cliff edge surveying the ruin, the wind blowing his trousers against his legs and disordering his hair. 'Chap who owned it gave it to the army to use as an artillery target. They certainly smashed it up proper.'

'What a thing to do! I couldn't do that with my house, could you, Etty? Oh my, it's a pull up them slopes!'

'Sit down a bit and get your breath.'

She found a broken wall out of the wind and sat, knees apart, fanning herself with her hand. Esther picked her way among the shafts and holes that honeycombed the cliff to where Raymond stood and linked her arm with his, leaning to him before the wind. 'Here we have a desirable, absolutely detached residence,' he said, 'fine views of the sea, no rent, rates or maintenance, room for expansion, bomb shelters, completely redecorated by the Royal Artillery, price only twenty thousand pounds, can I interest you, madam?' She squeezed his arm, laughing. 'Or should you desire something smaller, easily run by a staff of steeplejacks, compact, weatherproof, constant lighting guaranteed, I can offer you that unusual residence down there.' He swung her round so that they faced the sea and the lighthouse and she clung to him, the hair blowing in her eyes, while Gran called, 'Don't go too near the edge, now!'

The wind had stung the pallor from his usually pale face, his skin and his eyes seemed to sparkle. Ever since the holiday started he had been in high spirits – indeed, for some time before that. He had always been good-tempered and polite, but lately it was as though something danced inside him; as though,

Esther thought, he were both happy and excited, had found a zest in happiness. Could that be it? Could she have made life as different for him as he had done for her, filled it, enriched it, brought the discovery that one person alone was only half but two people together were a whole? She knew that to have a home, a wife – even a grandmother – a place that was his and where he belonged, had brought him a security he had long needed; but was it just these things that made him happy or was it she, herself? She could not tell; he would never say. Sometimes she asked him, when her arms were round him and his head on her shoulder so that he could not see the colour rise in her face as she forced herself to ask, 'Are you happy, Ray?' 'What do you think?' he answered, and if she persisted, 'No, can't you tell? I'm blooming miserable!', turning her question always with a joke. It was the same with love; he could not actually say the words, 'I love you', as though, she felt, the admission might in some way unarm him, take something from him that he had to keep.

She did not really mind. She understood how the uttering of words from the heart could be like the tearing away of a skin, a limb. She was not able to say much herself, even on that day when he had told her of his accident and she had found herself standing not by the scullery sink but by a chasm of terror and loss, a glimpse of fear so piercing that it pierced still to remember it. Even then she had been unable to express her love but had stood there, peeling the potatoes, while her whole soul shook within her. It was as well; Grandad had always said one mustn't give way. It was best to say nothing but to go on quietly, demonstrating one's love and happiness in the things one did. She showed hers by making a home for him, a haven after all his years of not belonging, of going from place to place and person to person, always without love; his father dying, his mother leaving, his aunt and uncle old, perhaps not really wanting him; and then the army, and then the travelling from town to town, belonging nowhere and with no belongings but his own obduracy. 'Look out for Number One,' he said, 'for no one else will.' He was right, it was the only way he could have survived; but she would look out for him now.

On holiday he was merry and teasing, masterful, paying for everything, treating her and Gran alike as if they were two inexperienced girls. His hair carefully brushed, a silk scarf carefully knotted inside the collar of his open shirt, a woman on each arm, he walked each morning down to the café on the front and bought them coffee. Not tea, not ice-cream: those were for tea-time. Coffee was proper in the morning and they accepted his ruling without argument, smilingly, as part of the right order of things. Actually Gran thought sometimes longingly of the Dick Whittington and a small gin and lime and it crossed her mind, when he had put her into her deck-chair on the middle promenade, paid for her ticket, seen she had her newspaper and then gone off for a stroll with Esther, to nip into the town and have one; but she never did. His discipline was upon her; such an action would have been outside the pattern of this holiday.

Esther accepted his discipline too, his strangely high spirits and the bracketing of her and Gran together, as part of his plan to make this holiday a happy one for Gran, to make her feel welcome and youthful, on a level with Esther herself. She accepted it but looked for a special intimacy from him when they were alone. She did not find it. Here on holiday, away from their shared domestic life, it was as if he hid behind the jocularity he wore for Gran and would not let Esther near him. He was confidential, gentle, gay, he talked of Gran as separate from themselves, they were he and she together, man and wife; yet somewhere within him was a guard, worn like the holiday scarf and crêpe-soled canvas shoes, a holiday Raymond. Perhaps – she had no means of knowing – it was because of what had happened their fifth night at Shinglenook. The first night it had been as usual, unheralded, quick, a courtesy. The next time, four nights later, he had not been able. Nothing Esther had ever heard helped her with his humiliation; she did not know if this happened to other men or why it should happen to him, but his hurt and desperation harrowed her. 'Don't,' she whispered. 'It doesn't matter, dear, don't try.'

His voice was the voice of a furious child, 'It never happened to me before,' and he turned away from her to the furthest edge of the bed, his breath coming loudly.

Without touching him she could feel his tense body. 'It doesn't matter, dear,' she said again, out of her own bewilderment, but no answer came from the desert of his.

That was the Thursday of their first week and he had not tried again since. Jaunty and neat, he seemed his own affectionate self again; he had not mentioned it and nor had she, for she had no idea what one should say, whether it was forever, whether it were her fault. So she too was outwardly as she had always been, acquiescing to his mastery, doing as he wished her to do, trying to show him that nothing was altered. Touching his hand, taking his arm on the cliff-top, she clung to him, trying by her body to reassure him and to reach him, shutting her mind to the leap of her own body that often now longed for his, telling him by her smile and her confidence that it did not matter, they were man and wife; but although he smiled and pressed her hand in return, no answer came back from him. He had shut himself off from her.

He was the same with her as he was with Gran but now, despite his tearing spirits, it was she and Gran who were together and Raymond who was outside. Esther did not know how she could reach him, and behind her smile misery and confusion began to creep, poisoning the holiday.

It was wild up there on the cliff with the wind beating at them and the ruins of the house stark under the shadows of the clouds. Not many people came as far as this; they stayed nearer their cars and merely crossed the turf to look down on the lighthouse below. When, on the Monday evening of their second week, Ray said they would go again Gran did not want to. 'I've been,' she said, 'you and Etty go. I don't want to climb up all that slippery grass again – that is, if you don't mind, Ray?'

'You're getting idle,' he said, teasing, 'a proper old layabout, that's what you are. Well, OK then, you sit here and make eyes at the boys.'

'Raymond Banks!' she shrieked – but quietly, because there were people about and she wanted to act like a lady. 'May you be forgiven for the wicked things you say!'

'I will be,' he said. They left her snug in her deck-chair out of the wind, with the *Daily Mirror* and *Woman*, and caught the bus up the cliff road.

It was not a nice day, with wind blowing grey waves and greyer clouds in towards the land. No one got off the bus at the top for Beachy Head, and only a couple of cars were parked on the road behind the cliff. The smell of wet grass and the sea mingled strongly as they climbed upwards and the wind blew her hair from under the scarf and whipped it about her eyes. Even Raymond's thick hair had torn loose from its brilliantine and flickered about his head. A pace or two behind him, she held to his coat as they climbed up towards the ruin, hot in her macintosh and out of breath but exhilarated by the height and air and the hope that perhaps in this lonely place he would take her in his arms and be with her again. They reached the barbed wire and stepped over, then went up past the broken bricks and juts of stone to stand at the peak in the shelter of a wall.

'Oh my!' she gasped, 'it's a climb. It's ever so high – how high is it, Ray?' for that was the sort of thing he knew and liked to tell.

'It's high all right.' He went a little way out on to the cliff and looked about him. Down the slope two children suddenly came in sight, running round and round like dogs, chasing each other in the wind. He returned to the shelter of the wall.

She tucked the hair back into her scarf, looking up at the sky. 'It's going to rain, I think. I hope the weather's not going to break.'

'It won't. I told you. Not at Eastbourne.'

'Do you like the sun? I mean, proper sunbathing and that like in the south of France? I never asked you.'

'I never tried it. I never had the cash.'

'One year – if we could leave Gran somewhere – we might go. I'd like to see the Riviera. It needn't cost too much, we could do it through Cooks or the Polytechnic. But with your fair skin you'd have to be careful, sunburn can be ever so painful.' She put out a hand and stroked his cheek. He jerked away, staring out over the sea as though oblivious of her. Flushing, she put both hands in the pockets of her raincoat.

A man appeared at one of the parked cars down the cliff, calling and beckoning to the children. Their shrieks, as they wheeled crazily over the grass, were blown up to Raymond and Esther like feathers on the wind.

They stood in silence against the wall.

'If it rains this afternoon we could go to the pictures,' she said presently. He did not answer. 'There's a good one on at the cinema by the bus station. Unless you'd rather have a sleep.'

'Why should I want to sleep?'

'I'm sorry, dear. Only I said I'd go round the shops with Gran sometime and as it's not very nice we could do that and leave you on your own.'

'OK.'

'But it may not rain.'

'No.'

She was silent, helplessly. He stood aloof from her, whistling softly through his teeth, watching the distant children get into the car, the doors slam, the car back, turn, and move away, going back towards the town. There was no one else in sight.

Raymond moved out, looking about him. She saw him against the amplitude of sky and sea, compact and neat in spite of his ruffled hair, and her heart trembled. His shape, his colour, the clothes he wore, all these she knew with all her senses; he stood before her in his blue blazer, the scarf at his neck was one she had given him; and she knew the tone of his voice and the shape of his lips, the roughness beneath his jaw which the razor had missed, the scent of his brilliantine, the way he liked his tea – all these things she knew, encased in the shape that stood before her, all these things she would always know, but himself she did not know. What she saw was merely a box whose colours and textures she knew; but what it held she did not know, could never know, would never. He had gone from her. The eyes he turned on her were china blue, opaque, blazing; she would never be able to see through them to the thought within. She had believed that to love was to know; now, on the cliff-top in the beating wind, she knew nothing, nothing . . .

He held out his hand and smiled. 'Come here,' he said.

She knew the smile but not the man who wore it. She took his hand; it was very cold – where had he left his gloves? He drew her up the cliff towards the edge but he was not with her; it was as if he stood alone in time, outlawed, cut off from everyone, consuming himself in the bitter fire of his own blazing smile. His hand did not hold her, his eyes did not see her, he was locked up for ever in the cage of his own self. Bleak and lonely as the lighthouse tiny below them, he stood on the cliff edge holding her with his cold hand.

'Ray?' she said.

He turned his unseeing eyes to her, smiling his desolate smile.

'Was it my fault?'

His voice was courteous. 'What?'

'The other night. Was it me?'

'You?'

'I don't know, you see. You must tell me.'

'Tell you what?'

'If it was me. If I don't . . .' She faltered and with astonishment felt tears thrust into her eyes. 'If you can't feel that way about me, it doesn't matter. I have to tell you – if we was never to – if you never wanted to again because I'm not, I don't . . .' With her free hand she tried to wipe the tears away, but they ran down again. 'It's not that important to me, Ray. If we were never to do it again, if I don't suit you anymore, it doesn't matter. You're all that matters, being with you, having you to love – only to love . . .'

His face dissolved in her tears; she turned her head away, groping in her pocket for a handkerchief. 'I can't bear it when you're alone. You go away from me and you're all alone – I can't reach you, can't help you. You're like someone standing out in the cold and there's a window between and I can't make you hear and bring you inside, its like a bad dream . . .'

He took her by the arm and with his other hand caught her chin and turned her face savagely to his. His eyes were no longer opaque but brilliant with anger and – was it fear? 'What are you saying?' he said in a hard low voice, and he shook her, 'What do you want from me?'

'Nothing. I don't want anything, Ray. I love you. All I want is to love you.'

She tried to twist her head away and since she could not, she shut her eyes, standing limp in his grasp with her face defenceless before him.

'Say that again,' he said.

'I only want to love you,' she repeated dully.

He was silent so long, his hand still on her chin, that she opened her eyes. He was staring at her, searching as a hungry man searches a table laden with food that may be poisoned, warily, greedily, suspicion struggling with hope, hunger with fear.

'It's true,' he said. 'You don't want anything, do you?'

He released her chin, smoothed her hair back from the wet face with an angry, caressing movement. 'You don't want anything,' he said again. His hands still hurt her arms but now they were warm. His eyes were the astonished clear blue of forget-me-nots.

A spatter of rain drove at them off the sea as they stood on their pinnacle, the stony beach laid far below them.

'We're too near the edge,' he said, and laughed. Back in the shelter of the ruined house he kissed her, gently.

PART TWO

EIGHT

THE GROVERS never went on holiday. For a week each September Mrs Grover went to her brother's farm in Norfolk and woke every morning of her stay at five o'clock, worrying about Mr Grover, who at that hour would be getting himself a cup of Bovril (it roused him more quickly than tea) before going downstairs to receive the deliveries from the newspaper offices and make up the roundsmen's orders. Mr Grover never went away, for he would trust nobody with the shop. The shop was not only his livelihood but his life; times had been bad when he first went to work for Mr Wilson there and in self-preservation he had burrowed his way further and further into the business; then in the flailing sand of the desert, man and tank stinking with their own hot grease, the shop had been what he dreamed of, clung to, the rock to which he must fight home. He and Nancy had taken over when Mr Wilson began to fail; and when he died they seemed to flatten themselves into the ground as birds or little animals do in an effort not to be flushed from cover.

They need not have feared. Esther was glad to have them. They grew bolder, had the flat above the shop redecorated, bought a budgerigar. Mr Grover compiled his scrapbook of strange or macabre incidents; Mrs Grover tried out crochet patterns and some embroidery. Snug yet always fearful, they had no other interests in life but the shop and each other. They had not loved each other particularly when they married; they had met at night class, where both of them were learning book-keeping, and had got into the habit of going home together since both took the same bus. After a while their marriage seemed to be understood; almost without anything actually being said they found themselves standing side by side in church, he in a new blue suit, she in white taffeta with a Juliet cap of artificial orange blossom, and if he had one last backward thought of the girls he might have chosen to marry but had never met, hers were all of the future, of a little home and a little family and a nice little business all their own.

It had not worked out that way, of course. They saved for the little home but it took a long time, and the little business as well as the little family eluded them forever. A daughter, Christabel Elaine, lived for four days and died like a little skinned rabbit. The Grovers were not framed for grief so elemental and they never tried again. Each felt guilty towards the other, which made them more tender, and they dared not risk hazarding anything else. They continued to save, but not for the little home, simply for each other. They had their home over the shop, and the shop was their business as much as if it had been bought with their own money. Flat, shop, each other: for these they would stand at bay if need be, a pair of desperate mice.

Gradually their fears at Esther's marriage quietened. They had not believed that Esther would betray them but, 'You can't tell what a woman will do when she marries,' said Mr Grover. 'Look at Queen Victoria, look at William and Mary. They take on the colour of their husbands.'

'She wouldn't, dear. Not Esther. She appreciates us.' Her fingers pecked at the crochet-work she held, a cascade over her lap, long ago begun, forever unfinished, a coverlet for their bed.

'They take on the colour of their husbands,' he repeated. 'No minds of their own. You just can't tell.'

But it had been all right. Esther had reassured them and interfered no more than she had ever done, and they had only seen her husband once after the wedding, when she had brought him round to see the shop. They all had tea together in the back parlour, with Mr Grover in and out dealing with customers. Mr Banks had been pleasant enough; he didn't say much and you could see he didn't miss much either, but the Grovers had nothing to complain about and were left in peace. Nevertheless, the threat to their security remained like a barb under their skins. In those few minutes at dawn before they got out of bed and drank their Bovril, each lay with their terror: the flat was not their own little home, the shop was not their own little business, they had no little family except the budgerigar and each other precariously held, a temptation to fortune.

All the time Esther was pregnant she continued to do the books. It was more than a year after she had married and the Grovers had hardly seen Raymond since; but the day after she went to hospital he came round. It was one of the few hot afternoons of that late summer, the heat throbbing up from the pavements, doors and windows wide as though to gulp the air. Little boys ran skinny in bathing trunks and dust, and their mothers' flesh was too apparent under thin cotton dresses. It was not too bad in the shop, for the Grovers kept the awning down outside and the interior was twilit. Raymond came in wearing an open-necked shirt but otherwise trim as always, smiling. Mr Grover rose when he entered.

'Good afternoon,' said Raymond. 'My word, it's hot! I just popped round to tell you the glad news. I know Esther would wish it. It's a girl!'

'A girl! Congratulations indeed. Nancy!' Pleasure at Esther's deliverance, anguish at their own memories, flashed through Mr Grover as he called. A little girl . . . 'Nancy! Mr Banks is here. He's a father.'

'No! When?' Mrs Grover darted out from the parlour, eyes alight with interest. A birth is a birth, no matter to whom, all women participate . . . 'Is she all right?'

'Fine, fine – mother and daughter doing well. Even father's not feeling too sorry for himself.'

'A little girl! Well!' said Mrs Grover, shadowed for a moment.

'Six and a half pounds and pretty as a picture. Arrived just about breakfast-time. I didn't feel much like bacon and eggs, I must say!'

'Well now,' said Mrs Grover. 'I do congratulate you.'

'Mrs Wilson wanted to come but I told her no. She's near off her head with being a great-grandmother, I can tell you, and in this heat and all. I told her to have a lay down before going round to the hospital with me later. But she said you'd be sure to want to know and I know Etty'd wish it too. She's a great regard for you, you know.' He looked at them smilingly over the counter spread with their livelihood, chinking coins in his pockets.

'Please give Mrs Banks our kindest congratulations,' Mr Grover said formally. Mrs Grover burst out, 'Can I go and see her?'

'Not for a week – hospital rules. Only family, see? After that I dare say she'd be glad.'

'I'll send her some flowers – or would she rather have fruit? Have you thought of a name yet?'

'Not yet.'

'Well now!' exclaimed Mrs Grover again. Christabel Elaine . . .

'It's kind of you to bring us the news,' her husband said.

'Well, I knew you'd be interested, knowing her such a long time and all. And I thought I'd pick up the books at the same time.'

'The books,' said Mr Grover flatly. The smile vanished from his wife's face.

'That's right. It's the end of the month, isn't it?'

'Yes.' The air hung heavily in the twilit silence. The Grovers stared at Raymond and he looked back at them pleasantly. 'No one but Miss Wilson – Mrs Banks – ever has the books,' Grover said at last.

'No? Well, there's not really been anyone *to* have them, has there, not until now.'

'I've no instructions . . .'

'I can get it in writing for you if you like,' said Raymond carelessly, 'if you really want me to trouble her the day she's just had a baby.'

'Can't it wait over?'

He gave him a sharp look. 'That's not how I do business, Mr Grover. It may be your way but it's not mine. It's the end of the month, the books are due. Of course, if you've some reason . . .'

Mr Grover coloured from his neck to the top of his bald head. Even his eyes grew pink. 'I've no reason, Mr Banks, except that this business belongs to Miss Wilson and no one but she has ever been entitled to see the books.'

'Well, she's Mrs Banks now,' said Raymond coolly, 'and her business is my business. You may not have understood that, Mr Grover, but that's how it is.'

'She never told me so,' said Grover, his voice shaking with rage.

'Leonard!' His wife pulled at his sleeve, 'It's the law, dear. Mr Banks is right, perfectly right.'

'Thank you, Mrs Grover.' Raymond smiled at her and she thought how brightly blue his eyes were. 'I don't want to make ill-will about this, you know. It's just that the books are due and frankly I don't want my wife to come out of hospital with a new baby and find her first job when she gets home is to try and get some sense out of books that have been allowed to run on. I'd rather she was able to take things easy for a while, see?' He was smiling steadily, secure in his rights.

'Of course,' she agreed, 'of course she mustn't do that. Get the books, Leonard.'

Slowly he turned and lifted the two ledgers down from the shelf behind him. Mrs Grover bustled to find a newspaper in which to wrap them – 'We always wrap them for Mrs Banks' – and without a word Grover handed them across. Raymond took them with a nod.

'Thanks,' he said, 'I'll let you have them back tomorrow. Sorry if I've rubbed you up the wrong way, old man, but honestly I'm only trying to spare my wife.'

'Of course you are. We understand that, don't we, Leonard? Give her all the best from us, do, and kiss the dear little baby for me. I'll take her some flowers in the morning.'

'That's good of you, Mrs Grover. She's in Willow Ward, end bed on the left when you're calling. Cheeri-bye.'

He went. The Grovers looked at one another, and it was she who coloured now. 'But he was right, Leonard. It's the law.'

'I shouldn't come round for the books the day you'd just had a baby.'

Tears came to her eyes. 'Oh Len,' she said, 'he was only trying to spare her.'

A boy appeared in the doorway. 'The gobstopper's stuck,' he said hoarsely. Slowly Mr Grover went out to see to the machine. They did not speak of the books again for a long time.

The day Esther had her baby, Terry got drunk. When he came back from work and lifted Kim out of the cot to kiss her good evening Gloria, at the table with a cup of tea, said, 'Well, she's had it. A girl.'

He turned with the child in his arms. 'Mrs Banks?'

'Who else? The old girl was so certain it would be a boy, too.'

'Hear that, pet?' He nuzzled his daughter's hair. 'A sweet little girl for Kimpet to play with, eh?'

'Sweet little girl my foot,' said Gloria and blew cigarette smoke across the table. 'She'll find out.'

So Terry went out and got drunk.

First of all he toasted the birth of the new baby, and then its mother, and then all new babies; by the time the pub closed he was mourning his child, his marriage and himself. He thought of his mother and all the things she'd said about Kim being only the first and how proud she had made him feel and potent and triumphant, of how Kim loved him and cuddled up to him and pulled his ears and said 'Dad Dad' when she woke each morning and how her hair curled at her moist pink nape and her body was round and firm as a – as a rose, he thought, and tears came into his eyes. My little rose, my little fairy doll – and only the one. Never no more, despite what his mother had proudly prophesied and he himself knew waited within him. Only the one, and it was Mrs Banks who was blessed today, whose health he was drinking, who held the pink miracle in her arms. He longed for his mother so intensely that when he finally reached home it was a shock to see Gloria and not his mother sitting in bed reading a magazine. He paused in the doorway, adjusting his sight to the small figure in cerise nylon, hair pinned, face creamed, instead of the full bosom he had been going to rest his head on and the strong hands he had been going to feel caressing his hair. The two images merged in a confusing way, leaving him with an overwhelming love, for both, for all, for himself. He came carefully across the room, avoiding the screen which shielded Kim's cot from the light, and dropped down on the edge of the bed.

'Gloria,' he said and took her hand.

Her voice was cold. 'You know what time it is?'

He shook his head, not attending, thinking how pretty she was, this woman, this mother . . .

'It's nearly twelve. Where the hell have you been?'

'I went out.'

'I know you went out. I didn't think you was hiding under the bed all evening, did I?' He shook his head again and she pulled her hand away. 'You might at least have the decency to come home when the pubs close. I need my sleep even if you don't. You needn't think I'm going to make myself late in the morning getting you to work on time, I've enough to do without that. Now for God's sake get to bed.' She threw down the magazine, turned her back and flounced down under the bedclothes. His return had banished her faint anxiety at his absence and left her with nothing but anger, anger that hurt like grief. She lay motionless while slowly he undressed, and when he turned off the light and got into bed she flounced the other way round again so that her back should still be against him. He put his hand on her waist but she shook it off. He smelt of beer. Had he persisted she would have fought him; but he turned his back to her too and with both hands pressed the pillow to his cheek and would have cried for his mother had he not instantly fallen asleep.

They did not speak very much next day. Terry had to be at work at half past eight and Gloria had to take Kim to the nursery before getting to Maison Alfredo, the hairdresser's shop at which she now worked as a receptionist. Times had changed since, more than a year ago, at Gran's suggestion, she had got a part-time job in Woolworth's. From there she had worked in a new self-service supermarket where housewives passed in a state of light hypnosis along the alleys of tins and packages, wire baskets on their arms, their minds ticking like meters to the stimulation of OUR PRICE and TODAY'S SPECIAL BARGAIN. She had worked two full and three half days then; now she worked five full days for Mr Alfredo, a friend of Madame Sheelagh's whom she had met in the Dick Whittington where she often went at lunchtime. Sometimes she saw Gran there but they seldom sat together now. Gloria had her own friends at the bar, Gran sat with Mr Phelps; Gloria had got more lively, Gran had quietened down; Gloria was fulfilling what Gran irresponsibly had set in motion.

Terry and Gloria had got out of the habit of talking to each other. Their conversation sprang from the child, who banged and clamoured in her highchair between them. 'Oog-oog!' she would cry, and Terry would say, 'She wants her sugar – Mum give Kimpet some nice oog-oog?' and Gloria would pop a lump into the child's wet mouth and say, 'Don't you spit that out now,' and Terry would say, 'Lovely oog-oog, yum yum! Dad have some oog-oog too?' and pass his cup and Gloria would fill it again with tea. Kim always cried when Terry left for work, for she loved his doting attention and his young bony face with the crest of hair he let her tug. As she cried Gloria whisked her out of the chair and on to her pot, and there she immediately grew silent, edging herself along the floor to forbidden things like the gas fire or the rubbish basket, to be whisked up again, washed, buttoned, brushed, put in the pram and left at the crèche with the other babies whose existence she regarded with curiosity but disbelief. There she stayed contentedly till Gloria fetched her at five. Sometimes she did not want to leave and screamed and grew rigid; sometimes she ran to Gloria and threw her arms round her knees, her red hair pushing against her mother's thighs, crying 'Mum Mum Mum!' in heartbroken delight; and then Gloria's anger could scarcely be contained and she lifted the child roughly, mad with anger at the spear to the heart wielded by this little creature.

Sometimes she and Terry went to the pictures or to the pub; occasionally they went and danced, making a four with a girl from Maison Alfredo's and her boy-friend, or an old mate from London Transport. These evenings they enjoyed; hearing the gossip, living again in the old world, they grew alive together again, forgot Kim, forgot the time that lay behind them, were back at their beginning. After these evenings they came home gaily and, if Kim did not waken, usually made love; but in the lovemaking the gaiety died, leaving distrust with her, frustration with him. Kim was eight-een months and the only one . . .

Every Sunday they took her over to Plumstead. On Monday mornings they hardly spoke to each other at all.

Terry bought a big bunch of roses, pink and yellow, at cost price from where he worked and left them at the hospital for Esther. Through the sweltering day and stuffy night he thought of Esther and her baby. His awareness of the new child never left him and on Friday night he took Gloria all the way up to Tottenham Court Road to a cinema whose façade was so thick with Xs one could hardly find the title of the film. In the darkness inside he pressed and kneaded Gloria's hand as shoulders were bared and bedclothes tumbled above the English subtitles. Obedient to suggestion, she put her head on his shoulder and let him feel her breast. They sang softly together as they walked home afterwards, undressed quickly and were soon in bed. Power, determination, even love, reared strongly up in Terry; and Gloria, lulled by the climate of the evening, responded dreamily as if she hardly knew who he was. Then: 'No,' she whispered sharply. He did not answer but pressed on. 'No,' she said again, closing and wriggling aside. He bore down on her implacably, impervious to all but his purpose. She raised her head and bit the lobe of his ear as hard as she could. He gave a cry and released her, then with the hand he had pressed to his ear he hit her full across the face. The slap and the scream of her indrawn breath were loud in the darkness. She jumped out of bed, snatched up her dressing-gown and ran out of the room.

For a moment he lay there, his flesh throbbing, wondering if his ear were bleeding. His fingertips tingled from the blow and the open bed began to cool at his side. He wondered where Gloria had gone; and then with a sudden terror wondered indeed . . . Had she run out into the street, thrown herself out of the window, gone down to hammer on Mrs Wilson's door? He, too, jumped out of bed and blundered in the darkness out into the sitting-room.

She was sitting huddled up on a chair by the table in the glare of the electric light. She looked shrunken and hard as a gargoyle and he halted in the doorway, hitching his pyjamas together with one hand.

'Don't you touch me,' she said, and her voice frightened him.

'Gloria – are you all right . . .?'

'If you lay a finger on me I'll scream. D'you hear, I'll scream!'

'I didn't mean to hurt you . . .'

'I'll scream so loud it'll wake Mrs Wilson and Raymond and the whole bloody street. I'll wake your precious baby so she can see what her dad has done to me . . .'

He saw the great red mark of his hand deepening across her mouth and cheek and he began to shake. 'Oh baby,' he whispered, 'I didn't mean to hurt you – I wouldn't hurt you . . .'

'No, you didn't mean to! You never mean to do anything, do you, except slobber over the baby and suck up to your mum. You never mean to do anything but run whining to your mum and try to get me in the family way again. That's all you think about, isn't it, getting your filthy hands on me so's you can get me caught again. Well I won't, d'you hear, I won't! I'll never sleep with you again as long as I live!'

'Gloria!' He came a few steps into the room and bent slowly to his knees in front of her. 'I love you, Gloria.'

She drew herself aside even from the space that still lay between them. Her mouth was beginning to swell. 'Love, love!' she sneered. 'All you ever wanted was to get yourself a good time. Bed's all you ever thought about, bed and getting babies!'

'I love you, Gloria. We had good times together, we was happy . . .'

'So long as you got what you wanted you didn't care . . .'

'Don't say that, baby, you was happy too . . .'

'Me – happy? What makes you think that? You was never any good to me . . .'

He shouted, 'That's a bloody lie!' and grabbed at her arms.

They struggled, their faces contorted with rage. 'That's a bloody lie!' he shouted again. 'I was all right. I did you all right and you bloody well know it! It's you that don't want nothing but pleasure, you bloody little

bitch! I did you proper and you was ready for it too. I'll
teach you, I'll teach you . . .'

From the bedroom came the waking wail of the baby.

Lying in the neat room below, wrists crossed
behind his head, staring up at the ceiling as though
he could see through it, Raymond thought placidly:
Those Masons will have to go.

The hot weather had broken and turned to heavy
rain when Esther came home from hospital. She ran
with the baby huddled to her from taxi to front door,
where Gran, forbidden to go with Raymond to fetch
them, waited distractedly. Her face with raindrops on
it was rosy above the little swaddled creature; laughing, she laid her cheek against Gran's lips as Gran's
arms enfolded her, her own enfolding the baby, crying
'What a day! What a homecoming!' while Raymond
paid the taxi-driver and carried in the suitcase.

'What a day!' echoed Gran. She was crying but
unaware of it. 'I meant to have everything shining –
and all the neighbours to see – and look at it!' The rain
beat down between sealed windows and shut doors.
They shut their own front door and stood crowded in
the gloom of the hall. 'Where shall we put her? Ow
bless her, the love!' Gran pulled aside the shawl and
looked at the sleeping baby. 'Oh Etty – oh dear?' The
tears ran faster and she groped for a handkerchief.

'Ray, take the case up, will you?'

'OK.' He edged past them and went upstairs. Followed by Gran, Esther moved down the passage.

'I've got the kettle on,' Gran sniffed, 'and I got some of that teacake. Oh my – there's currants in it.'

'Why not?'

'The milk?'

They stared at each other at the head of the stairs, astonished at Esther having milk, having a baby, having a husband, who for so many years had been a maiden. Then Esther laughed. 'You're old-fashioned, Gran. That's only an old wives' tale.'

'Is it?' She peered at her humbly, then followed on down the stairs. 'Mind them steps with the baby, it's so dark.'

'I know these steps, dear,' Esther said gently. They went into the front room and Esther laid the baby on what had been Grandad's chair and now was Raymond's. She knelt down in front of it and arranged cushions on either side so that the baby was supported. Freed from the hooding shawl, the face of a tiny Raymond stirred and yawned enormously, the eyes opened and stared about. 'Isn't she like her daddy?' asked Esther softly.

'But she's got your eyes,' said Gran.

It was extraordinary what a profusion of belongings so tiny a creature had, nappies, shawls, the crib upstairs with its blankets, the little bath on legs and the basket full of safety-pins and talcum, ointment and cotton wool. There was a smell of baby too, of newness made up of wool and milk and warm water that seemed very strange in the rooms where no child had been for so long, for Kim had never done more than visit clandestinely here for a moment or so. The newness and paleness of the baby's things showed up the lived-in mellowness of walls and furniture so that they too seemed strange. Only Esther seemed at home with old and new, dealing with both with the serenity of possession, while Gran ran back and forth, completing nothing, quite at a loss. She longed to take the baby in her arms but she was afraid; with Kim she had been heedless, but this one was Etty's. It was so small, so new; she was so old. All the things she had thought she knew were nothing now. Everything had changed, time had moved on and left her standing foolishly. It was Etty now who knew everything, even this ultimate knowledge of child and breast. Gran was afraid to touch the baby lest it cried at the sight of her.

It was Raymond who made the tea and served it, cleared it and washed it up. He did not talk very much. He filled the bath with warm water, set the chair ready beside it for Esther, watched as she tested the heat with her elbow as the nurses had taught her to do, and as she unwrapped the coverings that hid the tiny naked body of his daughter. Awkwardly, for she was not accustomed to it yet, Esther lifted the baby from her spread knees, the tiny shoulder and tiny leg like a bird's in her nervous grasp, and bathed her. The baby shut her eyes, twitched and whimpered a little. Raymond watched in silence, while Gran exclaimed and handed the wrong towel, dropped the tin of ointment, laid the nightgown against her cheek to feel if it were aired. The baby began its small bawling as Esther dressed her, her eyes pressed tightly shut, her mouth seeking and squalling for her feed. Raymond was emptying the bath and as Esther, after a moment's hesitation, began to unbutton her blouse, he flushed a swift bright crimson. 'Come on, Gran,' he said tersely. As they went down the stairs they heard the squalling stop abruptly.

They went into the sitting-room. Raymond began to read a newspaper, the sheets held before his face, but Gran sat on the edge of her chair by the television and wiped her face all over with her handkerchief. Still it was wet, for the tears ran out of her eyes, soothing as they fell. She sat and wiped them away as old women sit in the sun and wipe the sweat away, patiently, knowing its health.

After a little while she said, 'I can't help thinking of Winnie. She should have been here. Poor Win.'

He lowered the newspaper. 'I know about her,' he said gently.

Gran nodded. 'Yes. Poor Win. She tried everything to get rid of it. Pills I got her, and medicine – she went to a woman somewhere, Tufnell Park, somewhere, but it didn't do no good. She never had the joy of it, my poor Win-baby.'

Raymond stayed home that week; he said his firm allowed him the time off if he forewent a week's commission and Esther needed him to get settled into the new routine of home and baby. He was gentle and practical and although he would not tend the baby he would hold her in silence, studying this small shut face that was so like his own. He never said anything much about her but Esther had seen the pride, the arrogant protectiveness that lit his eyes when he saw the child, so that their blue was transparent, letting her glimpse the happiness within.

It was a great comfort to have him home, for she found herself easily tired and easily weepy, which was odd considering that she had been as happy only once before in her life, when Raymond had asked her to marry him. Then as now she had felt a great blossoming of fulfilment; then as now the end of one phase seemed to have been reached and the beginning of a new. Between his asking her and their return home with their baby were many happinesses, depths and richness of developing love and learning; now there were new things to learn, practical things, like how to bring a baby's wind up, and things beyond definition, like loving the child. It was beyond her how she could love so much; she would sit in the low chair quietly, herself alone with the baby, holding its body under her breast, feeling the tug-tug on her nipple, knowing that some milk would come back, nappies would be dirtied, she would have to wake in the night to still its insistence, her eyes wooden with sleep, and yet adrift with enchantment, spellbound by an instinct beyond explanation, a selfless passionate surrender.

On Sunday they took the baby into the park, walking together self-consciously for the first time as parents. There were plenty of other couples pushing prams but none seemed so new, none seemed to have so tiny and perfect a child. She tried to manoeuvre the pram smoothly, as though she were practised at it, and up and down the kerbs Raymond laid a controlling hand on the bars to help her and assert his share. They found a quiet place under the trees from which they could watch the people walking up and down the broad main path, and Esther spread a rug. The air was warm and Raymond lay on his back with his hands behind his head as though he were in bed, watching the clouds through the leaves above him, while Esther brought out her knitting.

'What's that,' he asked teasingly, 'bed-socks?'

'Silly. It's a frock for baby. See, pink? I'll go and see about the christening tomorrow.'

'You do that. Make it next weekend.'

'I thought the one after. If we're inviting people they'll need a bit of notice.'

'Are we inviting people?'

'It would be nice. Just a few for a cup of tea. I'd like them to see her.'

'OK. Whatever you say.'

'Will you write to your auntie?'

'She wouldn't come down.'

'But we ought to ask her.'

'OK.'

He reached out and stroked her cheek and she bent her head to press his hand to her shoulder, busily knitting.

'About the name,' she said, 'I think June's nice, like we discussed.'

'June. June Banks. Not bad.'

'It's nice to remember the summer in your name, and it's not too fancy.'

'No, it's fine.'

'But then there's the second name. I'd like Raymonde, you know, like they have in French, but perhaps it sounds silly.'

'It does a bit. Raymonde. Sort of like she might change her sex.'

'Don't! Then I thought perhaps – but I suppose you wouldn't want your mother's?'

'No.'

'So I thought what about Auntie's?'

'Auntie?'

'Yes. She's an old lady and you're all she's got now. I thought she might be pleased.'

'She wouldn't care about something like that.'

'She would, Ray, I'm sure of it. People do, you know, they take it as a compliment, especially old people.'

'What about calling her Victoria?'

'You can't have Victoria Banks, it sounds like a place. We might call her June Victoria and then your auntie. What is her name, you always just call her Auntie.'

'Matilda.'

'Matilda?'

'Aunt Matilda.'

'That does sound funny, like something in a play. Hasn't she any other?'

'No. You can't call the kid that.'

'It's a bit of a mouthful. Still, it's only for show. She'd never use it.'

'No, Ett, you can't.'

'Yes I can. I want to. I want to do something for your auntie.'

He leaned up on one elbow, staring at her hands

busily knitting. 'Ett,' putting his hand over hers he stilled them into her lap. She could see only the neat crown of his head. 'You can't do that.'

'Why not, silly?'

'Because – I haven't got an auntie.'

'What?' She stared at him stupidly.

He bent his head farther, pressing her hands. 'I haven't got an auntie.'

'But you said . . . She wrote . . .'

'I made it all up.'

Space seemed to whirl about her, as though she had jumped from an aeroplane and were floating without form or purpose.

'Whatever for?'

'To have something. You know, some sort of background. You had. When I first met you I didn't want you to think I had nothing behind me.'

'But you kept it up,' she said amazedly.

'I had to. The longer it went on, the more I had to keep it up. D'you see, Ett?'

'But there was no need. I wouldn't have cared.'

'I know that now. But I didn't then, did I?'

'All this time, all those lies . . .'

'I'm sorry, dear.'

'Did you ever have an auntie?'

He raised his head and looked at her before answering, 'No.'

'Oh, Raymond . . .'

'I was going to say yes. I was going to say yes I did have an Aunt Matilda when I was a kid, so's you shouldn't think I didn't tell the truth sometimes. But I never did have no one, not till now – and that's the truth.'

'Your mother and dad . . .?'

His eyes were unwavering. 'That's the truth too. But when my mother went off they put me in the orphanage.'

'Oh Ray! What made you tell me now?'

'Well – the baby, I suppose. I couldn't have her called after an untruth, could I? I'm not going to have that for my kid. She's got a family and a home and everything a kid ought to have. She doesn't need no make-believe.' He laid one of her hands against his cheek. 'You're not wild at me, Ett?'

'All those lies . . .'

'You have to lie sometimes. You've never had to, you've always been safe, but I had to. All I had was lies, what I made for myself. I never had nothing, only what I got for myself. Say you understand, Ett.'

'I don't know. I think I do.' She put her arm round his shoulders and drew him to her, stroking the hair back from his forehead. He clung to her, and she tried through the maze of conflicting thoughts to follow the thread of understanding to his heart.

'How old were you when you went in the orphanage?'

'Five or six. Till I was fifteen.'

'Was it – bad?'

'They did their best. I don't want to talk about it.'

'They weren't unkind to you, Ray?'

'No. I said, they did their best. We was all treated alike. Maybe the other kids didn't mind. I did. I made up stories about who I really was and what I'd do when. I was grown up – fairy stories, you know the kind of stuff. And later on, when I found if you hadn't got nothing, you didn't get nothing, I went on with it.'

'And the letters Auntie wrote to me, and the wedding present . . .'

He turned his face into her shoulder. 'I'm sorry, Ett.'

She sat in silence, stroking his hair, trying to steady herself in the whirling rearrangement of her knowledge of him. He was Raymond, whatever else he might pretend to or invent. Whatever make-believe he had imposed on himself and her, he lay in her arms and their baby slept beside them in the pram.

'You've got us now,' she said, 'now and always.'

His voice was muffled. 'I'll tell you something, something I never thought I should say to a living soul. It's hard to say. I love you, Ett.' She drew her breath and held him closer. 'I never loved anyone in my life and I never wanted to. I hated the lot. But you – you're the one.'

'Ray, Ray . . .'

'All the rest – I never cared that for them. They was all after what they could get, I never wasted a thought on them. But you and the baby – you're what I want. So remember it.' He lifted his face so that they could look at one another. 'Remember it,' he repeated, 'no matter what.'

The leaves dappled them. The baby in the pram did not stir. People strolled up and down the asphalt paths, taking no notice of the couples dotted about the grass, some lying, some sitting with their arms about each other, as Ray and Esther were. Indistinguishable from the others, they sat silently, absorbed in wonder.

NINE

FINDING GODPARENTS for June was quite a problem; it was a shock to Esther to realise how few friends they had. Finally they chose the Grovers and Norah West, the nurse at the hospital who had attended Esther in the labour ward and with whom a friendship had grown up. She was a pretty, sensible girl in her middle twenties, already wearing the silver buckle of her third year. She had been to tea twice with Gran and Esther on her days off, and, as Esther said, it would be nice to give the baby somebody young as a godmother. Raymond had not demurred, but he had been against having the Grovers.

'They don't like me, and I don't like them,' he said. 'They took a very queer attitude to me over the books.'

'If you'd told me what you were going to do, I would have written them a note, dear. You can't really blame them.'

'You can't because you're soft,' he answered fondly, 'but yours truly can and does. Who does Mr flipping Grover think he is? You and me could run that business ourselves.'

'We could, but we don't want to, do we?'

'Well . . .'

'Now go along with you, Ray – you know you don't want to be tied to a shop every day of your life. Up at five to see to the orders too, and stock-taking and open on Sunday mornings and never a day off.'

He grinned. 'I see what you mean. Only it puts my back up to be paying out good money and getting nothing but sauce back.'

'We get money back too, dear. Now you've seen the books you know for yourself. Don't be nasty about them. They were ever so fond of Grandad and they've run the shop like as if it was their own. I'd like them to stand for June, dear. And anyway, who else could we have?'

So the Grovers it was, with a silver mug engraved with the baby's initials, Ray's only stipulation being that Norah should hold the child and make the responses. Miss Burroughs was there too, and the Masons with Kim exuberantly kicking the pew, and at

Gran's invitation Mr Phelps. It had been a bit difficult to explain Mr Phelps but she had done it by saying she met him at the launderette. 'A man at the launderette?' laughed Esther and Gran flushed and said crossly, 'Why not? They have to wash their clothes, don't they? He hasn't got no wife to do it for him,' and this at least was true. Little by little in the past year she had learned that he was a widower, that his wife had drunk, that his daughter had married a double-bass player in a dance band and his son had emigrated to Israel. The mournful dark woman who took turns with him in his shop was his sister, Leah, and she too had her troubles, for her husband was a commercial traveller and unfaithful to her whenever he got the chance, which was often.

Mr Phelps did not come to the church but joined them at Handel Street for tea afterwards. He brought a tiny silver bracelet in a leather case which lay on the sleeping baby's wrist like the ring on a hoopla peg; and when they had drunk their tea and cleared the plates of sandwiches and cakes, he produced a bottle of champagne with which, diffidently, he suggested they should drink the baby's health.

The wine altered the atmosphere; Raymond and Esther were put out, Raymond angry that it might be thought he ought to have produced champagne himself, Esther flustered at having no proper glasses, the Grovers feeling themselves at a disadvantage, not used to parties where champagne was drunk, defensive and not much caring for the warm, faintly sour-tasting liquid. Terry and Gloria were drawn together by it, exchanging glances of complicity and patronage, remembering their own christening party where the drink and the glasses had been a matter of course. Gran was entranced by the generosity of her personal friend; Norah West and Miss Burroughs became festive, not from the amount but from the mere idea – champagne meant a celebration. What had been simply a tea party became a function at which people looked self-consciously at one another, turning the ill-assorted glasses in their hands and waiting for a speech. Finally Raymond made one, a few banalities, a laboured joke or two artificially delivered because he must hide his irritation. Gran led the applause enthusiastically, and Miss Burroughs called out, 'Well done, well done!'

'You ought to have done that really, you know,' Raymond said to Mr Grover as he stepped away from the centre of the room. 'It's the godparent's job, not the father's.' His smile was forced and he spoke to the Grovers simply because they were the people next to him; his mind was hot with humiliation and the feeling he had been shown up in some way by not providing wine himself. But Grover did not know this;

he flushed and answered coldly, 'I didn't want to push forward, Mr Banks, or take it upon myself . . .'

'Rubbish, what are you here for?' said Raymond roughly. He looked round for Esther, found Gloria's eyes upon him teasingly, and his temper hardened. 'We look to you and Mrs Grover to pull your weight, see.'

'If there's any complaint . . .' said Mr Grover, his bald head red with anger.

Mrs Grover broke in, 'We'll give little June of our best, Mr Banks. Sweet little soul, we'll take our responsibilities ever so seriously, won't we, Leonard?'

'We always have,' he muttered.

'OK, OK,' said Raymond absently. He had found Esther, exchanged a look of irritation and confidence with her as she talked to Mr Phelps, and felt better. He moved away to put his arm round Gran who was talking to Miss Burroughs and Norah. Under his breath Mr Grover said furiously, 'Did you hear that, Nancy? I won't stand for it – I won't stand for it!'

'Ssh, dear, ssh! We're guests.'

'I don't care. I won't be given orders by that – that upstart. He'll have us out, Nancy, you mark my words.'

'Ssh, dear.'

'He'll have us out. Out on our ears . . . Giving me orders!'

'Leonard, ssh! She'll hear you.'

'Her! Poor woman, I'm sorry for her . . .' But at the remembrance of Esther he calmed himself, looking round to see if his outburst had been noticed.

Miss Burroughs was rallying Raymond. She had not drunk all her wine but was spinning it out in little sips, like a pigeon flirting in a bird-bath. 'Such a clever speech – you travelling men have such splendid *savoir-faire*, a word for every occasion.'

'I was caught on the hop this time, though. Your Mr Phelps shouldn't have done it, Gran.'

'Shouldn't he? I thought it was lovely of him.'

'It was nice enough – only seeing we've only just met the fellow . . .'

'A slightly over-generous gesture,' said Miss Burroughs playfully, 'from one who is not perhaps quite of our persuasion?'

'Did he do wrong, Ray?' Gran peered up at him from the circle of his arm, her rouged old face anxious.

Ray gave her a squeeze. 'Forget it. He's all right.'

'It's a dear little bracelet,' said Norah. 'When she wears that and the corals I gave her she'll look like a queen.'

'How very well Miss Wils – Mrs Banks is looking,' said Miss Burroughs, nodding her head towards Esther. Esther did her hair more loosely now and shorter, and her face was relaxed and rosy as she tested the teapot for a last drop for Mr Phelps' cup. She had put on a little weight since the baby, which made her more, rather than less, shapely, her bosom was now full and maternal, her limbs firm. She looked as though she had bloomed into middle-age too early and would stay there, never growing old.

'It's the baby,' said Norah. 'Having babies agrees with her.'

'Such a happy home,' sighed Miss Burroughs, sipping. 'Three – four generations – and all under the same roof. I remember coming here long, long ago – one Christmas, do you remember, Mrs Wilson?' Gran gave her a dark look. 'One bleak and wintry Christmas, just we three women alone trying to share some Christmas cheer, and now ... Who would have thought that things would change so much, such a happy outcome, and all in the same four walls.' She looked about her vaguely, as though the furniture were friends. 'The old familiar pieces from those long years ago – and of course some new ones too – although I don't see the suite?'

'The suite?' said Gran.

'Mr Banks knows – don't you, Mr Banks?' She smiled at him archly but with a little uncertainty as to exactly where he was, then finished the warm dregs of champagne recklessly.

'Do I?' he asked.

'January – the sale!' she whispered conspiratorially. 'In green contemporary moquette. You didn't see me but I saw you – at least, I saw the invoice!' She wagged her finger at him.

He stared at her. 'That's between you and me, then,' he said.

'A secret?' She clapped her hand to her mouth. 'Oh dear – I did wonder, noticing the address wasn't . . . I won't say another word.'

'Nor you don't neither,' he said to Gran, who had been looking from one to another. 'Understand? This is something I had in mind that didn't work out, see?' Gran nodded. He tightened his grip on her. 'Not a word, see?'

'Not a word, dear.'

'Good girl.' He released her and sent her off with a little push towards the Grovers, who had joined the Masons and were trying to coax Kim to smile at them.

'I'm terribly sorry,' began Miss Burroughs.

He cut her short. 'That's all right, but I just didn't want it talked about – the old lady'd be disappointed.'

'But you did buy the suite . . .'

'For my auntie.' The words came out smooth as butter.

'Your auntie?'

'First of all I thought it'd do fine for here and then all of a sudden my old auntie had to move house – the Rent Act and that lark, see – so I didn't say nothing here but had it shipped straight away up to Leicester. They fitted her new place just right.'

'How kind . . .' murmured Miss Burroughs confusedly.

'So not a word now or I'll be in hot water.' He smiled at them both, and to Norah added, 'Keep my secret, nurse?'

'I'll keep more secrets than you'll ever have,' she answered tartly.

'Good girl. Let's see if there's any more christening cake left. Etty made it, see, and she cooks a treat. Put a bit under your pillow and you'll dream of Mr Right.'

'Not christening cake, Mr Banks . . .'

'Any cake full of fruit and covered with marzipan icing.' He moved away to speak to Esther, who sent him down to the scullery. Alone in the litter of milk bottles, heels of loaves, biscuit wrappings and buttery knives he stood for a moment staring down at the floor unseeingly before finding a knife and starting to cut the rest of the cake meticulously into little wedges.

Esther made another iced cake that year, in October for Gran's birthday. It fell on a Tuesday and there were only the two of them there to eat it, for Norah was on duty and Mr Phelps at the shop. Mr Phelps sometimes called in for a cup of tea in the evenings now and Norah came whenever she had an hour or two to spare. Being friends with Norah made Esther realise what she had missed by having no friends of her own age; Norah was younger than she was by several years, but her experience in the wards and Esther's innocence levelled them up. It was comfortable to hear Norah setting the things on the tray in the scullery or find after she had gone a folded copy of the *Nursing Weekly* in the chair where she had been sitting. It was comforting too to have her advice over June: was she getting too much or too little milk, why did her face turn blue, when could it be expected that she would no longer need to be fed at five in the morning? Norah, with her sturdy legs and eyes of a dark liquid blue, was capable and brisk, with flashes of gaiety that, when she chose, could make them cry with laughter, and her description of the night a famous actress was admitted to Casualty had to be told to Gran over and over again like a favourite fairy story.

Since Esther's marriage, and especially since the baby, Gran had begun to surrender a little to her years. She felt at once more childish and more ancient, letting herself lie back and drift on the tide of lives more virile than her own that were still obedient to the pull and flow of creation. When Esther and she had been alone it was she who had been the young one, the larky one, full of audacity and knowingness; but little by little since Raymond came, since the implacable cycle of marriage, pregnancy and birth had come close to her, she had relinquished her clutch on life. Perhaps it was Raymond's masculine presence that reasserted her old subservience to Grandad, except that in her heart she had defied Grandad and Raymond she did not defy. Perhaps it was just that she was growing old; but this she would not think about, would not permit her glance to stray down the shortening corridor of time to the closed door at the end, closer each year, each month, behind which was – what? Rather she told herself she could no longer be bothered, let them get on with it, they'd got Ray to look after them now; and with the baby her attitude was sometimes austere, as though the reaches between this new-hatched creature and herself were too long, too uncharted for them to launch themselves together.

She came to rely more and more on Mr Phelps. Two or three times a week at the Dick Whittington, once a week at home on the evenings when Raymond was absent, they would sit side by side, not saying very much, exchanging comment on the weather or Mr Phelps' business or something in the newspaper, secure in their maturity. Mr Phelps was not so old as she was, but the eternal patience of his race made him seem older and she sat with him in comfort.

Now she looked forward to her birthday with greed because of the presents, but also with aversion, for she would rather not think about the passing of time. She could not remember how old she was but deliberately spared herself a few years. Esther had laid the table nicely with the best china and the lace tablecloth and, although the day was sunny, had lit the stove so that Gran did not need to wear a jacket but could sit in her dress with the sequin snake down it and Raymond's lizard pinned at the neck. The cake was not a big one but iced in pink, with glacé cherries and pink icing rosettes on the top, and beside it was a little pile of presents. There was a tablet of soap from Miss Burroughs, at which Gran snorted; a shawl of pink and grey knitted by Norah; four handkerchiefs from Cousin Em ('Again!' exclaimed Gran); slippers with pompoms on the toes and a tin of talcum powder from Esther, a pretty card from the Grovers, and from Raymond?

'Well,' said Esther, 'he didn't know what to get you and he was a bit rushed, so I got you this from him. I knew you needed them.'

With pleasant anticipation Gran opened the parcel, for Ray always gave such classy presents. The paper revealed a petticoat and a pair of stout, locknit bloomers. Esther went on, 'It's something he wouldn't have cared to get you himself and I knew your size,' said Esther.

'He always gives me something pretty,' said Gran in a small voice.

'Well, these are pretty – at least, the petticoat is.'

'No, it isn't. All high at the neck, and the bloomers...'

'They're the kind you wear.'

'He always gives me something pretty.' She let her hands lie on the crumpled garments and the tears well out of her eyes. 'He goes himself and chooses me something pretty, a bit of jewellery or a bottle of scent, something I wouldn't buy for meself . . .'

'But Gran, I told you – he didn't know what . . .'

'He couldn't be bothered, that's what. Once it was a different story, when you was courting. Now he's got you and the whole blooming caboodle, he doesn't have to trouble himself with me no more.'

'Oh rubbish, Gran!'

'My best girl, he used to call me,' Gran went on drearily. 'Nothing was too much trouble, this brooch, lovely big boxes of chocolates, nothing but the best for his best girl, he used to say. And now he can't even be bothered to go in a shop and choose something pretty . . .'

Esther said impatiently, 'Oh honestly, Gran, don't be so silly! If there's anything wrong, it's my fault, I got the things. You can't blame Raymond.' She reached forward and took the parcel from Gran's lap, straightening and refolding the things in their paper.

'He's hard,' said Gran. 'I always thought so. There's a hard streak in him.'

'That's enough now.'

'The Grovers think so. The Grovers think he's after the shop.'

Esther flushed. 'Have you been discussing him with the Grovers?'

'I called in to thank her for the card. I don't have to ask your leave to do that, do I?'

'I won't have my business talked about.'

'She just passed the remark. She just said they reckoned he knew he was on to a good thing when he saw it.'

'Oh, what nonsense, Gran!' She struck the table impatiently with her hand. 'We did discuss it ages ago, soon after we married – whether it wouldn't be better, more practical, to run it ourselves. I told him it wouldn't, that the Grovers were part of the business and I wouldn't get rid of them. And he saw, he agreed. He can see the profit it's making, he's never referred to it again. They've nothing to worry about from Raymond, he'd have had them out long ago if he was going to. The same with the Masons. He thought we might let their rooms separate, but he's given up that idea too.'

'There's a hard streak in him,' repeated Gran stubbornly.

'He's had a hard life – more than you know. He's had to make his own way.'

'I'm not saying he's not clever . . .'

'He never had people behind him, not a home or parents or anything till he had us. He thinks the world of us, Gran, you can see it, the way he behaves. You know he does.'

'A packet of cigarettes even, or a box of sweets . . .'

'Oh Gran!' She was able to laugh now, coming round to the chair and putting her arm about the sulky old woman's shoulders. 'How d'you know he won't be bringing you something?'

'Will he?' She perked up.

'He might. I can't say. You know what he is, him and his presents. And there's Mr Phelps to look forward to this evening, he's bound to bring something.'

'Well – he said he'd pop in . . .' Mollified, cheerful again, she drank her tea. Mr Phelps brought a bottle of port and they drank everyone's health in it in front of the telly.

There was no doubt that life for Gran was easier now that she took her place as eldest in a family group. She even went sometimes now to the old age pensioners' evening club to boast there of the triple crown of her great-grandmotherhood. She indulged herself in ease, encouraged herself to be the crotchety old grandmother with her fads and fancies against whom the young ones were helpless because she was their responsibility and old. Sometimes she baited Esther in this way, deliberately acting a part; yet the acting sprang from something genuine, dissatisfaction, loneliness, fear. They were so busy with their lives that were so full, they had no time for hers which, by their care, was now so empty. Snuggling querulously into her comfort, she was both fearful and bored. She armed herself against them with the weapons of feebleness, said things she only half intended because she felt that no attention would be spared to her if she said nothing.

With Raymond, whose authority she would never question, she was good as a little tame cat: poor old Gran, timid old Gran. She kept on the right side of Raymond all right, yet allowed herself to resent him when she felt in the mood. Acting so masterful, forgetting her birthday, sitting in Grandad's chair like as if it were his own . . . She forgot how she had welcomed him, had wooed him for Esther, admired his knowledge and basked in the pride of having a man at home at last. She could summon either side of her feeling for Raymond at will, perversely, now doting on the grandson-in-law, now jealous of the usurper. She had built him up and now wilfully delighted in destroying him; both gave her pleasure and grief.

She did not see much of Gloria now, for in the Dick Whittington Gloria was always with her own friends, girls from Maison Alfredo's or the men with whom Madame Sheelagh did business. Got no time for me now, Gran indulged herself, she and her flashy friends. Not at all a nice type. If I was her hubby I'd be worried. No wonder there's still only the one . . . She often heard Terry come in when the pubs shut, alone and stumblingly, and Gloria much later, clicking upstairs on her spindle heels after laughter outside on the pavement, the slam of a car door. Often as she dozed off, she heard Terry and Gloria quarrelling; often in the mornings she was woken by Kim yelling for attention or thumping over the floor above. 'That child!' she would complain piteously. 'I can't get a wink of sleep.'

One evening she met Gloria coming down the stairs and barred her exit by stopping to exclaim, 'My word, don't you look smashing! Going out?'

'Just meeting some friends.' She looked like a tube of toothpaste, thought Gran, in that blooming sack dress.

'Want us to listen for your little darling?'

'Well, thanks ever so. Terry's in now but he may go out later.'

'Poor boy. He likes a bit of fun too, I expect.'

'Who doesn't?' Gloria screwed an earring tighter and tried to edge past.

Gran lowered her voice. 'I'd creep out quiet if I was you. Between you and me, Mr Banks doesn't like it.'

'Doesn't like what?'

'Us having to listen for Kim.'

Gloria flushed. 'You don't have to.'

'That's what I told him. "She never cries," I told him, "she's no trouble at all, bless her." "No trouble," he says, "with that yelling and carrying on and all that running about? She'll have the plaster down," he says, "if she's there much longer." He doesn't like it, you see.'

'You can't help noise with a kid.'

'That's what I told him. "It's not like business girls, nice and quiet," I said. I could see he was thinking something, so I thought I'd best tip you the wink. Places is hard to find nowadays, especially with a kiddy.'

'I'm sure no one's ever said anything.' Behind the make-up Gloria looked shaken. Gran moved aside and began to go upstairs.

'He wouldn't,' she said, 'that's not his way. Have a nice time, dear.'

She did not discourage the Grovers fears either, whenever she saw them, which was not very often. 'Ah,' she would say, 'he's a deep one, is Raymond. Thinks the world of us, of course, can't do enough for us. He doesn't say much, but you can see he's always thinking how to do the best for his home and his family,' and her bright eyes would range over the shop and come to rest compassionately on the Grovers.

Esther did not forget what Gran, in her birthday tantrum, had said, and she checked with Raymond when he came home that week. They had resumed their Thursdays out now that the baby was weaned, although with her ten o'clock feed there was no longer time for a meal and a double feature. Times had changed since Raymond borrowed Esther's *Evening Standard* over the fish and chips and tea of the tea-room. They went now to a glossy, streamlined place, all polished wood, plastic, and rotating spits. Everything was cooked where you could see it, by deft men encased in crackling, towering starch. 'Right up to the minute,' Raymond said, 'just my style.'

They laughed together over the catastrophe of Gran's bloomers (Raymond had brought her back a pair of earrings, so she was comforted now), marvelled at the way in which June was able to lift her head from the mattress and understand everything that was said to her, exchanged the grains of day-to-day happenings that formed the rock of their foundation and Esther said, 'Ray, you've never had second thoughts about the shop, have you?'

He shook his head, his mouth full of lemon meringue pie. 'Why?'

'Something Gran said. It seems the Grovers are frightened you want to take over the shop.'

'Who, me? They're off their rockers.'

'That's what I said. But you did think of it once, didn't you? Soon after we were married, when we were doing the wills and all?'

'Yes, I thought of it. I'd thought of it a long time, as a matter of fact, and I still do sometimes, especially when old Grover's got my goat.'

'But you've never said so to him, have you?'

'No, of course not. I wouldn't be such a fool. Besides, I don't want it.'

'You're sure, Raymond?'

'Of course I'm sure. Like you said a while back, I don't want to be tied to a shop every day and get up at five every morning. Let them do the work, it pays us off OK.'

But when Raymond had gone again three days later she called in at the shop to show them how June had grown and passed on her more tactful version of Raymond's words. The Grovers were not convinced. They smiled and said she was very kind and that of course a business like this must appeal to a business mind, that it was, of course, a little gold mine in which anyone would be bound to feel interest and that nothing lasted for ever and that June was a bonny baby. Esther did her best and went away feeling that at least Mrs Grover believed her; but she could see that somehow Raymond had antagonised Mr Grover and could only hope that time would calm his apprehensions. She did not know that when she had gone, 'Poor woman,' Mr Grover said, 'they say love is blind. It's easy for anyone else to see that somebody's sitting very pretty indeed, living rent-free and with a nice little business all ready for him.'

With her life enriched by Raymond and the baby, the friendship of Norah and Mr Phelps, the camaraderie with other mothers at the clinic, Esther could hardly remember what she had been like as little as three years ago. When she looked in the mirror, she saw the same pale, nondescript face, but with a different woman looking out from it, serene now, not with emptiness but completion. Her eyes were deeper, her lips fuller, still firmly set but inclining upwards into a smile. Her hands had always been confident as they went about their tasks but now they seemed to move zestfully also, whether washing or mending or tending the baby, helping Gran on with her shoes or brushing with delicate strokes the fair infant hair that would, she feared, too soon turn to her own uninteresting brown. Never for one moment was her heart or her mind left empty; even her reveries were full of tenderness, trances of blessedness in which, without words, she was grateful for all she now possessed. Regular and rich, the routine of her life had steadied itself again, even Raymond's absences accepted and useful, his return looked forward to, their days together content. There had been no recurrence of that lack in him which had so troubled her at Eastbourne. He was not a sensual man – so she gathered from listening to the gossip of her contemporaries at the clinic – but since that terrible uncertainty and fear, when the terror that she had lost him had pierced her beyond bearing, they had been truly together. Since those moments on the cliff top he had, little by little, become more open to her, less armoured; there were privacies, of course, he was a secret person. She still did not know in detail anything of his life away from Handel Street, and the long deception about his aunt had shocked her – it was so needless, he should have known her better – yet it did not hurt her, for she saw it as a shield against himself rather than her, another pitiful detail emerging from his solitary past as they grew closer together. For they were close. She could never doubt that. They were close in the habits of their lives, in their sleep, their occasional intercourse, their ordinary conversation, in tastes unspoken and looks exchanged, caught unexpectedly, a bent head lifted, a smile drawing another smile for no reason save that they were in the same place together. On Thursday afternoons he was glad to be home again, on Sunday evenings regretful to be gone; during their days together he gave off comfort like a warmth, sitting in his chair with his magazines or whistling out in the coal shed or playing with June as she wriggled and laughed on the rug in the sunlight. He adored June;

pride blazed in his eyes when he looked at her, and he always brought her some trinket or garment – seldom a toy – when he came home. He took pride in her fatness, good humour and health; he liked her to be dressed just so, spotless and cherished and happy. He often said, 'She's the image of me, isn't she?'

June was an added unity; and Esther remembered, although he never said it again, 'I never loved anyone in my life ... but you're the one,' and 'Something I never said before to a living soul – I love you, Ett.' Out of their lonely childhood, their emotions unused, hers by neglect, his by hostility, they had created this miracle of union, merging two separate deserts to form one richness. Little by little the sad secrets of his past would come out to her; she would draw their bitterness off by her own compassion, each fault and meanness in him becoming harmless because it was shared and open at last. Gran would grow older and die, June would grow older and live; there would be another perhaps, a boy this time, and perhaps a third if times stayed peaceful and the house and the shop and Raymond's job all flourished, and amid it all would be the two of them, quiet, close, understood.

She thought all this as she went about her chores, articulately, as one tells oneself a story: This is what I have and this is how it will be. There was nothing instinctive or unconscious about her happiness or her love for Raymond. She counted what she had and found it all that she needed.

She and Gran were at the shops one Friday afternoon in October, and Raymond sat alone in the sitting-room, reading the *Reader's Digest*. There was a knock on the door and Gloria recoiled in confusion when he opened it.

'Oh Mr Banks! I wouldn't have knocked if I'd known it was you. Is Mrs Banks about?'

'She's out.'

'Oh. I'm ever so sorry to trouble you. It was just – well, there's ever such a queer mark coming on the ceiling just by the front window and I thought perhaps she wouldn't mind having a look at it.'

'I'll tell her.'

'Thanks ever so.' She looked at him innocently, her mascaraed eyes round. 'It's only – I'm a bit worried. It seems to be spreading all the time.'

'What, now?'

'Yes. I noticed it when I come home dinner-time – Mr Alfredo let me have a half-day today, you see, because I worked extra late yesterday, a business lady with a perm and a henna and a manicure and I don't know what-all, so of course I hadn't any option – and as soon as I got in I noticed this big patch on the ceiling and I said to myself, "Oh my goodness, that looks like a slate's off or something, what with all that rain," so I thought I'd come down and ask Mrs Banks to look at it.'

'I'll tell her. She won't be long.'

'I suppose you couldn't come up and look at it yourself, could you? I mean, if it's spreading all the time we may have to get a plumber and it's the weekend tomorrow. I wouldn't like any bad damage to be done.'

He stared at her coldly, marking the elaborate blonde hairstyle, the blue sack dress that clung to her hips and tapered at her knees, thinking she looked a proper sight. 'OK,' he said.

She went up the stairs ahead of him, her little buttocks shifting, her knees pinched by the tight skirt. The Masons' flat was tidy and clean as rooms can be only when they have just been done. A stuffed rabbit lay on the floor by the fireplace and with a pettish exclamation Gloria snatched it up and put it in the toy-box before pointing to the window and saying, 'That's it – my word, I think it's spread while I was just talking to you.'

There was indeed a damp patch spreading between ceiling and window. Raymond examined it, then opened the lower half of the window and carefully leaned out, twisting himself round to look towards the roof. 'Oh, do be careful!' cried Gloria delicately. He drew himself in again.

'It's the gutter,' he said, dusting his hands together, 'blocked up with leaves, I expect. I'll get a man round in the morning.'

'That's ever so kind of you. I was frightened it might be a burst pipe or something and we'd all wake up in the middle of the night and find ourselves avalanched.'

'It won't get much worse, not unless it rains.'

'You never can tell, can you, not this climate? One minute it's sweltering, the next it's practically a snowstorm. I don't know how we all stand it, really. Down at Westgate where we were in the summer we only had four fine days – that's days you could really call fine, you know, to wear beach clothes and just lie lazing. I love to lie lazing, don't you, Mr Banks?'

'I never tried it.'

'Oh, you should. Although it's not everybody can stand a lot of sun and you've got ever such a delicate, fair skin, haven't you? That's what's so odd about me, I'm ever so fair and yet I can just stretch out in the sun and let it soak into me, just like a lizard, Terry, my husband, says.' She stretched her arms out and gave an ecstatic little wriggle. 'Still, I didn't get much chance this summer, I must say, even if I did get a nice tan. You and Mrs Banks didn't go on holiday this year, did you?'

'No.'

'Well, you'd had the baby and all. It does run away with the lolly, doesn't it, you can't give yourself any of the little treats you used to when you was single – that's what me and Terry finds. Still, we managed the fortnight. I had to have it, I felt I'd die if I stayed stuck up in stuffy old London and the stuffy old shop a minute longer. Everyone needs a break, don't they? Although of course it wasn't much of a break for me with Kim underfoot the whole time.'

He did not answer but moved across to the door, looking around him sharply for something to complain about. She followed him, playing with the long beads round her neck.

'I hope you think I keep the place nice,' she said slyly. He gave her a glance which recognised a sharpness equal to his own. 'It's hard doing it all myself and going out to work and all, and of course Terry's not much help, never has been. His mother never made him do a thing in the house and so of course he's practically useless. But I can't bear not to take a pride in the place. Some girls mightn't but that's not my style. Of course you can't help a bit of untidiness with a kiddy.'

'I don't see any.'

'Oh my!' She laughed, leaning against the table with her silky ankles crossed. 'You ought to see it by the time it's her bedtime! It's a good thing I take a pride in the place and of course one of the things I see to is that she clears it all up herself. You can't start training them too young.'

He looked at her with quite expressionless eyes. 'We was always made to clear away,' he said. 'I never found it did me any good.'

'It may not have done you any good but I bet it was good for your mum. After all, parents are owed some consideration, I always say. Who was it said, "Parents are people"?'

'I don't know – who was it?'

'Some American, I expect. They're ever so quick at putting things, Americans. I've got an American friend, he's only a simple sort of fellow, you know, just an electrician back in the States, nothing special about him, but he's got ever such a quick way of putting things, all with a straight sort of deadpan expression, you know, he kills me sometimes, the things he says, he really does.'

She looked at him, smiling, twirling her beads. He moved again towards the door. 'I'll get a builder in the morning,' he said.

'Thanks ever so. Are you sure you wouldn't like a cup of tea? I was just going to have one.'

'No thanks.'

'Or something stronger?' She followed him out onto the landing. It was dark out there, only half lit by the window at the turn of the stairs through which the afternoon light was fading.

'I don't drink.'

'What, never? Nothing at all? My goodness, I wish I could say the same of my husband. Everyone likes a nip now and then, I won't pretend I don't like to be in a jolly crowd with a drop of something to make me feel in the mood, but Terry . . . I don't know what's the matter with him these days, I'm sometimes half frantic with the worry, but of course I can't talk to anyone about it, it wouldn't be right. It's since Kim came, of course. Don't you believe what they say about kids binding people together, that's all my eye. Kids break people up, that's what they do – break them right up.'

For a moment her voice and her pretty face were alive with sincerity, piercing the make-up and the hairdo and the coquetry like a shaft of sun shot from an opening window.

Motionless in the twilight he said, 'Speak for yourself.'

Artifice reasserted itself. She laughed trillingly. 'Well, that's all any of us ever can do, isn't it? I mean, none of us ever really knows what goes on in another person's head. At least, only at certain times and then it's dead easy, isn't it?' She glanced at him under her lashes, moving a little closer. 'Are you sure you wouldn't like something?' she said.

He stood perfectly still, letting her move towards him. She could not see the expression on his face but knew that her perfume would be all about him. For a moment as she stood there in the half darkness, the anonymous male figure in front of her, feeling her own body stretched within its sheath of cloth and skin, hearing for a moment her own false voice, she could have cried aloud in pain, the pain of love and loneliness and the corruption of hope, for Terry as he had been three years ago and herself then, too.

'Seeing we're both on our own,' she said, 'I should like you to feel at home up here. Seeing that everything's nice.'

'Where's Kim?' he said. The choked sound of his voice pleased her. She moved nearer.

'Kim's safe enough. I can fetch her or leave her to suit myself. I don't let the kid bother me none.'

She felt a great heat escape from him and as she braced herself in the darkness to yield herself against him she felt his hands on her upper arms seize and grip and throw her sideways so that she lost her balance and her needle heels caught in the rug and she fell, screaming, tied by her narrow hem, the beads flying out and banging behind her neck, into and down the twilit staircase, down and round, banging and twisted, the stairs a nightmare of inversion, flying upwards past her, her head below her legs, flying and falling, catching at banisters that tore from her fingers, a shoe striking her face as she fell and the thin clatter of her overthrow making a silence round her one shrill scream.

She fell against the angle of the wall where the staircase turned, slid a little and lay, a huddle of spindle limbs and torn seams, the beads still intact but hanging down her back. There was a moment of infinite time, an eternity of shock and death; then a hurry of footsteps down to her and Raymond betiding over, his face anxious.

'Are you hurt? Did you hurt yourself? Are you all right?'

She drew a shrill wheezing breath, half sob, half scream.

'Are you hurt?' he repeated. 'Can you move?' He put out his hand and made to lift her. She recoiled against the wall.

'You beast!' she screamed in a whisper. 'You filthy beast!'

'You slipped,' he said. 'Your heel must have caught and you slipped.'

'You filthy beast,' she said again faintly and began to cry, turning her head away against the wall like a child in disgrace.

'You slipped,' he said again. 'Here, let's see if you can stand.'

He put his hands under her elbows and weakly she let him raise her, hobbling on one twisted ankle, sobbing and gasping. He supported her carefully up the stairs and into the living room. 'There,' he said, 'take it easy. You'll be all right. There. I'll get you a drink.' He put her into a chair, busy and helpful. 'Shall I make you some tea? Or shall I get you a nip of brandy from the pub?'

'In the cupboard – some whisky,' she said faintly. He found it and poured her a good measure, putting the glass into her hands. 'Drink it down,' he said. 'A nasty fall like that. You've had a shock.'

Shuddering, her teeth knocking the glass, she drank. He stood looking down at her, his face almost as pale as her own.

'You must have that rug nailed down. You came a real nasty cropper.'

She glared up at him in fear and hatred. 'I might have broke my neck.'

He nodded. 'You might indeed. That was a real nasty fall. How d'you feel now?'

'I've cut my leg.' Blood oozed through the stocking on her shin and her forearm and hand began to burn from a long, sealing graze. 'I might have broke my neck,' she repeated querulously.

'You're a lucky girl,' he said. 'We shouldn't have been . . .' he paused, considering his words, 'shouldn't have been playing games on the landing like that, should we? Not in the dark with the rug loose and all and those high heels of yours. There might have been a nasty accident.'

The whisky was steadying her and she took another sip, putting up a hand to straighten her hair, adjust her beads, finger the split seam of her dress.

'Will you be all right now?'

She nodded. Now that her panic was over, she could not look at him, wanting only that he should go.

'I'll get downstairs then. You're sure you're all right?' She nodded again, violently. 'If you feel queer, give us a shout. Esther and the old lady ought to be back any minute. You know they'll be only too glad to help. Take things easy now. OK?'

She turned her head away, lying back in the chair. When she knew he had gone she began to cry, very quietly, wiping her nose on her hand.

Esther herself came up next day to nail the rug down on the landing; and Gran, clucking and exclaiming, examined the staircase where a long scar in the paint marked the skidding of Gloria's heels. Kim ran in and out, pleased at the bustle but uncertain of its cause, supposing it to be herself. Outside the house a builder on a ladder warbled as he cleared the blocked gutter, looking in at the window each time he went up or down on a Gloria very silent and pale as she did the housework. She had not felt up to going to work this morning; nor had she sent Kim, as she could have done, to the woman round the corner who looked after her when both Terry and Gloria were at work. She had wanted someone with her, even Kim; anyone rather than be alone in the rooms at the top of that flight of stairs about which Esther and Gran and even Raymond had busied themselves. Kim, her own small, red-headed, demanding nuisance, provided by her egocentric presence protection against thought. For Gloria must not think; the injunction went round and round in her head like a squirrel in a wheel: I mustn't think, I mustn't think, each repetition emphasising the thought: He pushed me.

But why did he push me?

Because I was doing wrong.

It wasn't me doing wrong, it was him, wanting it.

He didn't want it.

All men want it.

He didn't. I was doing wrong and he pushed me.

I might have been killed.

Serve me right. He'd have been had up for . . .

Don't think. I mustn't think . . .

But he pushed me . . .

No, he didn't. I slipped. He went to put his hands on me and in the struggle I slipped.

Silently she went through the day, feeling the cold creep through her until by Kim's bedtime she could do nothing but sit shaking in her chair with Kim on her lap for warmth. She and the child clung to each other, the child sensing her mother's need and, in her response, becoming the older of the two. Terry found them like that when he came home at seven o'clock.

He put them both to bed, Gloria first. Kim went to sleep quickly but Gloria lay like a pinched monkey, watching him move about the room. He gave her some soup and two aspirins, which she swallowed down obediently. He sat on the edge of the bed and awkwardly took her hand. 'You've had a proper shake-up,' he said. 'It's the shock catching up with you. You'll be all right in the morning.'

She stared at him dumbly.

'You just lay there and don't worry,' he said. 'I'll see to everything. I'll ring Mum in the morning and tell her we shan't be over. You have a day in bed.'

He went away and did the washing-up, tidied Kim's toys, laid the next day's breakfast. Then he came back and sat on the bed again.

'Feeling better?' She nodded faintly. 'That's right. You'll be all right. It gives you a shock, a nasty fall like that. It's a good thing Mr Banks was there to help you.'

She clutched his hand and began to cry. He put his arm round her and felt her trembling, clinging to him as though in terror. 'Why, baby,' he said, 'here now, steady on. It's all right, it's all right.'

She put her arms round his waist, tying him tightly to her, her face pressed into his shoulder. 'Oh Terry! Oh Terry!' she gasped.

'What is it? What's the matter, baby?'

'Oh Terry! Oh Terry!'

'Here now – what is it? What's up? Tell me. Tell Terry.'

In his shoulder she shook her head violently. Even in his perturbation he could feel joy at her need for him. He stroked her hair and her shoulders. 'Was it something that happened? Did you hurt yourself bad somewhere?' Again she shook her head. 'Then what's the matter? Is it just remembering it?'

She nodded, her eyes closing. Against her cheek she could feel the warm cotton of his shirt and under her arms the heart beating steadily within its lean casing.

'Here, wait a sec.' He undid her arms and turned so that, putting his legs up on the bed beside her, he could cradle her at ease. She curled herself up to him once more, a hand tucked under his armpit, and was soon asleep. He stayed like that for a long time, getting pins and needles, thinking of nothing but that he comforted her.

Gloria's fall was a nine days' wonder, at Maison Alfredo's, among her acquaintances at the Dick Whittington, for Gran at the launderette and Terry at his fruiterers'. By Monday Gloria had recovered herself and was able to present the accident dramatically and show her grazed arm and the nasty place on her shin and hint of the enormous bruise that was coming out all over her left hip and thigh. There were also bruises on both her upper arms but these she did not mention; and although Terry noticed them he merely added them to the general list of injuries caused by her fall. Raymond himself had been voluble about the way he had just been coming downstairs after looking at the ceiling, with Gloria seeing him off, when the rug had shifted and caught her heel and before he could save her she'd gone head first down the staircase. Everyone said, he said it himself, what a good thing it was he'd been there to help her afterwards; and if Gloria, each time this part of the story were reached, was inclined to grow a little silent, no one noticed it. As her wounds healed and her nerve returned, she began to feel she would not mind if people did notice it just a little. Not so that they would think anything; but just to depreci-ate the credit he was getting to which, goodness knows, he was not entitled. Just to let people think maybe, after all, perhaps he'd been up to something. After all, he never had been up to their place before, had he? And his wife and the old girl had been out, hadn't they? And all men were the same, give them half a chance. Not to think that he'd tried to . . . Not that he'd deliberately . . . But it drove her mad to hear people praising him when she knew, all the time, only would not know and woke sometimes sweating with fear at the fall relived in a dream, till Terry soothed her asleep again as he used to three years ago when they were first married and Kim, unborn, had stirred her in the night.

'Quite got over your fall?' people asked her in the Dick Whittington. 'The better they are, the harder they fall, eh?' and everyone would laugh and talk about something else.

'Quite got over your fall?' asked Mr Grover when she called in for cigarettes on her way back from work.

'All but the bruises. I'm still like something in glorious Technicolor.'

'It takes a long time for a bruise to work out. You were lucky you didn't break your neck.'

'You don't know the half of it. I'll have one of them Poppets for Kim too, Mr Grover.'

'Of course, those high heels you young ladies will wear, they're asking for trouble.'

'The heels are safe enough – in the normal way, that is.'

'It beats me what ladies will do for the sake of fashion. I say to Mrs Grover sometimes, if you ladies were asked to paint yourselves blue, you'd do it, I tell her.'

'I pretty near am blue, I can tell you.'

'It's surprising what can happen,' said Mr Grover, resting himself on the shelf behind the counter. 'I remember seeing a Jerry once, about ten miles from Benghazi it was, the second time up, and there was this Jerry sitting in an armoured car, or what was left of an armoured car, and there wasn't a scratch on him. Not a scratch, yet the car and his driver were in a terrible state, they'd gone over a mine, you see, but not right over or there wouldn't have been anything left, but near enough to explode it, you see, and the other chap and the car were in a real mess and yet this chap hadn't a scratch on him you could see. I always remember that. All internal. Been there for days.' He looked at her gently, remembering, as she shuddered. 'It's a good thing you weren't left laying there without help. You must have been glad to see Mr Banks.'

She made her face expressionless. 'Well, I was and I wasn't.'

'Hm.' He sent her a look of complicity which she could not help returning. 'He's not everyone's cup of tea, that one. Of course, Mrs Banks thinks the world of him?' The question, hardly posed, evoked no answer. 'I suppose he handles all her business with you and your husband now?'

'Well, it's funny you should say that.' She fiddled with the rack of paperback Westerns that hung at the end of the counter. 'I hardly ever set eyes on him as it so happens.'

'Really? Doesn't he fetch your rent and so on?'

'No, Mrs Banks does that, like she always has. That's why it was so queer him being up in the flat just then, with me on my own and them out and everything.'

He gave her a sharp look but her eyes were hidden. 'I see what you mean. A funny coincidence, like.'

'That's right.'

'Still, it was lucky for you.'

'You could call it that. On the other hand . . .' her voice was casual, 'it might never have happened if he'd not been there.'

'How d'you mean?'

'Well,' she shrugged, 'I might not have tripped.'

'You mean him being there made you trip?'

'Well . . .' She raised her eyes and looked at him, intending to register the sex appeal which had perhaps drawn Mr Banks. Grover's whole round body seemed stretched to a quivering point as a mouse elongates itself in investigation.

'You mean, he made you trip?' he insisted.

'No. No, of course not.' The avidity in his face frightened her. 'I never said that, Mr Grover.'

'You said it mightn't have happened if he'd not been there.'

'Well, it mightn't. I mean, I wouldn't have been out on the landing in the dark and all . . . I wouldn't have lost my balance . . .' Her voice trailed off as she realised the possible import of what she was saying. She cried in a panic, 'Don't misunderstand me, Mr Grover. He come up in the ordinary way to see to the patch on the ceiling.'

'But uninvited?'

'No. Well, yes. I mean . . .' she floundered. It was only natural. 'Naturally, I thought it was Mrs Banks – she always sees to things like that.'

'It's funny he didn't leave it to her then, Mrs Mason, isn't it? I mean, she's never out long, I shouldn't wonder. But she was out, and he knew you was in, so he came upstairs and then you have this – accident on the landing and a terrible fall down the stairs. It's a chapter of accidents, isn't it?'

'Yes it is, Mr Grover,' she said determinedly. 'That's just what it is, a chapter of accidents. No one could possibly think it was anything else . . .'

'Anything else? Could it be anything else?' His eyes were keen, his smile jubilant. She felt her heart turn over with horror at what she might let slip, and in a flurry snatched up the cigarettes, the Poppets, an evening paper.

'I'll get a rocket from Terry,' she said, 'he'll be back by now and his tea not ready.' He would not be back and he always got his own. 'Cheeri-bye, Mr Grover,' and she ran from the shop, her cheeks hot, her heart thumping, feeling not only the terror of the fall upon her again but the terror of hands gripping and flinging sideways and the thick, blue blaze of eyes close to her own.

'Nancy,' said Mr Grover, going into the back room, 'take the shop a moment, will you?' She put down her crochet and went through the door obediently. Mr Grover went to the cupboard by the fireplace and from the shelves underneath brought out his scrapbook. He sat down with it on his lap and leafed through it backwards, skimming, stopping for a moment, discarding, skimming on again through the thick pages and their yellowing cuttings, breathing in the smell of paste. Presently he found what he was looking for. He read it through attentively, then turned to the cross-reference neatly written in at its foot. He read both stories through twice; then, holding the book open, he carried it out into the shop, waited till Mrs Grover's customer had gone, laid it down on the bright quilt of periodicals. 'Here, Nancy,' he said quietly, 'have a look at this.'

Together they bent over the scrapbook.

TEN

ESTHER GLANCED at the clock on the mantelpiece. 'It's time you were back in your prammy,' she said, resting her cheek on the soft hair of the baby held up to her shoulder. June gave a small screech and beat amiably on Esther's face.

'She'll hurt you,' said Norah over her teacup at the table, 'she's got ever such sharp nails.'

'Like a kitten. Aren't you, pet – a little, soft kitten.'

'Not house-trained yet, either.'

'Oh, unkind Auntie Norah!' Esther took one of the child's hands and shook it at Norah. 'We do use our potty sometimes, don't we? I read in a magazine how you shouldn't force training on a baby because they think they're giving you a present, you see, and if you scold them, then something awful happens inside to their natures.'

'Ah, get on with you,' said Norah pleasantly. 'If you'd carried as many bedpans as I have . . .' She turned a page in the newspaper spread beside her.

'That's a quarter past two already,' said Esther, listening to St Peter's chimes coming to them on the wind. 'You were quick getting here. More tea?'

'If it's stewed enough.' Norah held out the cup and with her free hand Esther refilled it. 'Gran gone to her rest?'

'What a way to put it!' laughed Esther. 'Yes, she's gone upstairs. She likes to go early the days Ray comes home so's she can look her best for him. Say ta-ta, Auntie Norah.' She held June down for Norah to kiss, which she did with relish, nuzzling the baby's warm neck.

'Ta-ta, me beautiful little darling,' said Norah fondly. Esther went out and could be heard talking to June as she carried her through the scullery to the yard where the November sun still made a patch of autumn for the pram to stand in. Sipping her black tea, Norah read the paper contentedly. IKE TELLS MAC OK she did not read, nor TEDDIES BAR X IN SEX; but FENELLA COLLAPSES, BABY NEXT YEAR SAYS HANK, she did.

'Honestly,' she said, 'they must be barmy.'

'Who must?' Esther came back alone.

'Fenella Forbes and her husband. She can't be but five weeks pregnant if the baby's not till July. And if she's collapsing now the chances she'll go full term aren't much. Who reads this stuff?'

'You do.'

'Only because it makes me so cross. Honestly, they might just as well put a piece in the paper saying, "We had intercourse last night and forgot to take precautions."'

'Norah!' She laughed, scandalised.

'Och, don't be such a prude. That's what it comes down to. Who cares if she's pregnant, anyway?'

'She's famous.'

'So what? 'Tis a personal matter. If the curse is a week late you don't rush out and tell the reporters.'

Esther looked at the clock again and sat down by the table. 'Are you due back at four?'

'Yes. But I've a bit of shopping to do before I get in, so don't let me linger.'

'It's early closing.'

'Not in the Multimart, clever.'

Esther laughed again, then stretched herself and sighed. 'Oh, I feel lazy today! It's Ray coming back. I never can settle to anything after the morning on Thursdays.'

'After three years of it?'

'Mm.'

'Well, I suppose you're lucky.'

'Only suppose?'

'Yes. It wouldn't suit me. No ties is my choice.'

'Nurses are all hard-hearted.'

'If we weren't, we'd be loonies. My first Sister said to me once, "It's the patients who do the suffering, Nurse, not the staff." Old bitch she was, too.'

Esther leaned forward, elbows on the table. 'You're as soft as marshmallow, Norah, thank goodness. I won't ever forget how you stayed with me when June was coming.'

'Oh, that! 'Twas the sadist in me coming out.'

They sat in contented silence for a moment.

'Ray likes you ever so much,' Esther said presently. 'He was saying the other day how glad he is I've got you.'

'That's good,' said Norah.

'It's made ever such a difference, Norah. I don't know, I never seemed to know anyone sort of to talk to and be silly with before.'

'Thanks very much, I'm sure.'

'You know what I mean. I mean, there's June and Raymond and they're all the world to me, but to have a friend on the top of it – I don't know, it just seems as much as anyone could deserve. Life seems so full, somehow.'

'Ah Esther, don't say things like that!' She crossed her fingers and rapped them on her chair-back. Smiling, Esther did the same. 'You can never trust life, that I've learned if nothing else. When everything seems to be going fine, whish! the roof falls in and you wish you'd never spoken.'

'I know that can happen. But at least you've had something to be grateful for. Better than never having anything.'

'What you've never had you don't miss.'

'Don't you? I did.'

'Only now.'

'No, then, before I met Ray. I knew I was missing – oh, everything.'

'I thought I had everything once,' said Norah, 'but it turned out to be only the half of it and it spoiled me for finding the rest. There was a man when I was eighteen – married, of course. For years he held on to me and I asking nothing better. And then one day there I was, twenty-two and him still as married as ever he was. Only somehow, after that, I could never be willing to trust to it happening again, one way or the other. He'd spoiled me for anything less, I suppose, or for anything more either. Or maybe it's just that I've seen too much of the miserable creatures lying in bed and calling, "Nurse, bring me a bottle".'

'Oh Norah, you are awful!' Esther's embarrassment at Norah's admission burst out in laughter.

Norah pushed back her chair and stood up. 'Ah, you're not down to earth enough, me darling, that's the trouble with you. Now, where's the washing-up?'

'You sit still. You're on your feet all day.' She got up quickly.

'Ah, fiddle!' said Norah and carried her crockery out to the scullery.

They were nearly finished when the bell rang. Wiping her hands, Esther went to the front room window and looked out. There was no one there in the area but she glimpsed trousers and feet standing on the front door steps. She smoothed her hair and went upstairs.

Two men stood on the doorstep.

'Mrs Raymond Banks?'

'Yes.'

'We're sorry to trouble you, Mrs Banks, but I wonder if we might just have a word with your husband?'

'He's not home yet.'

'No? We understood he came home on Thursdays.'

'Yes he does, but he doesn't get home till tea-time – between four and five. Is it from the firm?'

'No. As a matter of fact, we're police officers.' The man who had been speaking made a movement to his breast pocket and brought out credentials. She stared at them without comprehension, her palms suddenly wet. 'There's no need for alarm, Mrs Banks,' he said kindly. 'We just wanted a word with your husband, that's all.'

'What is it?'

'Just a few inquiries concerning his travelling, mainly.'

'He's all right, isn't he?'

'So far as we know he's perfectly all right.' The man looked at her genially, his solid face and form reassuring. 'You expect him back between four and five?'

'Yes.'

'You don't happen to know where he's coming from, do you?'

'Euston, I suppose. That's the Midlands, isn't it?'

'He's been in the Midlands?'

'He's based on the Midlands – Birmingham. I don't know what towns exactly he's covered this week.'

'He doesn't stay in one town, then?'

'No.' Suddenly she did not like this man and his silent companion, and his reassurance seemed to her false. She stepped back and made to close the door.

The man lifted his hat civilly. 'Sorry to have troubled you,' he said. 'We'll call again.'

They turned and went down the steps, marching away side by side without speaking. She shut the door and stood for a moment in the dark hall, wiping her wet palms down her apron. From her bedroom Gran called, 'Is that Raymond?'

'No, Gran.'

'Who was it?'

'Just two men.'

'What did they want?'

'Nothing. Just asking something.'

'Ow – one of them polls.' She was silent again. Esther went downstairs. Norah had finished the washing-up and was rinsing the sink.

'It was two policemen,' said Esther slowly.

'Policemen? What did they want?'

'Just to speak to Raymond.'

'Why, what's he been up to, I wonder?' She wrung the cloth out and spread it over the rack. 'Something to do with his National Service, I expect. It usually is.'

'Yes.' She began to put the crockery away, moving with her usual competence, her face and her voice calm. 'They said they'd call again.'

'Well, so they would. Don't look so glum, me darling. You ought to see as many policemen as I do, especially in Casualty. We think nothing at all of them now, I can tell you. It's just the idea of them gives you a turn.' Esther did not reply, closing the cupboard door and starting to put away the knives and forks. Norah looked at her keenly. 'It's a nice afternoon, so put on your coat now and let's get out in the air. I'll bring the pram through.'

'They might come back.'

'They won't be back yet and if they do, it's for nothing. Come along now and I can put my parcels in the pram.'

Talking and bustling, she got Esther and the baby out. It was mild and pleasant, with a taste of fog in the sunshine and the light fading towards four o'clock. Denuded by early closing, the streets shone with a gun-metal polish, the goods in the shop windows looked like dummies. Even the Multimart seemed unreal, glittering white and chromium with its shelves a mosaic. They did Norah's shopping then walked down the quiet street towards the park, Norah gossiping on. She kept them out till it was time to return to hospital, tickled the baby, put her arm about Esther's shoulders and kissed her cheek. 'If you want me you know where to find me,' she said and then wished she had not. As Esther walked away towards Handel Street Norah watched her, her expression that of a good nurse who senses an illness as yet undiagnosed.

Raymond was back when Esther got home; he and Gran were having tea together, the doors of the stove wide open and Monty, emerged from under the table, sitting between them with his tail wrapped primly round his forefeet. It was a scene of such domesticity, holding everything Esther cared for, that the chill left on her by the visit of the policemen was lost in a wave of happiness. Raymond put his arm round her as she bent to kiss him, the baby on her hip, and then he took June from her and held her up in the air so that she laughed fatly between his hands. 'How's my girl, eh?' he asked. 'How's my beautiful baby girl?'

'She's missed her daddy, hasn't she?' said Gran fatuously.

'Have you? Have you, my little sweetheart?' He cradled the child on his lap. Still chuckling, she seized his hand and carried it to her mouth. 'No, no, you can't eat that. Any sign of that tooth yet?'

'No. The gum's ever so hard and she rubs her cheek all the time. Have you had a good week, dear?'

'Not bad. How've you been?'

'I had the sweep Monday. You should have seen what he got down the front room chimney. Is there any tea left?'

'I'll fill up the pot,' said Gran, got up and went out to the scullery.

Raymond put out his hand to Esther. 'Did you miss me too?' he asked smilingly.

She took his hand and laid it against her cheek. 'I always miss you,' she said.

'How's Gran been?'

'Her usual – quite spry. She's beginning to think about Christmas.'

'The first Christmas for June, eh?' He looked down at the baby on his lap, drawing Esther closer to him so that they made a unit. 'Makes sense out of Christmas, doesn't it, having a kid?'

'Christmas is always sense, dear. Remember the first time you came here?'

'Do I not! And the panto . . .'

'I was in such a panic . . .'

'Ah . . .' He pulled her down to him and they kissed above the baby's head. 'Seems like a million years ago . . .'

Gran came back. 'You should see the way that Norah likes her tea,' she said, banging the pot down on the tray. 'Black as pitch, you could stand the spoon up in it. This won't be much better.'

'Oh!' Recollection came back to Esther. She lifted the baby from Raymond's arms. 'I must change June first. Come with me, Ray.'

'Ow, drink your tea now I've brought it!' cried Gran.

'No, I can't.' She saw that it was twenty past four. She had said between four and five . . . 'Come with me,' she repeated.

'Can't you let him sit and rest himself?'

'I'm rested already, Gran. Seeing you again makes me feel like a million dollars.' He rose and with a finger set her earrings swinging. Gran slapped his hand away.

'Give over, Raymond, you'll have them off,' but she was placated.

Raymond followed Esther upstairs to their bedroom, sitting on the bed and tickling the baby while Esther drew the curtains and got a clean nappy from the basket. She lit the gasfire, pulled up a chair beside it and held out her arms for June.

'You're a mucky pup,' he said, as he handed her over, 'a real stinking little mucky pup.'

'It's her teeth,' said Esther absently.

He sat on the edge of the bed, elbows on his knees, looking down at the floor while she dismantled the baby on her lap. He would not do this sort of thing himself; a squeamishness, almost a repugnance, assailed him at the baby's physical needs. He had never cared to watch her being fed till she was weaned; he would not change her nappies nor bath her. Only in the last few weeks had he consented to support her in the water and move her gently to and fro so that it lapped her body and she would splash and kick. Despite his pleasure and pride in her, her sex embarrassed him. It was a curious prudery in him which Esther thought must have its sources in the orphanage, a rejection of what was female; little by little she meant to cure him of it, by saying nothing but keeping him with her while she tended June.

But now she had brought him with them because she wanted to be free of Gran. Her hands busy, her voice casual, she could think of no way of telling him about the policemen that did not seem full of menace; she said, simply, 'Two men were here, dear.'

'Mm?'

'They said they'd come back. They want to ask you something.'

'What?'

'Something about your travelling, I think.'

'My travelling?' He looked at her, baffled. 'Who were they?'

'I think they said they were from the police. There were two of them,' she hurried on, 'very pleasant, sorry to have troubled me and so on, and said it was nothing important. So I said you'd be back between four and five . . .'

For a long moment he was absolutely still. Then he said, 'Why did you tell them that?'

'They asked me. They knew you come home on Thursdays. I suppose the firm told them that. They said it's nothing important.'

'What did they say?'

'I told you.'

He clenched his hands on his knees. 'I want to know exactly what they said.'

'Ray . . .' She stared at him, her heart beginning to labour. He was sitting rigidly on the bed, his face white and his eyes of a blind blue. 'Ray, it's nothing to worry about.' On her lap the baby sucked its fingers. 'Ray, they were ever so nice . . .'

'What exactly did they say?'

Her heart was beating so heavily she could hardly breathe. She sat the child up and held her tightly, trying to think. 'They said they understood you came home on Thursdays and could they just have a word with you.

And I said you didn't get home till tea-time, and they said did I know where you were coming from. And I said no I didn't but you were based on Birmingham. And they just thanked me and said they'd call again.'

'Did they say what they wanted?'

She tried to remember their words. 'They said just a few inquiries about your travelling.'

'A few inquiries about my travelling,' he repeated.

'Ray . . .' The words she was saying were unutterable. 'Ray, you haven't done anything . . .?'

'Of course not.' He spoke absently, as though to a child. 'About my travelling,' he repeated.

'Norah said it was probably about your National Service.'

'Norah was here?'

'Yes.'

'Yes, she's probably right. That's it, my National Service. Me travelling about so much I've forgotten to register every six months like you have to once you've been in the Forces, Z-men they call them. That's what it'll be.' His body relaxed a little and his eyes focused again on her. 'It gives you a turn though, policemen. They said they'd call back?'

'Yes.'

'When?'

'They didn't say. They know you get home between four and five.'

'Four and five.' He looked at his watch. 'It's twenty-five to now. Look – Etty . . .' He looked at her, his eyes clear and deep, clasping his hands together. 'I don't want to see them.'

Her lips opened but she did not speak. She just sat, holding the child.

'I don't want to see them and I'll tell you why. It's as I said, I've forgotten to register and although it's nothing to worry about, I don't want them going to the firm and chasing them up and all that lark, so if I just nip out now before they come I can get on the phone to a pal up in Birmingham who's in with the local police there and get him to go along and explain to them that it clean went out of my head and then when this lot check up again there, they'll say it's OK, I've registered after all and it's all clean and above board, see? Only I don't want to see them now and get involved in a lot of argy-bargy, see, when I've just got home, so if I just nip out before they come you can tell them I've been delayed and they'd better get on to Birmingham, see?'

She shook her head slowly. 'What have you done, Ray?'

'Done? Done? I haven't done nothing.' His voice rose and he got up jerkily, thrusting his hands into his pockets. 'It's like I told you, just one of them red-tape mess-ups I haven't got time for.'

'Is it money?'

'Why should it be money? D'you think I'm a thief? It's the National Service, Ett, just like Norah said. You tell them I didn't come home – tell them I rang up and said I wouldn't be home.'

'Rang where?'

'The Grovers.'

'They'd know.'

He stared at her and she saw fear creeping under his skin like a stain. 'Then I wrote. I'll write you a letter to show them.'

Downstairs the bell rang. Without knowledge she stood up. He caught her arm. 'Don't go,' he whispered.

'Gran will go.'

'Say I'm out. Say I didn't come home.' His hand clung to her. 'Ett. Ett. Say I didn't come home, Ett.'

She went to the door, opened it a fraction and listened. The bell rang again and they heard Gran come grumbling up the stairs into the hall. 'Etty!' she called as she came, 'there's someone ringing.'

They heard the front door open and a man's voice, Gran's answering. They heard footsteps coming into the hall, the front door close, and Gran shouting up the stairs, 'Raymond! There's two gentlemen to see you.'

Over the baby's head they looked at one another as one looks into the dark clear depths of a bottomless

lake; they looked into each other's hearts without sub-
terfuge, without passion, without hope. All the years
of her waiting were there, all the years of his stony
childhood, all understanding, all acceptance.

'Raymond!' Gran screamed again. 'There's someone
wants to see you.'

Esther saw him change under her eyes. His face,
his eyes hardened, his mouth set in the jaunty smile
she recognised now from their first meetings, acted
and false. He was still pale and his hands trembled;
but he straightened his jacket, ran his hand over his
hair. Then he smiled at her without seeing her and,
stepping carefully round her, went out onto the landing and down the stairs.

He was with the two men in the front room behind the
closed door for a long time. Mechanically Esther went
about her chores, washed up, bathed and fed June, put
her to bed. Her hands seemed to work without direction
from her mind; she lived solely, utterly, in the room
upstairs with Raymond, her ears stretched for voices,
movement, the opening of the door and the men
saying heartily, 'Well, thanks very much, Mr Banks,
you've been a great help to us.' 'Not at all, Inspector,
only too glad to assist in any way I can.' 'That's very
public-spirited of you, Mr Banks, I wish everyone was as
co-operative as you've been. We shan't need to trouble

you again . . . we shan't need to trouble you again – not again . . . no need to trouble you again . . .'

'What do them men want with Raymond?' asked Gran.

'I don't know. Nothing important.'

'They're taking long enough.' She settled herself into her chair and opened the *TV Times*. 'Oh, it's that Wally Wisely on tonight. Are you and Ray going out as usual?'

'I don't know. Perhaps.'

'Perhaps? You always do.'

'Why ask, then?'

'I'm sorry, I'm sure!' In a huff, she became absorbed in the magazine. She felt uneasy, on edge, as an animal sensing something amiss. It was always the same when Raymond came home; they shut her out, hadn't time for her any more. She and Ray got on fine without Etty – how cosy they'd sat there in front of the fire before she came in from her walk, with their tea and the stove roaring and Ray full of his jokes. Ray was fine when it was just the two of them, but as soon as Etty came back it was spoilt; it was as though he'd just been passing the time till her return, when she and the baby came in at the door.

And here was Etty going about the place with a face like an image, all shut up and her don't-touch-me-I-know-better-than-you expression that drove Gran mad.

Who does she think she is? grumbled Gran to herself; thinks herself so high and mighty, can't even spare a civil word or a smile for her granny. She ought to have more respect, hardly answering when I speak, shutting me up like as if I was a child; making me go all the way up them stairs to answer the doorbell just because she and her precious Raymond is shut upstairs canoodling, like as not. Can't hardly wait sometimes to get rid of me – go and have your rest, Gran; run out to the shops, Gran; I just want to speak to Raymond, Gran, like as if I was a child, not her grandmother; and where'd she be if it wasn't for me and all the years me and Grandad looked after her, with my Win away and no one but us to turn to? In a home, that's where she'd have been, in a home when the news came, the dreadful awful news of Win-baby up in Manchester – only twenty-seven and hair like barley-sugar, them curly sticks of clear dark gold you used to get in the good old days and crack it, splinter it between your teeth, laughing, chewing it with your mouth a little open, saucily, because the chaps were watching you, they'd only been passing the time before you come in at the door, and Grandad, broad in his best serge suit and his big hands quiet on his knees, watching, waiting till he could get rid of the others . . .

They could hear nothing from upstairs. They sat one on either side of the table, Gran in the past, Esther in the present, waiting. Once they heard a board creak over their heads and footsteps went unhurriedly across the floor. 'Should you take them a cup of tea?' asked Gran.

'They'll be going soon.'

She sat with her hands in her lap, hearing the clock tick and the stove crackle, cars whisk past in the street, footsteps go smartly by, echoing over the manhole. Monty woke up and started washing. The flames died down in the stove and ash began to feather the edges of its core. St Peter's chimed the quarter-hours on the wind. She sat, imprisoned in passivity, her lax hands sweating, past six o'clock, past seven . . .

'It's too late for you and Ray to go out now,' said Gran uneasily. 'Whatever can they be wanting?' Esther said nothing. 'Who did you say they were?'

'I don't know.'

'Something to do with his business, I suppose.' A little more silence passed. 'I was going to finish them sardines for my supper but there won't be enough for the three of us. What had we better have, Etty?'

'I don't know.'

'Well, that won't get us far!' but her tartness lacked conviction. She thought of turning on the telly but inertia weighed her down. She just sat there, the same as Esther, conscious more and more of the quiet room above their heads.

A chair was pushed back; footsteps moved quickly, stopped, voices mumbled; footsteps, slower this time, crossed the floor. The door upstairs opened.

'Mrs Banks?' It was the man she had spoken to, calling down the stairs. For a moment she stayed motionless, then rose and went steadily out into the passage. 'Mrs Banks. Would you come upstairs for a moment, please?'

She went up the stairs. The man was big and dark in the hall; past him the door of the front room was half open, brightly lit.

'Mrs Banks, I'm afraid I have to ask your husband to accompany us to the police station. There he will make a statement which will assist us to pursue our inquiries.' She stared at him, speechless. The man's voice was kind but studiedly impersonal. 'If you have a legal adviser, your husband is entitled to get in touch with him, should he so wish. Perhaps you might care to do that while we're on our way.'

Her throat was barred across. Her voice could hardly sound. 'Will he be long?'

'I'm afraid I can't tell you.'

The front room door opened and Raymond came out, the other policeman close behind him. Raymond was smiling, a perfectly meaningless smile as though his lips had been pinned upwards at the corners and stuck upon his face. He looked very small.

'I think perhaps if he might have his coat . . . It's turned quite nasty out. Is this it?' The inspector did not expect an answer but took Raymond's overcoat and scarf from the peg and handed them to him. Then he went to the front door and opened it. A dark car was parked outside and at the opening of the door the policeman at the wheel started the engine. A man and woman passing by on the other side of the street stopped to watch. There were already two children loitering by the kerb.

Raymond and the man with him moved forward. Raymond still smiled, but his eyes met hers as with a scream. She took a step towards him.

'I'll go with him . . .'

The big man interposed himself. 'Not at this juncture, I'm afraid,' he said. 'When your husband has made his statement the position will be a little clearer and then, of course, you will be notified. I'm sorry, Mrs Banks, very sorry indeed.'

The smile began to wobble on Raymond's face. With his overcoat clasped in his arms he moved slowly away from her to the front door, the man big at his shoulder. His eyes, shifting and returning to her again, were brilliant with terror; and yet, through the terror, dominating it as lightning dominates for an instant the enveloping cloud, a desperate stark love . . .

His voice croaked. 'Trust me, Ett,' he said.

The second man moved in beside him, they were down the steps, across the pavement, into the car. The inspector pulled the front door shut behind him, the car door slammed, the car moved off, was gone.

She stood in the dark hall, the barren oblong of the lit front room beside her. Slowly she began to shake. The tremor crept up her limbs, up her body, shaking her teeth, shaking the strength from her knees. She sank down on the stairs, holding her shaking arms about her body, hearing her teeth rattling in her head. She heard Gran's voice from very far away, exclaiming, asking, calling out. She heard Gran crying, 'Etty! What's happened? Where's Raymond gone? Where's he gone, Etty? What's happened? What's happened?' Felt hands on her and lips and someone else's tears and the voice going on and on, 'What's happened? What's happened?' She could only sit in the darkness on the lowest stair, clasping her cold body in the strait-waistcoat of her arms, and shake and shake.

ELEVEN

THE CHARGE was murder: that Raymond Cavendish Banks alias Roger Cavendish alias Ronald Brooks on 17th February 1958 did with malice aforethought wilfully kill and slay Olive Marina Forbes, spinster, of Putney in the county of London, having previously gone through a form of marriage with her under the name of Cavendish. The deaths of three other women were kept in reserve by the police; Olive Marina Forbes provided the most evidence. She had fallen from the top landing of a block of flats two weeks after her marriage. The other women had also fallen. All had possessed a few hundred pounds of their own, made over to their new husband.

The case burst on the newspaper public as a joyful change from Khrushchev, Africa, Nasser and the Bombs. Pictures of Raymond appeared, in uniform (he had been a batman in the Air Force Regiment, not a Regular infantryman as he had always said), on his wedding day, and as a pair of legs topped by a hooding overcoat scurrying into a police car between escorting plain-clothes men. Pictures appeared also of Olive Marina Forbes, a smiling, plain woman with large teeth; and the picture editors of newspapers held in a special file pictures of Mary Mabel Askew, of Birmingham, Georgina Rose Roberts, of Stoke-on-Trent, and Amy Drew, of Pimlico, until such time as they could be published in legal safety. Esther's picture appeared also – the one taken on her wedding day with Raymond.

Norah had come. Norah got leave from the hospital as soon as Terry rang her up that Thursday evening. He had come back from the shop – greengrocers' do not close on Thursday afternoon and he got home just after Raymond had been taken away – to find Gran and Esther crouched in the darkness on the stairs, Esther dumb and Gran hysterical. Gloria had come in soon after with Kim and, on hearing what had happened, had rushed upstairs and thrown herself on the bed, sobbing. Terry had run to the corner and telephoned Norah; Norah had summoned Mr Phelps; together they had taken over.

Police came during the evening and broke the charge to Esther. They were very kind and drove her round to the police station with Raymond's toilet things and a change of under-clothes. While she was gone two more of them searched delicately through the house; they took away Raymond's personal papers, diaries, account books, which Esther had never known he possessed, her fur cape and Gran's lizard brooch. Gran did not know this, for Norah had given her a sedative and she lay shrivelled asleep in her big bed, her lips without dentures collapsing in and out, her eyelids puffed and red, as though she decayed sleeping.

Upstairs, Kim at last fretfully fallen asleep, Gloria wept, throwing herself about the room, caught some-times in Terry's arms, sometimes within the arms of a chair. 'He tried to kill me – they asked me and I told them – it was me as told them. They'd never have got him if it wasn't for me – but he threw me, he threw me down the stairs! I wouldn't never have told if they hadn't come after me . . .'

'Who, baby – who came after you?'

'The police – one day . . .'

'When?'

'A few weeks ago. I came out of the house and they came up to me and asked me about Mr Banks.'

'Why you?'

'I don't know, I don't know! I never let on to a soul, not a soul. But then they asked me, bit by bit. They were ever so civil and gave me a cup of tea. They seemed to know what had happened already. I don't know how, I never told no one! Before I knew what I'd done, I'd told them about it.'

'About your fall?'

She laughed, rubbing her hands wildly over her wet face. 'It wasn't no fall! He pushed me, I tell you, he pushed me!'

'Why?'

'Why? Because he's a bloody murderer, that's why – he likes pushing women off things, that's the way he gets rid of them. He tried to kill me, Terry, he threw me down the stairs. And now they've caught him and it was me led them to it and there's his wife and baby . . . Oh, I wish I was dead, I wish I was dead!'

Silently he held her, absorbing into his own slender body the tremors that shook hers. Her face made a sodden patch on his chest and her hands with their long crimson fingernails clutched and dug at his jacket. When at last she was quieter she drew back her head and said, 'I can't stay here, Terry.'

'No. You can't stay here. I'll take you and Kim over to Mum.'

'It's late. How can we get there?'

'We'll get a taxi. Go and get packed.'

He kissed her gently and released her. Shuddering, she began to move about the room, helped by the task of gathering up her things. 'I'll stay the night and see you settled in,' he said, 'but I'll come back here tomorrow.'

She gaped at him, her mascara bleared, the rouge washed from her cheeks. 'Why?'

'They've been good to us, Mrs Banks and the old lady. Him . . .' His hands clenched slowly and relaxed, 'But he won't be here.'

At twenty-five to six the following morning Mr Grover came upstairs again to his wife's bedside, a newspaper in his hand. He was pale and his hand shook a little. He sat down on the edge of the bed, where Mrs Grover still lay swaddled, and held out the paper. 'They've done it,' he said in a low voice.

She half started up. 'When?'

'Last evening. It's on the front page.'

Together they read the account of Raymond's arrest. Mrs Grover seemed to shrink. 'Oh, Leonard! What have we done?'

'He's a murderer.'

'Miss Esther – and the baby . . .'

'It might have been their turn next.'

They sat in heavy silence, then Mr Grover said, 'They say a murderer always gives himself away, using the same trick once too often. I couldn't have done nothing else, not knowing what I did.'

'Guessing, Len – it was only guessing.'

He turned sad eyes on her in his pink mouse's face. 'It was knowing, Nancy. Something told me. Mrs Mason's fall and the other cases coming into my mind, it all tied in together. I had to go to the police.'

'Coincidence . . .'

He shook his head. 'The police wouldn't make an arrest on coincidence. I never liked him.'

'Will you have to give evidence?'

'I don't know. I suppose not, as there's nothing I know direct. I was only the link . . . I expect Mrs Mason will have to.'

She lay down, drawing the bedclothes up to her chin, her eyes big. 'We'll have to leave the shop, Len,' she said quietly.

'Yes.' He folded the newspaper carefully and got to his feet. 'But there was nothing else I could do, was there? I had to speak.'

He turned and went downstairs again. Under the bedclothes she clasped her hands together and prayed: Please God, help Miss Esther and the baby.

Time passed; at least, daylight alternated with darkness. Beyond that Esther did not know, for a dream has no time or place. There were things to see to, like washing up and cooking and caring for June; she was very rigid in her routine for June, everything had to be just so and to the minute so that the baby should know exactly what to expect and when. Real life had stopped days, weeks, perhaps months ago, the night they told her the charge against Raymond. Then had come a period when she seemed alone in a vast echoing scream, she herself dumb; nothing existed around her, she moved dead in a huge bell reverberating with screams. Slowly, like a sea mist, a great silence had enveloped and muffled the bell, and through the mist she moved now, bereft of place or time, putting one foot before the other on the small path of ordinary things. Beyond this she could not see or hear or think; in the bell she had thought, and the thoughts had made her long for madness. If she went mad, then nothing would be real. But she had not gone mad.

There had, she believed, been the hearing at the magistrate's court where Raymond had been sent for trial. There had been the occasions of her visits to him in prison, one on either side of a table and a warder present, with nothing to say but give news of June and ask if they fed him properly and stare across the table at Raymond, her husband, her love, as he stared back at her, with the monstrous questions and imperishable avowals alike impossible to speak. There had been, after the magistrate's hearing, the gentle departure of Terry Mason, who had stood between her and the public appetite as Raymond would have done had he been there; and there had been the arrival of Mr Phelps, who had moved into the Masons' empty rooms, dealt with the Grovers, run the shop, talked to the lawyers. There was Mr Fortescue, the solicitor drawn from the court like something from a bran tub, aghast but exhilarated by the nature of the case, for he knew he would live forever now in a volume of Famous Trials. And there was Gran.

Esther did not know where Gran had been while she herself had been in the bell. She saw her now through the mist and like everything else she seemed diminished and unreal. Perhaps it was because she was so quiet; but then in a mist everything seems quiet. The only sounds Esther really heard were those June made, for they were innocent.

But Gran was quiet. At first Norah and Mr Phelps thought she had had a little stroke, for she lay in her bed and did not move save to champ her gums, staring up at the ceiling; but presently she said, 'Where's my Etty?'

'Asleep,' they told her.

Gran nodded. 'That's good. That's my Etty. Let her sleep.'

Mr Phelps sat with her. After a long while Gran asked, 'Where've they taken him?'

'For a few days – to prison.'

Her jaws worked for a little. Then: 'What's he done?'

Mr Phelps laid his hand on hers. 'Rest now. Don't talk.'

She twisted her head round to look at him. 'What's he done?' she repeated.

He withdrew his hand. 'They say he's – made away with a woman. For some property and some money she had.'

Gran nodded, twice. 'He never got that car,' she muttered, and shut her eyes.

She was up next day, biddable and quiet. She sat in her chair in front of the television, ate and drank what was brought to her. She, who had avidly read so many newspapers, did not ask for them now, and since Raymond's arrest none had been brought into the house. She said she slept well, and she herself could not have told whether, or for how long, she woke in the darkness, the present entangled in the past. She was quiet with all of them, especially Esther; they said nothing to each other that was not a commonplace of domesticity. Mr Phelps used to come down and sit with them when Norah had gone back on duty and one evening, when Esther was upstairs with June, he told her, 'He's been sent for trial.'

A tiny gleam came into her eyes, to vanish immediately. 'Will we have to be there?'

'No. He doesn't want it.'

She nodded. 'He thought the world of us,' she said, and nothing more.

They thought she was shocked silly, but she was thinking. She thought all the time, absorbedly; there was not room in her life just now for anything else. She thought about the meaning of what had happened. What could it be? What could be its purpose? Why had Win died and Grandad died and this wicked thing come upon her and Esther? What were they supposed to make of it, what learn from it, how bear themselves? All her life Gran had gone from minute to minute, never thinking, alive only in the present, for even the recollections of her youth had been as vivid to her as though she lived them again; she had remembered them as a girl and a young woman, not as a woman grown old and looking back. Win had died and she had not thought, Grandad had died and she had understood nothing. Now something more terrible than either, something no other family she knew had ever experienced, had happened to them, and there must be a meaning. She sat quietly in her chair, the earrings still bright in her ears but the black hair growing grey at the parting, puzzling as though over a conundrum she could hold in her hand. She accepted what Norah did for them with gratitude, with Mr Phelps she was obedient and comforted; she knew that she could not help Esther, but that if she were

heedless as she used to be she could harm her griev-
ously. She sat quietly, thinking, learning to be still;
growing old.

The trial was to be held at the Old Bailey in the
New Year sessions. Mr Phelps and Mr Fortescue had
briefed Robert Haylett, QC, for Raymond's defence.
Esther had heard of him, he was often briefed in
murder cases, and it seemed very strange to her that
she should be employing him now. For she was
employing him, of course; everything she had would,
if necessary, go towards Raymond's defence; but it
would not be necessary. Raymond, they told her, had
a good deal of money in the bank in Birmingham,
more even than he had led her to believe when they
were making their wills long ago. There had been
offers of large sums from newspapers too, for his or
her own story; but Mr Phelps and Mr Fortescue did
not tell her of these. Mr Fortescue refused them rather
regretfully – money for jam, he thought irreverently –
but Mr Phelps did not think twice.

Mr Haylett's chambers were in King's Bench Walk
and on a fine January day Esther went to see him. She
had never been in the Temple before and its stillness, surrounded by the roar of Fleet Street and the
Embankment, seemed to mirror herself, a vacuum in
activity. She stood for a moment under the bare trees,

looking across the lawns to the Thames sparkling beyond. The river was full to the brim, jostling the walls as though it would overtop them, creamy and brown as stout. It would have given her pleasure long ago; she and Gran might have taken a steamer somewhere one summer afternoon . . .

She turned away and found the right house, mounted the stone staircase that echoed her footsteps, wondering at the prison-like bareness and the lists of names all painted up on the doors, such an old-world way of doing it. Through a double door like that of a safe, into an office full of leather and tape; a moment's wait on a chair rather like Miss Burroughs', another door opening into a room windowed with the branches of trees, walled with leather books and over the mantelpiece the portrait of a majestic bull. She stared at this in astonishment – it was an old picture, the man who rather warily held the bull's rope wore red breeches and his hair tied back – and only when Mr Haylett spoke her name a second time did she focus herself on him. She was like that now; details held her, the important things she found it difficult not to pass by.

He shook her hand and sat her down in an armchair. She refused a cigarette and learned that the bull was the ancestor of a bull Mr Haylett now owned on his farm in Suffolk. Mr Haylett was very keen on bulls and bemused her for a little by telling her of their various breeds and of how he had come to acquire the splendid animal of which he was so proud. She did not really listen but his voice enabled her to accept her presence here and to become accustomed to his.

He was a broad dark man with a humorous face, mobile and fleshy like an actor's. His hair was grey and carefully oiled and brushed into ducks tails over his ears, and he wore a plum-coloured velvet jacket with a very shabby collar. As he talked he swung gently from side to side in his swivel chair, soothingly as though he were lulling a baby.

'Well, Mrs Banks,' he said, 'I must confess I had great difficulty in shedding old Charlie Fortescue.' As she said nothing but looked at him wonderingly, he went on, 'It's very unorthodox to see you without your solicitor, you see – isn't really done at all, you know, so we'll keep it dark together, eh? But I find these lawyers, especially with ladies . . . and old Charlie will butt in. We were at Jesus together – Jesus College, Cambridge . . .' She doesn't understand anything, he thought, talking on, she's not going to utter a word. Pity she's not going to be a witness, they couldn't have shaken her . . . 'Of course, if you had been going to give evidence on your husband's behalf we should have to have had old Charlie here. As it is, this is strictly off the record, eh?' He swung gently, smiling.

She folded her hands in her lap, looking across at him steadily. Plain brown hat, plain brown coat, plain composed face – a good face, an honest face, he thought, seeing her in the box, convincing . . . Pity.

'Why am I not to give evidence?' she asked quietly.

'Your husband doesn't want it.'

'But you could make him.'

'I could advise him but I can't make him. If I thought your evidence would weigh powerfully in his favour, I could press him; but I can't force a witness on him.'

'I could tell them – how we lived together all that time, how he – how good he was to me and Gran. How he couldn't be – isn't the kind of person who could . . .' If she clasped her hands tightly they could not tremble and if they did not tremble, her voice need not either. She concentrated on this.

Mr Haylett stopped swinging, leaning forward and taking up a pencil from the desk. 'Mrs Banks,' he said gently, 'the case against your husband is very strong. I do not think what you could have to say would really influence the course of events in any way. Perhaps a juror might be touched, perhaps the public would believe for a little that there was not so serious a case to answer; but when your evidence was concluded and you had left the box, the process of the law and sober weighing of the facts would still prevail. You would have exposed yourself to little purpose, and that your husband will not have.'

She said nothing for a moment, her eyes steady. Then she asked, 'Mr Haylett, what is the truth?'

He was startled. 'The truth?'

'I know what he's charged with but I don't know why. People don't like talking to me about it and I . . .'

'Hasn't your husband . . .?'

'No. We don't talk about anything now, except just the baby. He told me a lot of things when I first got to know him but I know now a lot of them weren't true. About the firm, for instance. There never was a firm, was there?'

'Only at first.'

'Things like that, you see. I'd like to know the truth.'

He sat back in his chair and began swinging again. 'He was brought up in an orphanage until he was fifteen – that you do know, I think. His mother abandoned him at their lodgings when he was two years old. She was never traced and we don't know who his father was.'

Her voice was wondering. 'They weren't married?'

'No. When he left the orphanage he went from job to job – he didn't keep in touch with them as he could have done, as they like their children to do. He just disappeared. He turned up again in the RAF at eighteen for his National Service, just after the war ended. He

343

was batman to an officer whose wife – er – fell in love with him. From what I can gather she was a very silly, worthless sort of woman, who drank too much and had too little to do and from her I believe Banks conceived a contempt for women which was added to the resentment – hatred, you might almost call it – which he had grown up with because of the defection of his mother and his illegitimacy. This silly woman gave him a good many presents, even money. He has told me he found her "a soft touch". I think perhaps she continued to give him money after their relationship had ceased, whether from affection or from fear I don't know. The prosecution will say from fear, no doubt. They may even use the word "blackmail".' He looked at her sharply but she had not flinched. 'I am telling you the story as the prosecution will produce it in court. The facts so far can all be proved; it is in the interpretation of them that we must do our work.

'When his National Service was up, he went out into the world and as far as I can gather he repeated this pattern in varying degrees over a period of years. He does not dispute that he lived by his wits off women. They gave him gifts of both goods and money, very often they parted with their savings. I do not know, but I think it possible the prosecution may produce one of these women as a witness, and they will certainly allege that it was this which gave him the idea of marrying such a woman so that he could lawfully gain possession of her property by means of a settlement or a joint account or, ultimately, a will. Do you really want me to go on?'

She whispered, 'Please.'

He swung his chair right round so that his back was almost towards her. 'These women seem to have been always very much the same type. Lonely unmarried women with a little property, in their thirties usually, not very intelligent perhaps, hungry for love – rather too hungry very often, I think, for Banks's contempt for them is unbounded. Olive Forbes was of this type, I gather. His dislike of her is intense. Again, he does not dispute that he knew her or went through a form of marriage with her, but naturally he denies that he was in any way responsible for the fall that killed her. He does not deny that in the name of Roger Cavendish he married her with the intention of getting control of her capital, but says that she discovered this and in a fit of despair threw herself to her death. The fact remains that he proved her will as quickly as possible and disappeared. A report of the inquest, where an open verdict was returned, caught the eye of – er – someone, who made a study of queer cases, at the selfsame moment that he – the person – heard the story of Mrs Mason's fall. The two things together seemed too great a coincidence and he – this person – went to the police. They already had a file on the Forbes case and two other similar – er – fatalities. As a matter of fact,' he could not resist his own enthusiasm, 'it was very much the same sort of chain of coincidences that brought about the arrest of George Joseph Smith, you may remember. Pure coincidence, suspicion and someone with sharp eyes. Very strange. These things do happen. The law and coincidence both have long arms.'

She was perfectly still, her hands clenched on the handbag, dry-eyed, but her face and her lips were white. He threw down the pencil and leaned forward. 'My dear Mrs Banks, would you like some tea? My clerk makes a very creditable cup at this time of the afternoon. Coggers!' he bellowed. 'His name is Cogswell but Coggers sounds Dickensian and he is rather . . . Coggers, some tea. And some of those very nice biscuits. I find that almost anyone can make creditable Indian tea but not one in a thousand gets the hang of China. The whole approach to China tea should be different . . .'

He ran on as he had run on about the bulls. The tea came, he poured it and they drank it. He saw his chatter and the tea bring the life slowly back to her.

He was used to all sorts of visitors, the callous and the distraught, the shifty and the righteous, but the wracked composure of this murderer's wife roused his respect and pity. Murderer's wife? Haylett was going

346

to plead Not Guilty; guilty of fraud, yes, but the death of Olive Forbes was the desperate act of an unhappy woman finding herself betrayed – and of any other women he and the Court would have no cognizance. But, with the necessary schizophrenia of the advocate, whatever he might pretend to anyone else, Haylett did not see how he could hide from himself that the case against Raymond Banks was certainly a very strong one. He would do his damnedest to get him – off? Surely it would not be possible to do that – but to save him, and this good woman here, the worst punishment. And yet, if he were saved, would Banks appreciate it? Would he not simply accept it as one accepts a near shave, with a 'Whew!' and a sense of satisfaction? Haylett had seen too much of the glass wall that divides the abnormal from the normal mind, often in the same person; on the one side the ordinary emotions on ordinary subjects of an ordinary man; on the other nothing, a blank where nothing registered – not pity or conscience or fear, simply the cold vanity of expedience. A suspension of morality, where 'I want' becomes simply 'I will'. Poor old McNaghten – where did he begin and end?

He switched on the lamp on his desk, for the light was beginning to fade outside, and took up the pencil again.

'Now there are one or two things you can help me with, Mrs Banks, if you feel equal to it.' She nodded silently. 'Good. Splendid. It won't take long. Our friends the prosecution have certain facts, you see, so we have to know them, too, and put a proper interpretation of them forward. Tell me about your marriage.'

'We were happy.'

'Where did you meet?'

'In a teashop.'

'A chance meeting?'

'Yes.'

'He spoke to you?'

'Yes. He borrowed my evening paper.'

'And then?'

'He was there the next week.'

'By chance? Did he know you would be there?'

'No. At least – I may have said I would be. We went to the pictures.'

'Did he tell you about himself?'

'Yes. He said he was selling his car.'

'And you told him about yourself too, I expect?'

'Yes.'

'What sort of things?'

'Oh – where I worked, who I lived with – nothing in particular.'

Inwardly Mr Haylett sighed. Nothing particular, just every detail of her circumstances extracted with the skill of practice.

'And then?'

'We met every Thursday.'

'How long was it before you became engaged?'

'Not very long – two or three months, I think.' Her hands were bare of all save her wedding ring now; the turquoise daisy had not belonged to his mother.

'Did he ever try to borrow money from you?'

'Of course not.' The colour surged into her face. 'Never.' And as she spoke she heard Gran's voice long, long ago – 'Why couldn't you lend it him, Etty? His friend at the garage with a bargain . . .' 'Never,' she said again.

'You were married in St Peter's Church in March 1957. Whose wish was that?'

'Both of us. We both wanted to be married in church.'

'Did any relatives or friends of his come to the wedding?'

'No.'

'Didn't that seem odd?'

'No. I knew he was an orphan. I knew he hadn't anyone, not even an uncle or aunt.' She looked at him steadily. 'Lots of people have no one, no one at all. I didn't have anyone but Gran before I met Raymond.'

'Quite. So you were married in St Peter's Church and you went to Torquay for your honeymoon. Forgive me, Mrs Banks, but I have to ask these things: Who paid for all this?'

She opened her mouth and shut it again. Her account at Winters', a conversation echoing now . . . 'I can't stand not having the money, I'd pay you back . . .' and then the cape, Gran's lbzard brooch . . . 'He did,' she said steadily.

'Yes. Good. And then you came back and lived in Handel Street. Who paid the housekeeping?'

'He did.'

'Yes? You had lodgers in the top floor, of course. What arrangements did you make about the rent? I imagine it was paid weekly?'

'Yes.'

'You paid it into the bank then? Or did you use it for general running expenses?'

'Sometimes.'

'You had a joint account?'

'We both did.'

'Whose idea was that?'

'Mine.'

'Good, good. You know, do you, that in fact your husband's account was in his name only?'

She waited a moment. 'I never drew on his.'

'You couldn't have done,' he said gently. 'Did he draw on yours?'

'Never.'

'You would have known, of course, for it needed your signature also. And now there is this question of

350

the wills, and then I think I shall have done. Whose suggestion was it that you should make a will in his favour?'

'Mine.'

'I see. I ask you this because you must know, Mrs Banks, that the prosecution allege that this other woman was induced to make a will in your husband's favour and they will produce evidence to that effect. This is something I must know from you. It was you who suggested you should make the will?'

'He made one too.'

'Did you see it?'

'He showed it me.'

'Did you read it?'

'I . . . Yes.'

'I ask this because no such will exists among your husband's papers. If we could produce it, it would come in very useful. No? Well, perhaps it will turn up. Now only one more question and that, I'm afraid, is one I don't like asking you and you won't want to answer, but it has to be put. Has your husband at any time done or threatened to do violence to you?'

The world swung away again and for a moment she was back inside the bell. Her throat closed, she could not see, only feel the wind tearing at them on the cliff top, his cold cold hands, the awful loneliness . . .

'I ask,' said Mr Haylett gently, 'because you must know your husband is alleged to have induced women –

this woman – to make over her property to him and then to have made away with her by causing her to fall from a staircase. If having made a will in his favour, you nevertheless suffered not the slightest threat of such a thing, it would give me great confidence, Mrs Banks.'

Her lips were stiff. 'Never,' she whispered.

'He always behaved to you with perfect love and gentleness?'

'Yes.'

'And so far as you are aware has never benefited in any way from the financial arrangements you made for him?'

'No.'

'Good. Splendid. That really must be the crux of the matter.' And what good it will be to me I cannot at the moment conceive, against all the evidence of the others, he thought, not only the one – or the four – that died but the others that were defrauded. He swung back in his chair. 'Well, those are all the points I wanted to cover at this stage. You see, we didn't need old Charlie with us, did we?'

Her eyes were on her hands, clasping and unclasping in her lap. 'Mr Haylett, I want to tell them that.'

'He won't have it.'

'I want to tell them what you just said – that he has always behaved with perfect love and gentleness. Wouldn't it help?'

'You would have to stand up to cross-examination.'

'They couldn't shake me. It's the truth.'

'He has forbidden it. I did put it to him that a witness of your integrity . . .' – and the mere fact that you are alive at all, he thought wryly – 'might be of value. But he just kept repeating, "You don't drag Ett into it." I shall find some means of making it clear to the court that your marriage has been a happy and tranquil one, you can trust me for that.'

'I want to stand by him.'

'Of course, of course . . .'

'I don't care what he's done. I was just going along from day to day before I met him. He gave me everything. We were happy.'

'I believe he cares for you very deeply.'

She smiled, if the sun could be said to shine through cloud. 'Yes, he does. I suppose it sounds silly when there was all the others. Perhaps he didn't at first . . .' She shut her eyes, trying not to hear the echoing deceptions, 'Perhaps at first I was just another silly woman to make something out of. I can see that now, after what you've told me, but things changed for him and me. He loves me now, me and June and Gran. He's loved us for a long time.'

'Mrs Banks . . .' He hesitated, at a loss for once for the fluent, exact words. 'May I ask you as a purely personal thing from one good friend to another, not to come into court? I shall not call you and you would find the proceedings infinitely distressing. Things will be said, evidence produced, which can only hurt you deeply.'

'I want to stand by Raymond.'

'But he wants to spare you everything he can.' Rather late in the day for that, he added to himself.

'I'll see,' she said. 'I must think what would be best for Raymond.' She began to fumble with her gloves and handbag, not looking at him but with a faint colour staining her neck and face. 'There's just one thing . . . I haven't known who to ask. Somehow I couldn't Mr Fortescue. But I have to know . . .' She lifted her head and met his gaze with a clear and desperate steadiness. 'Mr Haylett, am I married?'

He felt the blood rush into his own face too and a sudden passion of rage against mankind assailed him, the misery, the cruelty, the dumb goodness . . . 'Of course you're married. Of course, of course!' he said vehemently. With the other three dead and you surviving, he almost shouted. How he loathed this part of it! Criminals were all right; he loved criminals as a collector loves his collection, entranced by the permutations of character so nearly like his own yet so perversely, fatally diverging. The people he defended, whether innocent or guilty, were by their very circumstances removed from ordinary life; when they breathed and suffered it was under glass. But their relatives, their victims . . .

'Thank you,' she said, 'I didn't know who to ask. I have to know, you see, because of June – the baby.'

'Quite, quite . . .'

'I expect Raymond excuses himself a lot because his parents weren't married. But that's not right. You can't blame other people for what you make of yourself, not in the end. There are hundreds of children brought up without parents and they grow up all right. June will be all right. So long as I know what to tell her.' She got to her feet. 'I mustn't take up your time, and there's June to see to. She has her orange juice at five.'

'If there's anything more on which I can advise you . . .'

'Thank you. You've been ever so kind.'

They were by the door and he held her hand in both his. 'Try not to worry too much, Mrs Banks. I'll do my best for him.'

He saw her eyes suddenly flood with tears as a bowl fills from a tap; but none spilt. She went out steadily, down the stairs, out into the sharp purple stillness of the evening. At five June had her orange juice and then she was bathed and put in her cot and then there was supper to get and bed and oblivion – oblivion. 'Oh God,' she said aloud, standing suddenly still under the plane trees, 'Oh God,' looking round in the emptiness. It was true, all true. She could pretend no more, lie to herself no more. The facts were there, he had done these things. He could do them, they were in him, she recognised that now that she knew the truth. He had chosen to do them, armouring himself in hate, choosing to live in hate. He had made his choice and then absolved himself, lied to himself as he had lied to everyone else: I was unloved, unwanted, my mother left me, I had no love, no home; it's not my fault, I couldn't help it, blame someone else, blame anyone but not me, I'm not responsible. But it was he, no one else, who had made the choice; it was he, no one else, who had yielded to the darkness in the heart, deliberately. When that first silly woman tired of him, he, no one else, chose not to be discarded but bought off.

She made blindly for the shelter of an archway but it led into another open space. Beyond the buildings the traffic of Fleet Street roared, but she could not go into it like this, the tears were running down her face, her breath coming in gasps. She stared round for refuge, saw that the building was a church, and blundered through its door. It was twilit inside and utterly silent. The silence heightened the sounds of her gasping breath. She sat down and covered her wet face with her hands, bowing down over the grief inside her, her whole being surrendered to despair.

He was gone, he was guilty. They would not kill him, for that was not now the law, but for years he would be locked away in a stony world to which she could never follow him. There would be letters; and once a month perhaps she would visit him and find him every time a little paler, a little more remote. Gran would die and June would grow and when the years had passed he would come back to them and they would go to some far part of England, change their names and start afresh, and always there would be the fear that someone would find out, that June would find out; and fear of the years lost between now and then.

'I can't,' she whispered, 'I can't.' I can't live alone with this knowledge, of the future as well as the past. I can't live knowing what Raymond may be, knowing what Raymond was; remembering the lies, foreseeing the pretences, carrying the corpse of love.

'I can't,' she said again, raising her head and staring round her. The walls and vaulted ceiling of the church arched over her like a ribcage. They housed a silence and a solitude so profound that for a moment she was startled, as though she had unexpectedly come upon her own reflection in a mirror. The silence waited. The wood of the pews was new and pale in the dusk, inanimate, offering nothing. On the bare altar stood nothing for beauty or comfort, only a plain bare cross. There was nothing enclosed in these arching ribs that could give response, nothing but herself and a solitude that waited as once before she had sensed a waiting, when she had knelt with closed eyes, Gran at her side, and had waited to be blessed.

Her sobs grew quieter. She no longer wept, though her face felt stiff with tears, and she laid her head back against the stone wall, the stillness calming her; and out of the stillness, like a fish coming to the surface of a muddy pool, came the memory of that time when Raymond had first entered her body with love; the day after Kim's christening and the confession, only half true even then, about his mother. That must have been the first sweetness he felt for her, the first loosening of his armour of hate, and it had drawn him back; she remembered how he had come back and said, 'I'd rather be here.' That was the truth, as much the truth as the things Mr Haylett had told her. Not only ugly things were real.

She remembered Eastbourne, how his body had not found it possible to lie to her when he had God knew what intention in his mind; and the cliff top, his hand roughly turning her face to his while he searched, searched for something whose existence he had denied till then and which was all she had ever had to offer. That was true too.

All of which he was capable, good and evil, made up the Raymond she loved. Without him what would she have to remember? Now, alongside despair and misery, were riches and fulfilment, equally true, equally indisputable. She had loved; she had been loved; how could she ever be poor again, while she had memory? Raymond was what he was and they had loved one another nevertheless. They had come to life in each other's keeping, broken the caul of solitude that enclosed them and become one flesh, one heart. She would remember that always; would always see the angle of his head when he shaved, the little hollow beneath his jaw, hear the tone of his voice when he was teasing Gran, remember the twitch of his slippered foot as he read the papers, the way he blew into June's fat neck and made her squeal, the smell of his clothes, the warmth of his hands, the back of his neck as he sat watching the telly. She would always remember his saying, 'You're the one, Ett'; remember looks caught and held deeply, lovingly; contentment, companionship, gentleness; him, his presence: love.

It was almost dark now. The altar was lost in shadow but she could still see the ribs of the church in which she was the living heart. She wiped her face with her handkerchief, tucked back her hair, rose to her feet. There was Gran to go back to and June; and always Raymond. Always Raymond . . .

Going out into the street again, she knew she had, after all, been blessed.

DAUNT BOOKS

Founded in 2010, Daunt Books Publishing grew out of Daunt Books, independent booksellers with shops in London and the south of England. We publish the finest writing in English and in translation, from literary fiction – novels and short stories – to narrative non-fiction, including essays and memoirs. Our modern classics list revives authors whose work has unjustly fallen out of print. In 2020 we launched Daunt Books Originals, an imprint for bold and inventive new writing.

www.dauntbookspublishing.co.uk